THE WICKED WALLFLOWER

#3 The Duchess Society Series

BY
TRACY SUMNER

WOLF PUBLISHING

The Wicked Wallflower by Tracy Sumner

Published by WOLF Publishing UG

Copyright © 2022 Tracy Sumner
Text by Tracy Sumner
Edited by Chris Hall
Cover Art by Victoria Cooper
Paperback ISBN: 978-3-98536-054-3
Hard Cover ISBN: 978-3-98536-055-0
Ebook ISBN: 978-3-98536-053-6

WOLF Publishing - This is us:

Two sisters, two personalities.. But only one big love!

Diving into a world of dreams..
   ...Romance, heartfelt emotions, lovable and witty characters, some humor, and some mystery! Because we want it all! Historical Romance at its best!

Visit our website to learn all about us, our authors and books!

Sign up to our mailing list to receive first hand information on new releases, freebies and promotions as well as exclusive giveaways and sneak-peeks!

WWW.WOLF-PUBLISHING.COM

Also by Tracy Sumner

The Duchess Society Series

The DUCHESS SOCIETY is a steamy new Regency-era series. Come along for a scandalous ride with the incorrigible ladies of the Duchess Society as they tame the wicked rogues of London! Second chance, marriage of convenience, enemies to lovers, forbidden love, passion, scandal, ROMANCE.

If you enjoy depraved dukes, erstwhile earls and sexy scoundrels, untamed bluestockings and rebellious society misses, the DUCHESS SOCIETY is the series for you!

#1 The Brazen Bluestocking

#2 The Scandalous Vixen

#3 The Wicked Wallflower

Prequel to the series: The Ice Duchess

THE WICKED WALLFLOWER

Carla —
Happy reading!
xoxo
Tracy

Foreword

Every young lady has at some time or other known the same agitation. All have been, or at least all have believed themselves to be, in danger from the pursuit of someone they wished to avoid.
Jane Austen, *Northanger Abbey*

Prologue

Leighton House, Hertfordshire, 1824

L ady Philippa Darlington placed the gift on the bed as if the contents would detonate upon opening.

Crawling atop the mattress, she crossed her legs and stared at the small wrapped parcel with angst, indecision, and anticipation. X.M. was scrawled on the back in elegant script, taunting her. As if she'd not known *immediately* who it was from.

Careful, Little Darlington, as you navigate these treacherous waters.

Xander Macauley's words rolled over her like a wave, as they seemed to at least once a day. Sometimes at night, alone in her bed, it was the biggest secret out of all the secrets a duke's sister was forced to keep.

Along with the memory of their stolen moment in the gaming room came the *feelings*.

Heat thrummed through her limbs. Through her head like champagne. Her pulse skipped, heart bumping against her ribs. She felt drunk. On a *man*.

Why, why, *why* did it have to be him?

Her brother, Roan Darlington, the Duke of Leighton, would never allow it. Xander Macauley would never ask. He thought her a bothersome fly buzzing about his face. Less than a fly, an ant he smashed beneath his boot. He had his choice of every chit in London. Why would he want her? An unsophisticated sister of his best friend?

She refused, simply *refused*, to be bothersome. A burden. A nuisance. When she married, *if* she married, the pitiable sod would be absolutely besotted, out of his head, *gone* for her. Tripping along like her brother tripped along behind Helena. The Duke of Markham with his duchess, Georgie. Tobias Streeter with Hildy, perhaps the worst case of lovesick behavior she'd ever seen.

Gads, there were men, hundreds, for her to choose from. Duke to baronet, solicitor to vicar. Her heart didn't have to set its sights on the most unreachable in status and demeanor. A confirmed, nay, *sworn* bachelor. A man born in the rookery of all places. A blackguard. A scoundrel. A *rake*. Hildy Streeter had done it, of course. Married a rogue who'd climbed from the slums then gone on to love him with all her heart.

Nevertheless, even after observing these beautiful relationships, Pippa wouldn't follow their example merely because of a fickle attraction.

She had a sister, two of them now, and the eldest, Helena, the powerful Duchess of Leighton, said she didn't have to marry if she didn't want to. But she'd also said Pippa had to *try* to make it through another season, at least, for her brother's sake.

Pippa was going to be the grandest wallflower who'd ever *lived*. She'd fade into every room she entered like mist. Prop up columns and disappear behind ferns. They wouldn't even know she was there. Her only spot of despair was missing out on the waltzes, but miss out, she would. Signing her dance card would be the most challenging feat in England.

Pippa caught her tongue between her teeth and touched the package, then traced her index finger over the twine wrapped twice around it. It was simply presented, like the man himself.

Echoes from carriages circling the front drive fluttered through her open window, along with a healthy dose of the crisp evening air. Fall was upon them in gorgeous measure. She heard the children first, shouts of bedlam after hours of forced containment. All arriving for her birthday celebration.

She loved when Leighton House's hallways rang with mischief and merriment. They'd not been so lonely, she and Roan, since he'd allowed these interesting people into their lives. Since he'd opened his heart and let Helena into its protected confines.

Pippa fiddled with the package for another minute, then sighed and tugged on the bow, the twine unraveling in her hand. The paper, similar to what would be wrapped around meat delivered from the butcher, fell open to reveal a bejeweled knife. Not in a fancy box or packed with additional trimmings. Just the knife. Tiny enough to fit in a fob pocket. Or her boot.

With a laugh she wouldn't have been able to contain had the man who'd given the gift been sitting in the chamber with her, she picked it up and brought it close to her face.

An inscription was etched in silver.

To help navigate the waters.

That was what he'd told her the night he found her with her nose jammed in the velvet collar of his coat, struggling to catch his scent.

When he'd recognized her attraction.

Pippa flopped to her back, the present clutched in her fist. The metal heated against her skin like an ember plucked from the fire. With a vulgar growl the Duchess Society had said she must *not* utter in public, she punched the mattress in frustration. Xander Macauley remembered their stolen moment as well as she.

She'd not imagined his breathless wonder, the bounder.

It would be the best gift she received, the most personal. Damn and blast. Somehow, he'd seen her for one brief moment. The real girl.

Closing her eyes, she wondered how she would ever forget that fact.

PART ONE
REVELATION

Chapter One

Where a hero decides he must act to save the heroine

A soon-to-be-fashionable gambling establishment
Limehouse Docks, London, 1826

"The lass is at it again. The hulking bloke you assigned to follow her sent round a note."

Xander Macauley let loose a curse that rang through the deserted main floor of his hell, his gaze roaming the candlelight and dense shadow to settle on his factotum's deceptively angelic face. Xander had appointed the canny young Scot to oversee the hazard tables, luring him away from a thriving business teaching aristocrats how to cheat at dice and cards. Sharps and Flats, Dashiell Campbell had called the crooked enterprise. News of it had swept the *ton* like the stinking mist rolling off the Thames, with men traveling hundreds of miles to sit in the frigid back room of a rookery boarding house for instruction. Xander had taken a lesson or two himself and been amazed by his ingenious deceit. He didn't even want the lad to cheat; he wanted Dash to keep others from milking *him*.

"What did you tell him?"

Dash warmed a pair of dice between his palms and shifted from one scuffed boot to the other. "I dinna send the messenger away. Waiting for an answer, he is."

Macauley wiggled a cheroot from his pocket and jammed it between his lips, with no intention of lighting it as it was a habit he was breaking. He wished he could say he'd employed Dash only for profit. In truth, he'd not been able to imagine anything but a bleak future for a young man making formidable enemies by schooling others in the art of swindling. Overconfidence and base connections were a detrimental mix. It took power to keep the knife from your throat—and Xander was willing to share his. He'd come from less than nothing and would never forget his desperate struggle to climb out of the slums.

Even if he ruled from within them.

"Where is she?" he finally asked because there was no use avoiding the problem. Or the woman, apparently.

Dash clicked his tongue against his teeth, a tell that suggested he had unpleasant information to impart. "Right fine cauldron she's dipped her toe in this time. *Cor*, I'm nae judge on what's suitable for a duke's sister, but I reckon this ain't it."

Riled, Macauley shoved to his feet from his spot by the roulette wheel he'd been repairing, drawing a breath scented with the linseed oil used to polish the maple trim of the *vingt-et-un* tables. He didn't have time for this. Next week, The Devil's Lair would open with a private event for select members of society. He had menus to review, croupiers to train, a final checklist of construction items to approve. Macauley expected word-of-mouth following the gathering to bring nobs beating on his door, the only crimson door on the block, for acceptance he wasn't going to easily give. When he'd said he was opening an exclusive club, he meant *exclusive*.

The Devil's Lair would make White's look like a bordello.

His stomach danced with anticipation when it'd been *years* since he'd been excited about anything. Particularly a business venture. Money came easily now, as did women. Challenges were few and uninteresting when he stumbled upon them. Even smuggling had become tedious, mostly due to the repeated requests from his closest friend and partner, Tobias Streeter, to give it up.

"Too little return on the risk" was the common refrain. Falling flat on his face in love, and the marriage and children that had subsequently followed, had made Tobias, former rogue king of the Limehouse docks, a dull boy indeed.

Macauley was *never* going to be a dull boy. He'd made a promise long ago, and he wasn't reneging for love *or* money.

"Where?" he repeated, though he didn't want to know.

"Some masquerade rout at a bloke's named Talbot."

"*Talbot*," Macauley whispered, appalled despite himself. Lord Talbot was a degenerate of the worst sort, a wealthy baron on the ladder's lowest rung, who had no hope of climbing higher. And because of a roomy bank account, rare for the aristocracy, he had no need to.

Pippa Darlington had outdone herself this time.

Getting a dismal idea of how *this* evening would end, Macauley yanked a rag from his back pocket and wiped a streak of grease from his palm. The wheel had begun making this maddening squeak on the final turn, and the Lair, as Macauley had come to think of it, would be nothing less than perfect.

"Summon the Duke of Leighton. *Immediately*. I won't tell him how I know where his darling sister is, only that Lady Philippa has again gotten herself into a jam."

"Your partner, ain't he?"

"In the distillery. The shipping venture. And a steam locomotion gambit that's going to secure enough blunt to smooth every wrinkle from His Grace's brow for the rest of time. It will fund every estate resting on his ducal shoulders and buy him a fancy new one should he be of a mood. He's happy with me at the moment. No matter having a sibling who is the most troublesome in London. I can't do much for him there."

"The duke is in Bath. Remember? His duchess is expecting another wee bairn, and the waters are supposedly good for expectant mothers."

Macauley tossed the rag to the floor. How many godforsaken children was Leighton planning to *have*?

"Truthfully, you've got a gang of high-steppers in your life. Not one but *two* dukes. I dinna see the need meself."

Macauley scowled, unwilling to explain that there were three men he trusted with his life, and yes, two of them were sadly a rung below prince. "The Duke of Markham, then. His wife, Georgiana, is Lady Philippa's etiquette tutor. God help her. Markham's townhouse is on Curzon. If you leave now, you can be there in ten minutes. Expect the duchess to be disappointed about her charge's misstep. Disappointed, but not surprised." He scrubbed his hand over the back of his neck, his stomach giving a slight, anticipatory tilt. He wasn't going after her. He *wasn't*.

Dash tossed the dice from hand to hand, his expression as flat as his words. "Duchess Society. I heard about 'em. Matchmakers. Meddlesome lasses. Calling them tutors is putting a shine on a grimy piece."

With a snort, Macauley turned to skirt the baize-covered tables that were going to make him and this spirited young man he'd invited into his world blindingly wealthy. He was already blindingly wealthy. But the change in status would be a revelation for Dash, one Macauley couldn't help but wish to witness.

"Of a sort. The Duchess Society polishes off the rough edges for those who've gotten themselves in dire straits. When marriage with a dowry sizable enough to choke a horse attached to it is the only way out. They make sure the men are respectable, and the women are educated about the legalities. Frightening dealings when a chit has the upper hand. Get my meaning, mate? Stay on the good side of your finances, and you won't have to adjust your ways for *anyone*. I've never had to."

Dash raced to catch up with Macauley's long-legged stride. He was a strapping lad, but Macauley was nearly the tallest man in London and could outpace anyone. "No one's about, guv. That's why I'm coming to ye. Dukes Leighton and Markham, Tobias Streeter. All gone. I tried them when I got the message, seeing as ye were with your lady friend." Dash's gaze rose to the upper reaches of the hell, his brow arching in wicked masculine delight.

Macauley halted so suddenly that Dash's shoulder knocked his and threw them off balance. "You mean they left Lady Philippa alone?

When she's managed to entangle herself in one predicament after another this entire season?" Dumping ratafia on a handsy earl's head, which had caused the Duchess Society to recommend she skip *last* season, was nothing compared to what she'd done during *this* one.

"Aye, they did. After all, you've cleaned up the messes, so how is her family to ken what a disaster she is? No one has any fair idea of her mischief." Dash scratched his nose with the pointed edge of the die and shrugged in puzzlement. "Where I come from—Glasgow way, Paisley, if I'm putting a dart on the map—most lasses her age are already married with a babe or two clinging to their teat. A grown woman canna be left alone with a hundred servants at her beck and call and keep from tomfoolery?"

A prickle of alarm skittered along Macauley's spine. From somewhere down the corridor he heard Fast Fingers Eddie, who called himself Pierre, the chef who would make the Lair a destination for gambling *and* food, shouting orders to his staff. Why he was unhappy when Macauley had built him a kitchen that would rival Carlton House's was anyone's guess. Part and parcel of pretending he was French, Macauley supposed.

"What's she doing anyway that ye have to worry about?"

Macauley shook his head, bringing himself back to the conversation. "Lady Philippa is working behind the Duchess Society's backs. She's investigating prospective bridegrooms, then providing information as if it's been passed to her in a parlor along with the rest of the day's gossip. Why does no one understand what a danger she is to herself? Reckless termagant."

Dash tapped the dice on the rosewood-paneled wall. "They're buying what the lass is selling, that's why. The wallflower bit. I seen what the scandal sheets wrote about her. Uninspiring sister of a duke, etcetera, etcetera. They ken she's harmless. Just another wearisome society chit bleeding into the fancy fabric covering the plaster." He tilted his head to the side, his frown one of proper study. "It's the spectacles. And the hideous garb. That putrid yellow gown she wore to the dinner ye invited me to at her brother's house? Ghastly. The marquess there thought to pair her with left marks on the cobbles, he raced away so quickly."

Macauley gave his coat pocket, and the spectacles a physician had requested he use for reading in dim light, a vicious tap. As if he needed a reminder of how damned old he was getting. At least he actually required them. He bet Pippa's were clear glass. He'd love to take them from her just once and peer through them, proving his theory. "They're a ruse, like the rest. She's a raffish irritant with perfect eyesight and better taste than she's letting on. I knew her before she thought to play this insipid role." He couldn't understand how the *ton* missed the girl even with the ugly clothing and dull smile. Her eyes alone were enough to halt a man in his tracks. Macauley had only seen that particular shade of green in a gemstone. Often on some woman's trifles that lay glittering on his bedside table.

Society disregarded Philippa Darlington's vibrancy because they preferred she not have any.

And her hair...

No one in London could claim strands resting between burnt honey and freshly shorn wheat. A multitude of shades that sunlight *loved* to play with whenever she happened to step into a broad beam.

She was deluding herself if she thought a mere mask could hide her identity. He would know her *anywhere*.

"Heedless nuisance," Macauley said between clenched teeth, then stalked into the room he was using as an office until final construction on the space upstairs was complete. He had a mask in his desk somewhere, probably the bottom drawer where he kept the useless items.

"Wouldna made a good cardsharp, your nuisance. Nae so wise gigging about at parties where she shouldna, especially since her brother is a duke, and everyone wants her to fail for their amusement. But she's got guts. Guts can carry ye far in life."

"Or they can end it." Macauley shouldered into his coat, checked his boot for his knife, his pocket for his pistol, and wrenched open that bottom drawer to grab the mask. It was onyx with bright crimson etchings around the eyes. The memory of why it was in his desk—an exuberant opera singer with a penchant for games and coitus in chairs —made his stomach twist into a hard knot.

Pippa was getting worse. Set to either give up the ghost, marry someone she would end up hating, or implode from pretending to be a typical girl when she was *not* a typical girl. Playing a role she was wholly unsuited for, covering her true self with a shroud that was weighing her down like an anchor.

Macauley knew all about pretending.

He was getting worse, too, exhausted from living this life he'd built for himself. Women, fisticuffs, contraband, blunt. He felt all his thirty-two years and ages more as he gazed in the cheval mirror above his bureau on the odd occasion and wondered who the hell he'd become. When it had started out differently.

Christ, he didn't want to think about the past now.

"What do ye care if the girl ruins herself?" Dash asked from his negligent slouch in the doorway, lingering like a guest not actually invited to the party.

Family, Macauley thought before he could stop himself. Or close to it. He and Leighton were friends. Partners. And the man's little sister was making terrible choices without anyone to pull her back. Macauley's attraction to her—and in the whispery depths of his mind, he admitted there was one—wasn't the reason he was going after her. It was the bloody reason he ought *not*.

"Be careful, guv. The blue-blooded ones love a bit of the stews. Dangerous, that, for both of ye."

Macauley yanked on his gloves and brushed past his factotum, who stepped aside with raised hands as if his counsel had been retracted.

"It isn't like that," Macauley murmured. When it wasn't.

Although it was. A little.

Damned if he hadn't had this argument with himself before.

Philippa Darlington was too young. Too impulsive. Too clever. Although he *liked* clever women. But not this one. Leighton, friend or not, would return the favor from years ago and toss him in the Thames if he dared touch her. And Macauley was never—*never*—attaching himself to a person in the way Leighton had. The way the Duke of Markham had. Hell, Tobias Streeter, was his best friend and the last man on this earth he'd have expected to fall. They were all sunk. Marriage was like the pox; something he was terrified of catching.

Macauley had tried to stay out of Pippa's path since the troubling incident two years ago—when she'd stumbled upon him in the gaming room at Leighton's country estate, and he'd had an insane, half-drunken urge to kiss her. He'd been stunned to catch her with her nose pressed against his coat, her lids fluttering like they would when she came. The sad truth was, his heart raced ahead of him on the rare occasion when they were in the same room.

He'd avoided her so often Leighton thought he was avoiding *him*.

Add to this catastrophe the impulsive birthday gift he'd given her last year. That silly knife he'd searched all over London for. Why he hadn't been able to simply disregard the day, he wasn't sure, although he'd disregarded the party. The invitation to the ball in her honor had sat there like a smoking pyrotechnic until he'd gotten drunk and pitched it in the hearth.

It was the startling way she watched him during the infrequent instances when he could *not* escape her. Like the moment mattered, like *he* mattered.

Maybe it was a game to her, this wordless flirtation. When she'd thought to teach him to play chess that night in the country, her fingers all over those marble pieces had made him imagine them wrapped around his—

He spun to face his factotum, his knees weak. When Macauley was not a man used to being weak-kneed, even with a blade pressed to his neck. "Escort Lady Bergeron home, will you? With my apologies."

Dash coughed into his fist, his cheeks firing. "She'll wait for ye. They always do."

Macauley bumped open the door to the alley entrance with his shoulder and stepped into the stormy night, an ache of what he suspected was loneliness zinging through him. A bitter gust blew past, tugging at the lapels of his greatcoat and sending the swollen aroma of London into his nose.

Someone he didn't truly desire in his bed, both of them wishing it meant more?

Aye, a lifetime of that brand of despair was what he feared most.

Chapter Two

Where a reckless heroine gets the hero into trouble

Attending Talbot's masquerade ball had been a dreadful mistake. An impulsive decision. With good intent but still a disaster.

Lady Philippa Darlington pondered this as she peered around the sculpture at the foxed couple who'd stumbled into view, their wobbly steps almost sending them into a thicket of hydrangea shrubs. In an effort to avoid the unwanted attention of a debauched viscount with a reputation as vile as any in London, Pippa had stolen away to Talbot's side garden.

While she debated what to do, the couple found a vacant bench and started making titillating use of it. Pippa's lips parted, a jagged edge on the stone nicking her taffeta gown as she leaned in to get a better view. Her cheeks heated beneath her mask.

Who would have guessed one could do that *outside?*

Intrigued by the amorous display—when she should look away, *run away*—Pippa chewed on her gloved thumb and weighed her options. *Damn and blast.* If she left her hiding spot, they would see her. Which wouldn't be cricket since the couple was going to the trouble of changing positions. Pippa tilted her head. The man had moved behind the woman, mounting her like her brother's dog, Darla, had mounted that hound they'd come across in Hyde Park last summer. Now, Roan and Helena had five half-hound, half-terrier puppies running loose on their estate grounds.

When the ardent groans and whispered entreaties began to escalate, Pippa searched for a means of escape. There was only one way out, a twisting gravel path leading directly past a carnal display no lady should witness outside her marital bedchamber.

Perhaps not there, either, if the stories she'd heard were true.

If Hildegard Streeter or Georgiana Munro, the Duchess of Markham, could see her now, the proprietresses of the Duchess Society and her occasional instructors would faint dead away.

This entire debacle had simply been Pippa's way of trying to help.

Wouldn't Georgie and Hildy want to know that Lord Dane-Hart had a predilection for certain activities that meant he could never be a proper husband for one of their clients? As risky as it had been, attending this ball was the only way to determine if what was rumored about the man was true. After all, he'd lied about everything on his application to the Duchess Society.

The wind ripped at her cloak, and Pippa glanced at a sky leaden with the promise of a brutal storm. How much longer would the couple take? Pippa had heard in hushed comments that the act was thankfully brief.

She'd imagined three minutes, perhaps five.

Closing her eyes, she pressed her cheek against the sculpted sandstone chest of a Greek god of uncertain origin, wondering how to get herself out of this mess.

This was what she got for stepping outside her brother's Mayfair terrace, where she supposed she belonged even if she didn't want to admit it. Disaster occurred whenever she tried to elude her banal existence. But a masquerade was safe, wasn't it? Even one where clothing was optional and the host was rumored to be partial to engaging in relations with anything—man, woman, or beast. No one would recognize her. She'd worn an appalling gown and padded her otherwise petite form in all the right places. She'd even taken the extreme but necessary measure of darkening her hair with powder she'd been saving for such a mission.

Perhaps it was fate, being stuck watching a couple tup on a bench, her hair smelling like an old codger's mustache, the sky minutes from raining hell down on her. Her maid, Viviette, whom she'd paid two pounds to keep quiet about the night's festivities, had finally convinced her of the insanity of this pursuit and gone in search of their footman. This occurred after a woman dressed as a shepherdess had shown her breast to the crowd bordering the ballroom's glossy marble floor. A perfectly round, pink-tipped breast. Against good judgment and sound sense, Pippa had been mesmerized by the sight.

As had most of the men in the room.

Mournfully, Pippa realized her breasts were not as bountiful.

Like the whack of a ruler across her knuckles, her mind went to the advice of her tutors, Georgie and Hildy, who reminded her to repeat it daily.

I am refined. I am elegant. I will someday be a fully baked cake.

When Pippa was none of those things. She was a *half*-baked cake, crisped on the edges and gooey inside, unrefined and inelegant. She had a curious thirst for life that no one in society outside her family seemed to share. Thrust into the role of duke's sister too late in life, after her opinions and habits were formed, she was wading through the morass as well as expected. When the expectation was *perfection*. At least to herself, she'd proven to be a hopeless girl playing a pointless game with society.

A game that had begun to feel like her actual *life*.

Mercifully, the season was coming to a close, and she'd survived without scandal. Or an unwelcome proposal being placed before her. Thanks in part to the vigilant efforts of the Duchess Society and her sister-in-law, Helena, who believed one should marry for love or not marry at all. But she didn't feel successful or particularly happy. Pippa had played a wallflower so convincingly, even she wasn't sure who she was anymore. Posing as a feather-wit—when only those who knew her understood it was a con—had started to turn her into one.

Exasperated, restless, and unfulfilled, Pippa dragged her thumb over a chipped spot on the statue and blew the ostrich feather dangling from her hat out of her eyes. She was taking chances no woman in her set would ever dream of taking to wake herself up.

However, it wasn't only her reputation on the line anymore. Pippa was an aunt and, unbelievably, a sister. Roan's marriage to Helena had changed everything. Helena had brought her half-sister, Theodosia, to live with them. A bookish, charming girl Pippa loved with all her heart. And there were children in the house, too, along with puppies. In another four months or so, there would be another. Helena had announced her pregnancy last week. A little girl, Pippa hoped. A sister for her nephews, Alexander and Alistair.

Except for her love for her brother, the emotion was a comfort Pippa had never allowed herself to fully embrace. Her parents had been cruel and unlovable—and then they'd been gone—their union leaving a wisp of bitter memories. Her brother's marriage, however, was giving her hope.

Nevertheless, even with the sound of laughter spiraling through the townhouse, the scent of sugar biscuits rippling through a nursery brimming with love, a shiver of dread shook Pippa when she gazed in the mirror.

Why couldn't these people, the first family she and Roan had ever had, fill the gaping chasm inside her?

Somehow, they could not. Not completely.

The hair on the back of Pippa's neck prickled, and she turned her head in alarm.

There was only one person in the entire *world* she sensed before she actually saw him.

"Hello, Little Darlington," Xander Macauley whispered as he stepped through the dense copse of azaleas bordering the garden, his broad body crowding hers against the chilled stone. It must be wonderful, she seethed, another boon to being a man, to be able to wear clothing that allowed one to arrive without a whisper of silk or lace sharing your confidences.

His silvery eyes glittered beneath his mask as if he read her thoughts, his smile a feral twist. "Imagine finding you here. At a masquerade where, as I noted while searching Talbot's manse for you, is getting more fascinating by the minute. *Ruinously* fascinating, if you take my meaning. I'm relieved to find you away from the debauchery and not wallowing knee-deep in it. That is tonight's meager windfall and one I shall seize."

Pippa let a pained breath slide free, her blood shimmering as it always did when he stepped into view. The knife he'd given her for her birthday came to life in her boot, the metal seeming to pulse against her skin. She'd had a custom sheath made especially for an item she never left the house without. Distressed, she turned her gaze away before she began to pick apart the splendor of him, his long body looming over hers in the shadows.

Unlike any man of her acquaintance, he was a wonder, pure brawny magnificence. A fact he didn't need to know. Beautiful but rough around the edges. His hair was thick and slightly curly, not a lot, merely enough to encourage the wanton need to tangle your fingers in the strands.

She would think the attraction only hers, an oddity. However, enough women in London desired him, invited to his bed with disturbing regularity. Once or twice a week, according to the scandal rags.

Warmth radiated from his skin to strike her back like sunlight as he moved closer. Through layers, she could feel his heat. Then making it a hundred times worse, his hand brushed her hip, padded beyond any hope of him touching her, but enough of a caress to make her breath seize. "*What* are you wearing?"

She swallowed hard, shaking off the sensation gripping her. "It's a disguise."

"Disguise." He snorted softly, an unflattering assessment, and gave a lock of hair at the back of her head a tug. A gesture that sent awareness twisting through her. "You missed a strand. It's glimmering in the light like a stalk of wheat lying atop coal dust."

"No one recognized me, I swear."

"I'm guessing Leighton has no idea about this hobby of yours. His sister attending raucous celebrations with the underbelly of society? I know what you're up to, you reckless chit. Gathering information for the Duchess Society when I'm fairly certain Georgie and Hildy never asked for your assistance. I'd make a bloody able investigator. Fetching simple, innit?"

She stilled in stunned bewilderment. How did he know? But he knew. And there was no use arguing with the most pigheaded man in England. "Talbot is a *baron*, Mr. Macauley. Hardly underbelly." She waved her hand negligently toward the terrace. "My maid, Viviette, is awaiting my return. My footman as well. This is utterly appropriate. Although your attendance may make me change my opinion."

"Sorry to rescript your fairy-tale narrative, but I sent your faithless maid home in that rented hack. She was quaking in her scuffed boots, ready to tell Leighton everything. I discharged your leased coachman, paid him five quid to forget his mistaken conviction that he'd squired the Duke of Leighton's hellion of a sister to a ball where women are *paid* to attend. Viviette was a babbling brook of information. Incredibly helpful. Directed me right to you. All I had to do was double your kickback to guarantee her silence. Honestly, not the cheapest night's entertainment I've ever had between the two of them."

Pippa cursed faintly, praying, *oh*, just *praying* he heard her.

"Don't be vexed with your maid, Blondie. She's a smart businesswoman, our Viviette. Merely demanding what the market is willing to pay. As for this event being acceptable, your upstanding *baron* is currently sprawled atop his billiards table being—" Macauley's words evaporated as he stepped forward, his boot striking the sculpture's base with a thud.

"Oh, *hell*," he hissed through his teeth, his gaze settling enough in the dim light to see the couple who'd again, remarkably, changed positions. The man was now standing, the woman's legs wrapped around his waist like a bow tied around a present. His large hand was cupped, holding her up by her bottom. They'd even decided to use the trunk of a nearby cedar for support. They were an ingenious duo, that was certain.

With the raw image burned in her mind and her secret obsession trapping her between his hard body and a stone god's, it wasn't Pippa's fault, really, it *wasn't*, if the image changed to one where *her* legs were wrapped around Macauley's lean waist, his hand curved around her—

With a rush of exhilaration that took her breath and weakened her knees, Pippa sighed and knocked her head against the sculpture, praying for deliverance.

Hearing her response, Macauley's hand flew up to cover her eyes. "You're leaving. *Now*." His voice was deadly. But beneath the anger, it trembled.

She wasn't experienced enough to examine what could cause this to occur. Could he be affected by the scene unfolding before them, with his veritable overabundance of knowledge? The mere thought warmed her in places Xander Macauley should *never* reach.

But reach them, he did. As he always had.

For several seconds, neither of them moved. Their delicate exhalations mingling with the echoes of revelry flowing through the terrace windows and the sound of a couple tupping a short distance away. Macauley hadn't shifted his hand from where it lay over her mask, so she couldn't see anything. His fingers smelled of tobacco and soap. His breath stirred the damp hair clinging to her skin. His body muscled and firm where it touched hers, affected in ways he was apparently finding it impossible to hide.

Yearning, fierce and powerful, rose in her, a rolling tide of recognition.

He was the biggest secret of the many she held locked within her. Xander Macauley, king of the underworld, a thieving, rookery scoundrel, was the only man who had ever made her feel *anything*.

She curled her fingers into fists. Why, why, *why* did it have to be him she wanted to do unspeakable things to her? He was entirely wrong for her, her attraction a disaster should it be exposed.

The list was endless, one she'd fashioned a thousand times in her mind.

He was a rake, a smuggler, a *commoner*. Rumored to have been raised in a workhouse, which must be true because he rarely stepped far from the Limehouse docks. He was too old for her. He raced phaetons down darkened city streets. Tossed men he brawled with, her brother once, into the Thames. Entertained light-skirts and changed mistresses as often as he did his greatcoat. Created the finest whisky in the country at his distillery while managing a flourishing shipping enterprise with what she'd heard was brilliant efficiency.

His life was every last thing she wanted hers to be. Meaningful. And *exciting*.

He seemed to know who he *was* when she'd never been sure of this.

However, his unsuitability was truly established because he was her brother's best friend. Or close to it, outside of Tobias Streeter. Macauley was Roan's business partner. The man who was going to help a reluctant duke free himself from the financial obligations weighing him down since he'd unexpectedly assumed a title no one had expected him to assume.

She couldn't wreck their partnership by exposing a preoccupation that had as much chance of surviving as a banana tree in London. Not when the Duke of Leighton needed Xander Macauley more than she ever would. Not when he found her to be a nuisance, a bothersome gnat, a gopher tearing through his flower beds. Not when his lips turned low every blasted time he looked at her. If he knew her heart skipped every time she saw *him*, he would laugh his gorgeous head off. It was enough to be mildly infatuated and have to watch him romp around town like a hungry canine.

Infuriated with herself as much as him, she attempted to step free of him. "Let me by, you cur. I'm not taking a dressing-down from you of all people."

With a snarl, he turned her in the loose circle of his arms. Forced her chin high with the calloused tip of his finger until she could only open her eyes and look at him. Let his heat consume her like she'd stepped into a steaming bath. He had a streak of grease on his cheek. He was unshaven, his stubborn jaw covered with grainy stubble as dark as the sky above them. His chestnut hair lay in tangled disarray across his brow, no cravat about his neck, no hat upon his head. Except for the onyx mask, he didn't look like a man who'd planned to attend a masquerade this evening.

Pippa jerked her head from his grasp. "How did you know I was here?"

Tearing his smoky gaze from hers, he glanced over her shoulder, his exhalation fast and furious, his body tensing, telling her the couple had not yet finished the race. "I've had you followed for weeks. Call it intuition on my part, but a high-spirited chit roaming the streets at great danger to herself made the hairs on the back of my neck stand up every time I.thought about it. For lack of a better way to phrase it, my surveillance mission began after that idiotic musicale at Lady Pontheiu's, which I only attended because he's buying what I'm selling. Lord Wilmington-Biles made sly mention of meeting you in a parlor of infrequent use for what he termed 'great fun,' as if I'd support his efforts to corrupt my business partner's little sister." Macauley tapped his temple, white teeth flashing with his savage smile. "In an instant, I caught your plan. To trap him and play hero for the Duchess Society. You foolish, foolish girl."

Pippa chewed on her gloved thumb while debating how to respond, slightly encouraged when his molten gaze tracked the movement. His smile flattened as a charming pleat appeared between his brows.

Although he didn't look away, not for one second.

Losing patience, his hands grasped her shoulders, giving her a gentle shake. "Who do you suppose caused the diversion that allowed you to flee the Earl of Kinsley's orangery before being found crouching behind that mound of potting soil? I had to send the bloke five citrus trees in payment for the window casing I shattered with a well-placed and timely kick. Citrus is quite costly, as most die during shipment.

"And because I disrupted his passionate interlude instead of *you* disrupting it, your plan, I gather, he thinks I have a fixation on his soon-to-be departed paramour. Departed, because the Duchess Society is going to demand he leave Miss Danbury if he hopes to gain their assistance locating a suitable countess. Suitable as in deep pockets and leagues of tolerance with masculine absurdity. Thanks to my helping you *and* keeping your brother out of this confusion, I might add, Miss Danbury has shown up at my townhouse twice in the past month. She believes that *I*, as an interested party, should be *her* next patron."

Pippa's belly twisted, and she shot him a hostile glare. Evelyn Danbury was radiant beyond description. Enough to make men overlook her humble beginnings as the daughter of an opera singer and a dockworker. "Maybe I did you a favor then, sending a stunning woman to your door. Delivery of the finest London has to offer without any effort on your part. She's your style from what I've heard."

He didn't comment. Merely continued to watch her until the air around them ignited with the startling recognition it had that night at Roan's country estate. The gears of time ground to a halt until it was just the two of them. Unbidden, Pippa's gaze dropped to his lips when they parted. The lower chapped, as if he routinely brought it between his teeth in contemplation. His jaw hard, his body magnificent. His broad chest rose and fell on a sigh.

He was the most attractive man in all of England.

She had this stolen moment with him, so why not take it? The gentle whisper of his breath against her cheek. The unique scent of soap and something she couldn't quite place drifting from his skin. The pulse beneath his ear flickering in time to the passing seconds. His long lashes lowering to hide anything his steely gaze might reveal. Thunder sounded in the distance as a profuse mist swirled past.

A raindrop hit his cheek, rolled down his jaw, and he scrubbed it away. "Maybe I'll take her up on her offer. Miss Danbury *is* my style, come to think of it."

Why had it sounded like a dare a man issued when cornered?

If he moved closer, just a hair. If she followed, brought her arms around his neck and—

The echo of shattering glass had them jumping apart, turning toward the townhouse to see flames shooting from a window on the ground floor. The next gust brought the acrid aroma of burnt fabric and charred wood that she'd somehow missed in her Xander Macauley-induced trance.

Macauley swore and shoved her back against the sculpture as the passionate couple scurried away from the madness after much straightening of attire. Then with shouts of dismay, a crowd of drunken carousers poured from the terrace's French doors, scattering as they made their way across the lawn, spilling into the street fronting the manse.

Macauley tunneled his hand through his hair, debating his role in this muddle she could see. "Candles, liquor, and carousing make for anarchy," he whispered mostly to himself.

Another window shattered, this one on the first floor, and Pippa instinctively lifted her arm to shield her face.

"Bloody *hell*," Macauley gritted between clenched teeth. Then like the brute he was, he hooked his arm about her knees and hoisted her effortlessly over his shoulder, much like he would a sack of dirty clothing.

She beat soundly on his lower back, impressed by the arrogant display but unwilling to accept it. The rain had slicked his woolen coat to his back, his linen trousers to his tight bottom. She couldn't help but admire the taut muscle as it shifted with his ground-eating stride across the lawn. Shards of glass cracked beneath his Wellingtons, and he skated over a muddy patch before righting himself. "Macauley, put me down this *instant*."

"I have an idea, mate. Why don't you tell your brother I've handled you so disrespectfully?" He laughed, sounding anything but amused. "*Ah*, dear me, then you'd have to tell Leighton about your ridiculous secret life. And I'd have to disclose my ill-advised involvement and suffer as his fist smashes my jaw."

A violent gust obliterated her chignon, sending bejeweled hairpins into the muck. Her mask tumbled free to be crushed beneath his next sodden step. She socked his hip and struggled within his tight hold. "I'm not your *mate*."

The wind howled as he stepped off the gravel path and into the street. The rain had begun to arrive in sheets, which would make any travel they attempted very difficult. "You're damned right you're not," he growled and paused only long enough to wrench open the carriage door, then he tossed her atop the velvet squabs without care. Hauling her ruined skirt past her knees, she whipped the drenched mass of hair from her face to find him standing by the conveyance, muttering to himself. Drumming his fist on the side of the carriage in an indignant rhythm as the coachman watched in trepidation.

"I should have known. My bloody payment for getting involved." Macauley threw a quick glance at the blaze erupting from an upstairs window and released a furious breath. Thankfully, Talbot's house was a standalone dwelling, or the city would have been at risk of going up in flames.

A parade of soaked partygoers were streaming out like rats from a sinking ship, their garish costumes plastered to their bodies, feet mired ankle-deep in mud. One of them, a footman in wrecked attire, skidded to a halt beside them. "Xander Macauley, ain't you? Tobias Streeter's smuggling partner?"

Reaching into the carriage, Macauley snatched a lap blanket from the floorboard and tossed it over Pippa's head. "Shut it," he ordered. Turning to the servant with a sigh, he ripped his mask from his face and flung it aside.

Incensed but understanding she, for once, needed to follow orders, Pippa peeked from a rip in the blanket to see the footman gesturing wildly and wringing his hands. "Sorry to expose ye during this madness, sir. It's the height, it were. Yet, no man can match ye in London. And no mask can hide ye either." He jacked his thumb toward the smoldering townhouse with a pained grimace. "There's still some inside. My darling girl, Janie, a scullery maid come up from Brighton just last month, is nowhere to be seen."

He wiped his nose and sniffled, rain streaking down his flushed cheeks and over his parted lips. "Talbot raced out like the flames was eating through his polished boots, he did. Just said 'run' and caused the greatest panic. Coward of the worst sort, the man is. My cousin works for ye and Streeter at the distillery. Says you're a hero to the Limehouse folks, contributing to the neighborhood like ye do. I thought to ask because I don't know who else to. Some are trying to locate the lord's hand pump, but this dwelling being only part stone means it won't last long. I say focus on the living and breathing still inside and let the house go."

"*Johnnie*," Macauley shouted, "come down. I need assistance."

The coachman obeyed immediately, lumbering off his seat and to the ground. He had the face of a pugilist who had lost many a match but the brawn of a man unafraid of being opposed.

Macauley pointed to the carriage interior, his gravelly voice rising over the distant peel of thunder and the crackle of a building being consumed by flame. "Keep this troublesome brat inside this vehicle. No matter what she says or offers to pay you. If I don't come back in ten minutes, take her home. She'll tell you where. Back entrance, for

God's sake. At all costs, we want to avoid her family knowing about this. She's a lady, so-called, if you can't tell, which after this evening, you might not be able to. Dashiell Campbell is here in this chaos, *somewhere* in this chaos. If he comes back before I do, leave. As you know, the boy is quick on his feet. Follow his instruction."

Johnnie saluted, the turmoil unfolding around them not overly concerning it seemed. "Aye, aye, Mac."

"We're not on the high seas," Pippa intoned from beneath her shroud.

Macauley leaned in, his tantalizing scent sneaking in behind him. *Oh,* the man smelled like a slice of heaven. She tried to scoot out of reach, but he caught her. Hooked his long finger under the worn edge of the blanket, lifting it just high enough to catch her gaze. Raindrops glistened on his lashes, highlighting eyes the color of the sodden ash raining down around them. His lips were set in a solid, dogged line. He looked fierce, powerful and, admittedly, exquisite. Nothing new to her mind.

Unexpectedly, Pippa had the desperate urge to keep him from leaving. To keep him safe.

She grasped his sleeve in her fist, mouthed *don't*. Swallowed and tried again. "Macauley, it isn't safe."

"Indeed, that *is* news." He stabbed his finger in her face. "Stay here, and I damn-well mean that. I'll tell Leighton every horrid detail of this season if you challenge me. Every. Horrid. Detail. Not one inch, luv. I'll only be distracted if you come. What do you hope to do, put out the blaze with a bucket of ratafia?"

Then he turned, and along with the frantic footman in search of his love, raced toward the inferno without looking back.

Pippa sat motionless, tears stinging her eyes, the blanket that had begun to smell of hell fires and spring squalls falling to her shoulders. The arrogant cur would bring up the ratafia incident. Was she not allowed to protect herself from an ogling earl, using the only weapon at her disposal?

She yanked the blanket away and tossed it to the floor, feeble protection against the disaster she'd once again brought on herself. This time, disaster brought upon Xander Macauley as well. A man who never refused a challenge. He was mad. Except for her blasted Lime-house hero and a lovestruck footman, men were *fleeing* the doomed dwelling, not going in.

As the roof of the townhouse partially collapsed with a wheezy gasp, Pippa released a prayer for a man she had no reason, aside from a clandestine enthrallment, to pray for.

Chapter Three

Where a reckless heroine rescues the hero

The quick-on-his-feet boy showed up fifteen minutes later. A year or two younger than Pippa, more a young man than a lad, Dashiell Campbell had a face that, once seen, was not easily forgotten. Arresting good looks she guessed were more trouble than they were worth.

Dash peered into the carriage with a puzzled expression, his pale blue eyes brilliant amidst his sooty skin. "The guv works quickly, he does. Come alone but willna go home as such. Gathers 'em up even amid misfortune."

Pippa scowled. She *bet* the rotten knave worked quickly.

"It's not like that," Pippa said, without disclosing who she was or why she was sitting unchaperoned in a profligate's vehicle in a storm unlike any London had seen in years.

The ferocious rainfall had doused the fire, although the building smoldered, releasing a milky, blackened plume into the sky. The hand-pump engine never arrived, and the paltry crowd surrounding the house wandered the lawn in confusion, carrying items they'd taken from the house. Lord Talbot was nowhere to be seen.

"Dinna he come back yet?" Dash swiped his wrist across his cheek, leaving a streak of inky ash. "I saw him nae five minutes ago, he and another hulking bloke hauling some portly toff to the back lawn. They've gathered the injured in the stables. No one dead, at last count. Ripping good luck if that's the end story. Though the house is nevermore."

A deafening crash sounded, and Pippa twisted her fingers together. Her gloves were as much a goner as Talbot's manse. Stripping them off, she tossed them to the seat with a sigh. "Why would he do this? Run into a burning building of all things?"

Dash swallowed hard, his gaze searching the seared ruins. He looked worried, which didn't make Pippa feel better about the situation. "Bleeding heart, he is. Whether he admits it or nae. Why I'm working with him, truth be told. Trying to save me from a horrid fate when maybe the horrid fate is mine to own. Anyway, my gran always said ye canna change the core of a man, you ken?"

"Bleeding heart?" *Xander Macauley?* Prince of the Limehouse docks?

Johnnie piped in from his resumed perch on the coachman's seat. "Quit your philosophizing and get in, lad. I was instructed to shove off once you arrived. Quick like, no delay. Them's the boss's orders, and the boss's orders are the ones I follow. I've already waited past what I shoulda."

Dash propped his muddy boot on the step, clearly hesitant to relinquish his post. "This ain't a vessel lolling in port, my friend. You're on land now, nae the sea. I dinna feel good leaving the guv like this."

Pippa didn't either.

"My lady," Johnnie said, appealing to her as Dash seemed immovable. "We need ta leave. I can't promise to manage on these mud-pocked roads even. If she gets stuck, we'll have to go on foot. I can scarcely see five paces in front of me as it is. So deliver ya' home safely, I'm gonna do."

Pippa leaned out, straining to see through the gray wash drenching the world. "Five more minutes. Just five, then we go."

She was about to argue for Dash returning to look for Macauley when he stumbled into view, appearing through the rolling layers of mist as he made his way down the gravel drive. The wind tore at his clothing, rain washing down his long, lean body in rivulets. He'd lost his coat and part of one shirtsleeve somewhere along the way. When he got closer, she noticed he held his right arm carefully against his belly and the missing sleeve had been burned off. Dash made to go to him, but he shook his head.

When he finally reached them, he halted, pressing his brow to the doorframe, breathing heavily, his body shaking. He had a gash on his temple, trailing blood down his face. His skin glowed unnaturally from the blaze, scorched beneath a thick layer of soot. His hair was filthy, covered in ash and grit.

The carriage rocked as Johnnie twisted to look at Macauley. "The roads are nigh impassable. We'd best shove off if we hope to make it Limehouse way, boss. Ya did all ya could with this pile. Leave it to the lord of the blasted manor. Raced off down the lane in a rented hack, I seen him with his doxy on the seat next to him. Didn't even try to help his domestics find their way out. Posh coward."

"I located the scullery maid," Macauley whispered, his voice raw. "Cowering under an escritoire... in the back parlor. Rescued three more from a linen closet before part of a wall, I think it was... tumbled on me." His words ended with a brutal coughing spell that tightened her belly. Smoke inhalation could be deadly.

As could a wall tumbling on you.

Before she could stop herself, Pippa slipped her hand under his elbow and drew him gently into the carriage, rain trailing in around him to puddle on the floor. Macauley's erratic pulse bounded beneath her fingertips. His helplessness, something she'd never witnessed, squeezed her heart.

Looking over his head, she caught Dash's gaze. *Help me.*

Dash swiftly stepped in to assist. They both realized how weak Macauley was when he didn't argue, merely let them support him, then sprawled across the seat with an anguished groan, his long legs spilling into the meager space between them. The arm he cradled against his side hung at an odd angle. His shoulder was dislocated if Pippa had to guess. Roan had done the same to his one summer after falling from his mount. He'd passed dead away from the pain and had been unable to ride for weeks.

Dash banged on the roof to alert the coachman and perched warily on the seat beside her as Macauley took up the entirety of the squab across from them. They jerked into motion, the conveyance swaying as it encountered the ruts in the road caused by the storm.

"When we get him home, you need to go for a bonesetter immediately. When injuries like this are allowed to heal on their own, it can be detrimental. Especially with the primary arm. I believe he's right-handed." A fact she should not have known but did.

Dash nodded, composed but pale, his boot tapping out a nervous ditty on the floorboard. "Aye, busted shoulder from the look of it."

She hoped it was only the shoulder. He possibly had a concussed brain, too.

Macauley's lids fluttered, his gaze meeting hers across the distance. His enlarged pupils flooded his eyes, turning them a compelling, murky gray. He looked bewildered but typically unyielding. "No bonesetter." This pronouncement ended with a flurry of coughing that seized his body. He swore and tucked his injured arm tighter against his belly, his eyes closing.

Dash grasped the leather ceiling strap when they hit a brutal rut, the carriage tilting ominously. "I ken of one. Two streets over from the hell. A croupier got his hand smashed beneath a hazard table last week whilst we tried to move it. The minute we arrive, I'll be off to get him. He willna dare refuse a request from Xander Macauley, prince of the docks. Or the Duke of Leighton, if we have to use a fookin' nob's name to get the deed done. Supposing your brother willna mind, you ken?"

Pippa turned to stare at the lad, her lips parting on a stunned exhalation. Roan was going to kill her. This disaster was worsening by the minute. If a young man she'd met perhaps twice in her life recognized her as the Duke of Leighton's sister, everyone she'd seen this evening had.

"We're headed to Mr. Macauley's gaming hell? I assumed we were going to his Hanover Square terrace. That's a few streets over from my brother's. I could make a run for it, sneak in the servants' entrance with none the wiser." She wasn't above paying anyone she encountered for their silence with the pin money stuffed beneath her mattress.

Dash glanced at the rugged cityscape swimming past the rain-streaked windowpane, as if she should have known the direction they traveled toward wasn't Mayfair.

"We can't make it that far... in this weather," Macauley murmured in a pained whisper. They hit another furrow. The transport floundered, rocking back and forth before the coachman steadied them, and they were able to continue. "Hold on to her..."

He pushed a heavy breath through his nostrils, his fingers folding into a fist. A trickle of blood trailed down his cheek, and Pippa's heart hammered against her ribs. His cuff was crisped and curling at the edges, a sinister reminder of this night. "Listen to me, mate. I can't have her bruised on my watch."

Dash's gangly arm locked around Pippa, pulling her into his side. No one was going to argue with Xander Macauley.

"Ollie," he whispered, his gaze going to Dash.

Scooting forward, Dash leaned over his employer. "Guv, you're nae expiring. Those were expiring instructions. I dinna think we're near the end."

Macauley took a rattling breath and, with his good hand, tapped his temple, then his chest. "It only feels like it. With smoke, one never knows." He laughed softly, his tongue coming out to moisten his lips. "If the lady should still be there... at the hell..." He gestured weakly to Pippa. "Remove her."

Oh, she thought. *You lousy cur.* He'd left a woman in his bed. Pippa hoped against hope he'd gotten the message from his spy about her activities *before* he'd completed the act. She'd love to know she'd ruined one passionate interlude out of the thousands he was rumored to have had.

Suddenly, she recalled what Macauley had murmured moments ago. "Ollie?"

Dash's arm tensed around her. Then they hit another rut and bounced, landing hard enough for Macauley to cry out from the force.

"It's nae my wee secret to tell, lass."

Secrets.

Pippa settled against the squab, her gaze locked on the man who would finally share a piece of his life with her.

Even if entirely against his will.

Pippa traversed the room she'd been escorted to moments after they arrived at the gaming hell. She'd barely had time to record anything about the place as a husky majordomo of the criminal variety dragged her across the main floor and up a back staircase without a word of explanation—when her mind was buzzing with curiosity. Women of her class never, *ever* got to see the inside of a gambling den. Velvet and brocade, gilded columns, gilt-embossed leather paneling, handsome mahogany cabinets, damask armchairs in various pleasing masculine colors. Crystal decanters on every ready surface, chandeliers much grander than any in her brother's townhouse hanging above baize-covered tables arranged in an improbably poised display. The scent of cigars and brandy and, unbelievably, roasted duck and plum sauce in the background.

It was unlike anything her imagination could have conjured, more palace than club. A palace in the middle of a *slum*. A newly constructed castle that she knew in her bones would turn this town on its ear. The gossip rags were brimming with stories about the opening and how the nobility were begging for entrance before they'd stepped foot inside.

Pippa laughed softly and spun her birthday knife in her hand. When Xander Macauley set out to rule the world, he set out to *rule* the world. Or perhaps, in this filthy little district, he'd set out to change it forever.

Halting by the window of her temporary gaol, Pippa nudged crimson velvet aside with her blade to see the woman she presumed they'd booted from Macauley's bed scramble into a carriage. The fancy feathered hat smashed atop her head a soggy mess. There wasn't a speck of moonlight to soften her visage, make the scene one of romance instead of humiliation. Only the warm glow of the transport's sconce. And a ripping gale sending rubbish and other unmentionables tumbling down the alley past her.

She looked expensive and enraged. As Macauley probably liked them.

Pippa fingered the silk tassel circling the drape, dragging the blade's pointed tip across glass free of so much as one streak. She breathed deeply of the tidy fragrance of beeswax and linseed oil. Trailed her hand across the glossy surface of a massive rosewood desk, the centerpiece of the room, as she passed it. This was a study she'd have expected to find in a lord's residence, not in a rookery gaming hell. Tasteful, every piece in the place. Circumspect wealth and masculine elegance on display. Pippa had grown up humbly. She remembered what poverty looked and *felt* like. This wasn't it.

She paused by a bookcase crammed with cracked leather spines, her mind recording fact, not fiction. Macauley owned books he actually *read*.

Who was he if he was not the ruffian society assumed him to be?

"He can read," a rueful voice sounded from the doorway. "Quite well, in fact. He presents a convincing ruse. More convincing by the day."

Pippa turned with a startled breath, her hand going to her throat, the knife almost nicking her skin.

The man dipped his head in apology and stepped inside the study. "Careful, sprite. Remarkably, or not for someone associated with Macauley, you're armed for this discussion."

Pippa lowered her hand as his visage and name collided in her mind. Air seized in her lungs until she felt lightheaded. "Lord Stanford?" Her situation unfolded like stained linen tossed to the floor. A duke's sister in a gaming hell in the middle of the night. Rain-soaked and disheveled. Recognized by an earl, holder of one of the oldest titles in England. A hard-nosed, antisocial peer known not to suffer fools gladly. She was a mere daybreak away from being the city's latest scandal should he whisper one word of this.

She was doomed, absolutely doomed.

Oliver Aspinwall, Earl of Stanford, halted beside her, where he gently removed the knife from her grasp. Snapping the blade closed, he tilted the spine into the candlelight and read the inscription. "*To help navigate the waters.*" His jet-black brow winged high. "Odd piece for a duke's sister to carry."

Pippa held out her hand. "Haven't you heard? I'm an odd girl."

Stanford laughed and placed the knife on her outstretched palm.

His gray eyes shimmered in the light, calling to Pippa from the depths of her memory. "Indeed."

She stared at him, a puzzle piece sliding into place before she fully realized her search for it.

Stanford scrubbed his hand across his jaw, disconcerted. Blowing out a breath, he crossed to a sideboard that was only partially stocked, despite the gaming hell's impending opening. He poured a scotch and tossed it back, then poured another. "It's the eyes," he murmured, his voice gravelly from the liquor's burn. "A remarkable color, I've been told. Unique. Inherited from my father, unfortunately. All he ever gave me and more than I wished for. However, women like them, so I suppose that's one benefit."

Pippa blinked, struggling to pull herself together. The only other person she knew to have eyes that color was Xander Macauley. She stared, rummaging for details like she would items in the bottom of a trunk. Stanford was tall, though not as tall as Macauley. His hair pitch-black where Macauley's was a myriad of shades close to the hue of the satinwood sideboard the earl leaned against. He was handsome, maybe on the edge of pretty. His noble stance brought to mind a bearing she'd noted in Macauley during the rare instances where she'd gotten a close look. Refinement a boy raised in the rookery shouldn't have.

Refinement the man across the room had in spades.

Ollie. Short for Oliver. She formed the question in her mind, halted, stumbled. "Are you...?"

Stanford shook his head woefully as he eyed her over the glass's beveled rim. "He only asked for me because his head is cracked and disorder of thought set in. Besides, those are his secrets to tell, not mine."

Again, someone was mentioning secrets and Xander Macauley in the same breath.

Pippa flipped the knife between her hands, wondering how much the earl would be willing to disclose if she asked nicely. She could bat her lashes and play the pathetic fool the *ton* thought her to be. Instead, she went with the blunt truth, which was her way.

"That's the second time I've been told that tonight. The Lime-house Prince has a multitude of secrets, doesn't he? And guises. Smuggler, rake, industrialist, shipping magnate." She snapped her fingers. "Let's not forget whisky-maker."

Stanford smiled, his face lighting with it. Fondness and emotion she wasn't sure she wanted to define crossing his features in lightning speed. "A man sometimes grows into his destiny, grows into everything you'd expected he would. Not often in this life, extraordinary when it happens, but sometimes it does. Though it's distressing to be held back, punished for a mistake made when you were twelve years old."

Pippa looked up from where she'd dropped to her knee, sliding the knife into its sheath in her boot. "My lord, I don't understand."

The earl poured another drink, his shoulders slumping, bringing his proud bearing low. "Sprite, it's simply not required that you do."

Pippa frowned, supposing that was true. At least he wasn't calling her "my lady," a reminder of her elevated place in society now that Roan was a blasted *duke*. She'd liked being the sister of a lowly baron much, much more. Even if they'd not had funds to pay the bills each month. And before the dukedom, they'd not had a family, either.

"How is he?" she finally asked when it appeared she'd have to.

With a weary sigh, Stanford turned to lean against the sideboard, facing her, his stance both negligent and tense. "The shoulder was dislocated, the forearm possibly fractured. He's been bandaged, given a splint, laudanum, and enough gin to kill an elephant. Luckily, arm muscles offer less resistance and can be set without too much exertion. Meaning, we didn't have to hold him down for long. It wasn't pretty."

Pippa swallowed and rose to her feet. *Hold him down.*

"The good news is, I've arranged for a duenna of sorts. The bone-setter's widowed sister, as it were. Polly Pilhouse, I believe she introduced herself as. The best I could secure with this storm raging. She'll find you as soon as they finish treating the patient and not leave your side once. Don't argue," he said when she started to and crossly gestured with his glass to the window. "The roads are treacherous, my carriage almost cracking a wheel on the mad dash here. My coachman near to being thrown from his box once we reached the docks, where roads are, I realize it's elitist to say, inferior to those in Regent's Park. However, I can't have anyone on my staff injured, so I'll remain here until the lanes are passable."

She thought it worth trying, her own gambit. "You're here. Isn't that enough? Why involve this Polly person?"

"Truly? That's your reasoning? Housed up with two unmarried men in a gaming hell? Sprite, what would your vaulted Duchess Society think of *that* decision? I pity your brother his obligations now that I've met you." He smiled tightly and polished off his drink. "Surprised I've heard of them, are you? Hildegard Streeter and the Duchess of Markham. Sorry to say, all of London has heard of them. So in deference or outright fear, I'll choose not to leave you stranded due to fate's mercurial whimsy, your reputation snuffed out like a dying flame. I don't know Leighton well. I don't have friends like this. But if I did, I'd want—" He glanced away, then back, his ashen gaze spinning with emotion. "I'd want my sister taken care of should she find herself in such a ruinous situation. In fact, I'd make damned sure she was safe at all costs."

Pippa's temper caught at the base of her spine and moved north until it filled her chest with heat. She didn't like being told what to do —even if the advice was correct. "My lord, I'm trying to tell you I don't need your assistance. Or a bloody chaperone. Once the storm lets up, I'm sneaking home. Surely, some bruised felon in this fine establishment will escort me."

"Lady Philippa, impulsively charming chit who swears like a sailor, you *do* need my assistance. In keeping my mouth shut if nothing else. If your reputation is cast aside without thought, consider your nieces and nephews, that bookish half-sister sure to take your place holding up walls at every ball she attends once she starts attending them. I met her at a musicale recently held for Baron Ardley's cousin or sister or some such. Theodosia Astley didn't lift her lovely gaze from her book the entire performance." He tilted his empty glass into the light and traced the toe of his Hessian along a scuff in the floorboard a servant had yet to buff out. "Although I can't say I blame her. It was atrocious."

Pippa took a fast step forward. "Theo isn't like that. She won't play the *ton* false simply to serve herself. She's like a rare jewel in this city of demons. Lovely and kind and quite... wonderful."

Nothing like Pippa.

Spent, her words died away. She wasn't used to having a sister, having a family. Being an older sibling. Protecting anyone. Aside from Roan, love was a new emotion. She would lay her life down for Theo, but the young earl with the sorrowful eyes didn't need to know it.

Stanford deposited his glass on the sideboard with the care he would if he held an egg. "I understand your angst only too well, sprite. Though I wish I didn't. It's hard to love family, and even harder when they reject it."

As he crossed the room with a long-legged stride, and it looked as if their conversation was coming to a close, her words tumbled out. "Macauley went racing into that fire when he didn't have to. We thought someone was missing, but still." Her voice dropped to a whisper, the man's actions eternally baffling. Her fascination even more baffling. Maybe the earl could provide answers. "I don't know many men who would do that." As in, she didn't know *any*, except for her brother Tobias Streeter or possibly Dexter Munro, the Duke of Markham.

Or they might have stood and watched the townhouse smolder. There was courage—and then there was foolishness. Masculine arrogance, Xander Macauley style.

Stanford halted in the doorway, tossing a sly glance over his shoulder. "Macauley's done it before. The hero bit. You'll have to ask him." He shrugged as if it didn't matter when she could tell it mattered greatly. "Maybe he'll tell you, maybe not. Regarding the feelings of— what did you call him, the Limehouse Prince?—no one is ever certain. He likes it that way."

Chapter Four

Where a couple feels puzzled by an intense attraction

Pippa escaped the clutches of her bone-setting chaperone four hours later. She'd simply had to wait her out.

Dawn was fast approaching, and if she wanted to check on that thug Macauley, which she'd no reason to aside from a maddening longing the likes of which she'd never experienced, she'd best do it before the Devil's Lair awoke. Although, when a gaming hell came to life was likely much later than when a household did. Perhaps the occupants slumbered until noon in such a place. But as she wasn't a morning person, this happenstance sounded dreamy to Pippa.

Theo had her up for tea and crumpets by seven, followed by a walk around the garden and discussing the latest books Roan had purchased for his library. This was followed by trips to museums and political debates and all manner of things Pippa found absolutely uninspiring. Having a brainy sister was delightful but exhausting as Pippa was only moderately clever.

She tiptoed past the closed door of the bedchamber she suspected was the temporary residence of the Earl of Stanford, past another, this open to reveal a space decorated in shades of lime green. Each room on the floor was exactly like the one she'd been given, modest in size, the furnishings in the same elegant style as the main floor below. All had numbers on each door, like a hotel. Hers was number three.

Why so many bedchambers, Pippa wondered? Did gaming hells commonly house men who couldn't find their way home after an over-abundance of drink? Was that a usual service, providing a place to sleep off one's indulgence?

Pippa arrived at an industrial metal staircase at the end of the hall. Pausing only a moment, she took the steps leading to Macauley's private world before she could talk herself out of the impulse. Her curiosity was undeniable, and she generally made decisions without too much deliberation. A maid had brought her tea and, when asked, had told her where her employer was before realizing she spoke of things she'd best not and scurried from the room.

The building had been a warehouse in its previous life, tobacco perhaps from the stale aroma lingering in the air. The rush of the Thames could be heard clearly on this floor, along with the creak and sway of ships docked at the wharf, the patter of rain insistent for hours, slapping the roof in soothing thumps. Only a man with abundant confidence would build a showplace in the stews and know those who'd never once stepped into such a repellent district would come to court him.

Pippa paused at the top of the staircase, her whispery sigh filling the air. *Oh.* The space was unlike any she'd ever seen. A cavernous expanse taking up the entire floor of the dwelling. On the opposite side, a wall of glass and iron windowpanes spilled what little moonlight there was into the room from floor to ceiling. One area was cordoned off as a study of sorts, two massive leather armchairs situated in a semi-circle around a rosewood desk. Another housed a sideboard and gaming table with a chess set that looked new sitting atop it. Book-shelves lined one wall, the volumes contained within stacked in unor-ganized, well-loved tumbles.

And then... there was the bedchamber.

Pippa crossed the room, a delicate footpad over worn planks and then the Aubusson rug as she neared him. Her crumpled gown, destroyed from this evening's festivities and hideous to begin with, trailed behind, doing little to halt her.

Pippa paused by the bed, a high mattress that brushed her hip, knowing this was, without doubt, the most scandalous thing she'd ever done. Alone with the underworld prince in his domain, a man she feared because of how he made her feel when he gazed upon her. The way he watched her, silent and predatory, but as if he could not care less, made her blood sizzle. Her appetite burn.

She stared down at him, searching for explanations.

Even when ill, power radiated off Xander Macauley.

It was clear why his enemies kept him close.

Why women adored him.

She'd not participated in settling him in the room and wondered what he had on underneath the midnight blue counterpane.

His brass and iron bed was massive. She ran her finger over a ball-shaped finial and inched closer. Light from an oil lamp on the side table played over his hair, the ruby glass bringing out hints of ginger in the coffee-colored strands. His skin was darker than hers, sun-bronzed and swarthy. His cheeks were flushed, the stubble blackening his jaw and making him look more sinister than usual. He had shallow burn marks on his neck, shoulder, and the uninjured arm lying by his side. The other arm was tightly bandaged, the strip of white linen serving as a sling looped around his neck. Her attention focused on the dusting of hair trailing down his chest and beneath the sheet that rose and fell with his gently rasping breaths.

He'd invited women into this enormous bed. Laid their bodies down and climbed atop them. Dozens if one believed the scandal rags. He'd allowed them, strangers even, to touch him, *see* him. Parts hidden to reckless duke's sisters who habitually overstepped their bounds. Why, he practically ran the other way when he saw her striding down the street toward him.

Pippa exhaled sharply, her cheeks finally, *finally* coloring as a lady's should. Sadly, it was awareness of the man, one she feared she wanted, not propriety in any fashion that affected the response.

Her behavior wasn't a surprise. She'd heard it from her father, the condemnation often accompanied by a bruising slap. So why not live out the prophecy?

She was *not* a good girl.

The urge to lay her hand flat upon Macauley's chest and soak up his heat was almost overwhelming. The vision riding on the heels of this longing was clear. She wanted more than her next breath to lift the coverlet and slide in beside him. Wrap her arms around his wounded body and let her vitality seep into *him*.

She could see it. Bright as day, in fact.

Which went back to how horribly unsuitable she was for the life fate had presented to her.

Go. Now.

Pippa followed the voice in her head, spinning away from Macauley to circle the room. Hildy Streeter, the daughter of an earl who'd snagged her own underworld king. Co-proprietress of the Duchess Society and a firm believer in following society's rules, although Hildy hadn't followed them herself. It was a devious endeavor. And took a person with the finesse Pippa didn't have. Bulls in china shops and such.

She understood both the gravity of her situation *and* the hypocrisy. Unfortunately, women had few choices—most suffered along without her brand of unwanted good fortune.

However, she was in a genuine fix. Being true to herself meant disappointing everyone.

It meant *failing*.

Her family and friends wanted her to choose. Even if they—Hildy, Georgie, Helena, Theo, Roan, the dukes Markham and Leighton, Tobias Streeter—said she didn't have to choose, they expected a choice. What else was there for a woman in this life? Either she would stick with being Pippa, a disaster in every way, or develop into Lady Philippa, the forlorn but proper wallflower the *ton* approved of.

Her ploy was working, the-butterfly-going-back-into-a-cocoon ruse. Everyone loved silent women. Some poor fool of a soul would marry that version of her without thinking twice about what he was getting. He'd ignore the sparkle of wickedness in her eyes that meant he didn't have any clue who she really was. He'd never care enough to ask, with her sizable dowry now his to manage.

Pippa halted by an exquisite bureau fit for Buckingham House. The items displayed atop it were typical but wholly personal. A comb, tooth powder, razor, and strop. Before touching anything, she glanced back at Macauley's slumbering form. He wouldn't be using a razor for days with those burns on his cheeks. He'd look like a veritable pirate by week's close.

There were dice. Cards. She smiled. His new scheme. She traced her finger along the cracked leather spine of a book on whisky distilling, one of his other passions.

The man was an unexpected bundle of contradictions. How many miscreants had shelves stuffed with books?

She looked to the mullioned windows and the dull pewter dawn working its way past a steady rainfall. Her time was limited. Someone was sure to check on the patient soon. And the roads were only going to be wrecked for travel for so long, keeping her captive in a gaming hell. With Xander Macauley. The most thrilling thing to happen in her twenty-two years.

Five more minutes, and she'd sneak back to her bedchamber. Maybe six.

After evaluating the contents of a desk across the way that beckoned, one last bit of snooping, she'd go back to being that blasted lady everyone wanted her to be.

It was a lovely piece, the desk. She didn't know furniture terribly well but guessed it was walnut. Roan had a similar one in his study. She scratched a ragged nail over the emerald leather top and tilted her head to view the correspondence lying there, open for her inspection. Not her fault if she happened to accidentally read it.

Macauley's handwriting was bold but circumspect, like the man. Pippa squinted, then reached to slip on the spectacles sitting beside a pile of ledgers. They were made for a wider face and drifted slowly down her nose.

She held them in place, and his words leaped out at her.

London borough, Tower Hamlets. Arcadia Street. Orphanage. Workhouse exchange. Two thousand pounds initial investment.

Giving up any suggestion of indifference, Pippa circled the paper into view. Xander Macauley, who likely had a connection to the *ton* that he'd hidden from, well, everyone, even his closest friends, was funding an orphanage. Pulling children from a vile workhouse to fill it.

At that moment, she understood. And hated him for a brief instant for it.

His life held all the meaning hers *lacked*.

She burned with envy and such admiration it took her breath.

Breaking her reverie, a broad shadow fell across the desk, and she spun with a cry of alarm.

Macauley stood pale and swaying, holding the counterpane he'd yanked from the bed tightly to his chest. His injured arm lay somewhere beneath. He looked like a knight, battered and bruised, his steely eyes narrowed in fragile vexation. His gaze landed on the spectacles resting on her face, and his lips tightened. Parted, as if he was set to say something. Whatever he'd seen, whatever he was *thinking*, seemed to captivate him enough to seize his speech. Finally, a guttural curse she could have sworn was French slipped out before he could stop it.

It was then she recalled he was half-drunk on laudanum and gin.

She nudged the spectacles high, burning with curiosity. He was revealing details to her faster than she could gather the information. "What did you say?"

With a muffled groan, he grabbed the book from his bureau, with a hand that was not his dominant, and slammed it over his correspondence lest she hope to read more.

"The Wicked Wallflower nosing through my personal papers. This must be hell, although I'd have reckoned the flames last night were enough to crisp me. *Christ*, there's not enough laudanum in England to erase the vision of waking to find you here." Bumping her unsteadily aside, he wrenched open the top desk drawer, grabbed a flask, and awkwardly thumbed the cork off. Leaning heavily against the wall, he lifted it to his lips. "I'd hoped it was a nightmare, but it appears you're real."

She slipped the flask from his feeble grasp before he could take more than a short gulp. His words were charmingly edged with cockney, something she'd never once heard from him. He must have worked incredibly hard to lose the accent. "You look ready to drop. More of this"—she held the dented flagon to her nose and sniffed—"isn't going to help."

His lashes lifted, his penetrating gaze piercing hers. The Earl of Stanford's eyes stared back at her, near the shade of the dirty mist that hovered over the Thames most days. Those eyes held power over her, a secret she'd never reveal to anyone. Even as her body fired with the knowledge.

Macauley dabbed a bead of sweat from his temple and swallowed hard. "A doctor now, innit?"

Pippa gestured to the desk. "A philanthropist now, innit?"

"Here you thought I was purely a jaded lothario."

"That, and a no-good smuggler."

A muffled laugh slipped free, surprising them both. Faint grooves diffused like sunlight from the corners of his mouth, etched by many episodes of merriment she'd not seen. "I hate to ask for assistance, Little Darlington, while we hash out who's a meddlesome trouble-maker and who's a wrecked libertine," he murmured, sucking a sharp breath through his teeth, "but I think I'm about to black out."

Pippa raced to his good side, slipped her arm gently around his waist to avoid jostling his injured arm, and guided him back to the bed. The counterpane fluttered to the floor behind them, their only chaperone gone. Macauley wore no shirt, so beneath the thin silk of her gown, his muscles rippled and flexed as they moved carefully across the room. It was an intimate caress, sparking a carnal awareness Pippa had never experienced before. The scent of charred wood clung to his skin. The crisp aroma of gin and man. Nothing that should have weakened her knees or made her want to press her nose into the tantalizing hollow at his throat and take the deepest breath of her life.

She couldn't help but turn her head, just a little, and graze his bicep with her cheek.

Her body quivered with need, the beating of her pulse resounding like a church's bell in her ears.

Halting by the bed, both of them shaky but for different reasons, he stared down at her, his body going rigid where she touched him. But he didn't pull away. He didn't even blink. It was a measured appraisal, a judgment she had no chance to debate. The strained moment reaffirmed everything she'd suspected. Some curious thing, a dashed bit of bad luck, connected them.

Xander Macauley could deny it. He could lie. She could deny it. She could lie.

But the charged air surrounding them could not.

Such was life when one desired a most improper person.

"What's that smell?" he murmured.

"Motherwort tea. They've been giving it to you since—"

"No, beneath that." He sniffed. "Vanilla."

Pippa's breath caught. Her sister-in-law, Helena, had given her a set of soaps imported from Spain. "It's clover," she whispered.

"I'd wondered," he said, a statement no gentleman would have ever made. Yet the thrill was startling.

He'd wondered.

They stood for what could have been hours but were mere minutes, enveloped in a forbidden attraction fostered by a dawning twilight and the sound of rain striking windowpanes. The two loneliest people in London she imagined for some mad reason.

Why, Pippa asked for the thousandth time this month, why *him*?

Ultimately, Macauley shook himself out of his trance, braced his broad palm on the mattress, and wrestled into the bed with an aggrieved groan. "Where is your damned companion? I told Dash to find someone, a female, *anyone* aside from the light-skirts patrolling the block. Apologies for the indelicacy of the sentiment but your situation, if you cannot see this, is as dire as a light-skirt's."

He settled upon his back as gingerly as an old man, then yanked a sheet over his chest before she got another good look. Thank heavens, or *not*, he still sported the trousers he'd worn during his rescue. However, his feet were bare, and one had escaped the sheet for her perusal. They were nicely formed. Long and slim, sleek jutting bones and curved arches.

She'd never found feet enticing before. Her fingertips burned to touch.

Instead, she chewed on her thumbnail while dragging her gaze higher, a leisurely crawl up his broad body. "Your assistant, Dash, found someone. The bonesetter's sister."

"Brilliant, I'd say, except you're here in a bachelor's chambers, and she's not. And while we're at it, may I ask that you quit inspecting me like a horse you're set to purchase?" The skin around his lips was pale as foolscap; sweat beaded his cheeks and brow. His lids fluttered, and she feared he'd slipped away. "Laudanum, please," he whispered hoarsely. "My shoulder feels like it's being carved from my body... in slow, sure degrees. Your scalding stare is not quite enough to dispel it."

Shocked at her transparency and unable to dispute the charge, Pippa played nurse, locating the opium tincture on the bedside table. Uncorking it, she poured an amount she deemed adequate, but not too, in a glass and added water. Then leaning in, she touched his jaw lightly to let him know she was there. With a weak murmur, he drank, then sank back. Tossed his good arm over his eyes to shut out the sight of her.

"You'll be ruined, Blondie, bloody well and rightly ruined if it gets out where you've spent the night. Polite society will rip you apart for coming here when they're set in a few short days to beat the door down to get in. Although a scandal, any, even yours, will be a fine bit of marketing for the Devil's Lair. Wolves with razor-sharp teeth who have no trouble spilling reputable blood. And when your brother finds out..." His words died away with a growl.

Pippa dragged a lattice-backed chair close to the bed and dropped cautiously upon it. She settled her ragged skirts about her ankles, an utter farce of a gesture. "Roan can't argue with the weather. This situation is beyond our control. I couldn't leave you bleeding and broken on Talbot's lawn. You're practically his closest friend."

"To save yourself, you could have. It's what *he* would have wanted. What were you thinking, attending that degenerate's masquerade? Hell's teeth, if it were anyone else, I'd have trouble believing it. You dare more than any woman I've ever known." Macauley lifted his arm, his gaze snagging hers, and she couldn't help but note the pleasing ripple of muscle across his chest.

My, he was finely formed.

"Do you not know of Leighton's infamous temper? Your brother throws his fist first and asks questions after. I'm half a head taller and two stone heavier, luv. I grew up in the stews. He won't fare well, his beat-down resting on your delicate shoulders. And he is, I'm almost reluctant to admit, a business partner *and* a friend, so I'll gain no pleasure from the fray. But I won't back away from it, either."

Pippa shrugged and nudged his spectacles up on her nose, wondering at the hitch in Macauley's breathing when she did it. This could get interesting if she had enough time to think about it. *Act* on it. When he was set on running her out of his private space, sending her *home* any second. Leaving her with the image of him wrestling with her brother, his skin gleaming with sweat, his muscles popping.

"Whatever you're cooking in that clever brain of yours, stop it. *Cor*, don't tell me you actually need eyepieces. I thought they were part of the wallflower travesty." He grimaced and jammed his arm back over his eyes. "How anyone thinks *you're* demure and sensible, I will never fathom. Bleeding into the wallpaper, my arse."

Pippa forced her gaze away, back to the desk. Why argue fact? "Is it true? The orphanage? The workhouse?"

He sighed, a sound so fatigued she nearly felt sorry for him. Although her desire to know more about him was more potent than her benevolence. "Tobias Streeter and I were in that workhouse for a time as boys. After life dealt us what many would consider cruel blows. Conditions have only gotten more deplorable, so I stepped in. I have the money. And the might. The will, too, I suppose. The younger children will go to the orphanage, the older lads directly into apprenticeships at the distillery, on my ships, at the warehouse. Maybe the gaming hell if I can keep it respectable enough. I haven't figured out what to do with the young ladies once they grow out of the orphanage. But I'm thinking on it. There must be a multitude of domestic positions in households, plus jobs with milliners, hatmakers, and the like. I can't begin to list the people who owe me in this town. I'm going to start calling in markers, and they better ante up."

She dusted her hand down her wrinkled bodice, hoping the idea sounded logical upon presentation. "I could assist in finding these young women suitable positions. I have contacts at almost every millinery and haberdashery in London. Entre into the *ton's* households.

Roan's staff as a start. Imagine how many connections a duke's sister has. You only have the modiste or two from which you purchase items for your harem. A jeweler, I'm sure, but that's not of much assistance except to get you underneath skirts."

His reply was vulgar.

Pippa's cheeks fired, her hands going into tight fists. "How rude of a brute you are, Xander Macauley, when I'm only trying to help."

"You nosy scamp, this isn't help any man needs." He snorted, then groaned, and reached to rub his shoulder. "When the hell is that opium kicking in? Can I be transported to delirium, please?"

"The Duchess Society, if not me, then. Hildy and Georgie are becoming quite progressive. Funds are rolling in from various anonymous parties as well. Grande dames and such who believe in the society's tenets and have the freedom to toss blunt wherever they choose. They even have scholarships. We could make arrangements for a certain number of girls to arrive under their guidance. I have pin money I can donate to help pay fees. I could assist with smoothing over the rough edges before the girls are placed—"

His laughter rang through the room, deep and, regrettably, sensual enough to curl her toes. Inside her right one, her birthday knife sat in its sheath, a brand burning her skin. "That is *grand*. The girl currently in a rakehell's bedchamber discussing how he uses baubles to get beneath women's drawers is certainly the one to polish off other young ladies' ragged edges." Clutching his side, he ended the burst of amusement with a pained grunt.

"You'd best not knock yourself off the bed laughing at what is a superb idea. A man of your advanced age with this injury should take care."

His arm lifted, his eyes, the pupils starting to swim from laudanum, meeting hers. "How old do you think I *am*?"

She pursed her lips. "Forty?"

He exhaled hard through his nose and dropped his arm. "Thirty-two."

She mouthed the words. *Thirty-two*. Only ten years older. *Hmm...*

"Don't even think it, Little Darlington. I would *never*."

Pippa skidded the chair back and jumped to her feet. "I'm not thinking anything, you ancient toad!" When of course, she was. Why get so angry otherwise?

"*Sit*," he whispered, startling her and likely himself. The catch in his voice was devastating. She would have done anything to soothe him at that moment.

Weak, infatuated Pippa. Weak, obstinate Macauley.

She reclaimed her seat, deciding laudanum might help ease the way into a delicate topic. Plucking his spectacles from her face, she folded the silver metal arms and laid them on her lap. "Are we going to talk about the earl in the bedchamber downstairs? Number five, I believe."

Macauley grunted, the fingers of his good hand flexing into a fist.

"You asked for him," she hedged. "Your Scot complied. Quite readily, in fact."

"I wasn't in my right mind," he returned when she'd expected him to deny everything. His words were slurring slightly as the laudanum took full effect. She liked the hint of cockney and wondered what he'd sounded like as a lad. "I told Dash to contact Stanford if I *died*. No pulse, chilled to the bone, knife-protruding-from-my-gut dead."

"Why were you speaking French?"

His lips turned up in the barest of smiles. "Why? Did you like it? I don't often get to trot that out. Doesn't match the hoodlum rig, don't you know."

"You have his eyes," she blurted, stunned to hear the words leave her. But what better time to pump the underworld prince for information when he'd likely never speak to her again after this debacle?

"I'm three bloody years older, so he has *my* eyes." He turned his head on the pillow and pierced her with them. They glowed silver-blue in the rosy circle of light cast from the oil lamp. "Don't tell a soul about this. Not now, not ever."

Pippa leaned in, her breath rushing out. She twisted her fingers before her lips in a locking motion. "Our little secret."

The intimacy of the moment vibrated between them.

Then he closed his eyes, his dark lashes dusting his skin—and the sensation of sharing their lives disappeared. Yet the memory remained like a punch to the chest.

"Don't be mindless enough to take anything from this, luv." His words crawled sluggishly from his throat. He always seemed to know what she was thinking, cutting her off at the pass. "You just happened to be there when a burning building fell on my head."

The seconds ticked by, a mantel clock across the room matching her rapid heartbeat. "I won't."

She knew when she said it that it was the biggest lie of the night.

Chapter Five

Where two headstrong men do the reconciliation dance

L ater that afternoon, boots sounded on the staircase leading to the lodgings Macauley liked to think of as his hideaway. He'd never had a soul up here except his construction team.
Until *her*.

Pippa damned Darlington. Before, he'd appreciated the vast space's inspired solitude, the chill in the air, the wash of the Thames against the shore, boats edging a wharf he could view from his perch high atop the world if he searched hard enough. A sweeping sense of freedom overtook him in this spot, something cities, *slums*, often deprived a man of.

Now the scent of vanilla lingered like a bad memory. The image of that troublesome brat leaning over his bed, her hair a golden shroud, the silken tips brushing his skin and sparking an inferno inside him.

He wanted his hideaway back. Wanted the scent of her *gone*.

He wanted to not want her, truth be fucking told.

He gazed around at what he'd created. This, *ah*, he'd seen the beauty in the crumbling warehouse on Limehouse's mucky banks immediately. Had signed the papers to purchase the derelict structure without thinking it through first, not his way. Then he'd gone about filling it with objects he loved, personal items he didn't want housed in his sterile Hanover Square townhouse. A dreary dwelling he'd purchased simply because he *could*. He likened that decision to a woman he finessed into an assignation, then forgot about entirely on the ride home.

Although Hanover Square provided pleasure of a unique variety. Watching his neighbor, a nob of plentiful titles but modest blunt, frown in dismay every time he saw Macauley striding down Oxford Street did make him smile. When smiles were rare. He knew what the *ton* thought of him, and he frankly loved it. The neighborhood was going to shite with the arrival of men of industry. Of new wealth. Macauley had spent fewer than five nights there in the two years he'd owned the place, preferring a tattered sofa of grand proportion in the distillery and now this comparatively luxurious spot atop the gaming hell. Although Westminster was an excellent locale in which to woo prospective clients, so keep it he would.

It showed well when he did not.

Hell, he could afford to keep twenty such townhouses. Could buy the entire street should he wish to.

He realized he sounded petulant.

His heart raced as the footsteps closed in on him, but he forced himself to calmly lift his teacup to his lips, his gaze focused on the sodden streets below, the scent of whatever vile medicinal concoction they were putting in the tea drifting past his nose. The rain had finally settled into what could be described as a typical London spit. But the streets were a catastrophe, pitted and mired in knee-deep muck. He'd seen a carriage take a tumble and land on its side not an hour ago.

Few were traveling; however, they soon would be.

His adorable pain in the arse needed to go home before reality caught up with her.

Two pains in the arse, actually. One linked by blood, the other yearning.

The knock on the doorframe was perfunctory. As if Macauley

would refuse entrance to an earl from one of the loftiest peerages in the land.

Even one who'd betrayed him in the harshest way possible.

Showtime, Macauley thought, taking a damp breath of London's leaden pall as he turned to face his half-brother.

"I thought I was dying, mate, or I would never have summoned you." Macauley landed the first blow as Gentleman John Jackson had taught him was often necessary to win the round. "Out of my mind, barmy with pain. I'm fine, as you can see. Except for this sling I'm stuck with for weeks and a shoulder that aches so badly I want to cry. So once the roads are clear, you can scurry back to Mayfair and your afternoon musicales and the like. As you can well see, Limehouse isn't fit for toffs."

Oliver Aspinwall, the Earl of Stanford, stepped into the room as if the floor was littered with blades. Which in a way, it was. Cautious, but inside he came. When he wanted to move into Macauley's life and stay there, there was no uncertainty on this point. There never had been. "Dislocations hurt like the devil. Known to temporarily take a man down for the count like a hard kick in the bollocks. I remember the one, that day we were riding through the meadow trail in Derbyshire, and I took the hedge too fast. Until you popped my shoulder back into the socket, I sought to let agony take me. I passed out at your feet, so I suppose I let it take me."

You cheeky bastard, Macauley fumed, his fingers clenching around the teacup until he feared it would shatter. Somehow, *scarcely*, he kept his smile even. "Fond memories, those." Forcibly, he closed his heart to his one-summer boyhood adventure. Two lads from vastly different worlds finding commonalities exploring the grassy meadows and river streams of Derbyshire. Late nights spent studying a vast horizon, hoping to see just *one* shooting star. He'd realized his love of astronomy then, something only two people knew.

The two breathing the chilled air in this very space.

The earl leisurely circled the room, taking stock of the bits and pieces of Macauley's life scattered about. Stanford had been a timid boy. An isolated aristocrat Macauley had quickly tried to gift his courage. Nevertheless, Macauley had cared greatly about him that summer.

Macauley suffered silently through his brother's appraisal. He kept his gaze from settling on the stacks of books littered across every available surface. A tell Stanford wouldn't miss.

His brother made no comment, only turning to give Macauley a thorough examination, his gaze guarded but not closed. "You look like you lost the brawl. Spot of flecked blood." He touched his finger to his temple. "Congratulations on a reasonably refined accent, by the by. The summer we spent buffing out the cockney helped, I suppose."

Macauley gulped tea when his lungs felt like they would burst from his held breath. He'd caught sight of himself in the cheval mirror above his bureau and knew he looked like a mutt dragged through the streets. "I never lose brawls. Even the verbal ones. You should know."

Stanford smiled in his poignant way and crossed to the sideboard. Going for liquor, not tea. Which shoved a dreadful, hated thrum of concern through Macauley, an emotion he couldn't deny if he tried. The earl had encountered issues with addiction in the past. The broadsheets were full of his exploits.

Added to this vulnerability was a stout wave of anger when Macauley's heart gave a familial, brotherly spasm at the sight of Stanford swiping his overlong hair from his brow. A gesture that was too bloody familiar. He wished he could say he hadn't kept up with his brother's every move. The weekly missives received from his investigator during his brother's idiotic fight in another war England didn't need had about done him in.

Anyway, they shared little aside from a horror of a father they both loathed. His brother was lean, whereas Macauley was brawny, built like a commoner when Stanford resembled a knight. Hair color, different. Faces, different. Temperaments, different.

Two extremely different interpretations of a man.

But their eyes were *exactly* the same, which was a most revealing fact.

The feature that had his father finally accepting he'd sired a bastard. His mother's pleas during her short life were never enough.

Only when Macauley was dragged into his father's study, a candelabra brought close to his eyes, that the venomous cur had given in.

As if he could hear Macauley's thoughts and wasn't quite ready to participate in the discussion, Stanford raised his glass and peered into it.

His brother had been a sickly child. Asthmatic, like the Duke of Leighton. Like most of his set, the last man anyone would have imagined would choose to fight a war in India instead of Mayfair. Macauley had experienced the protectiveness he was known for, combined with an actual blood connection, for the first time ever. It had been terrifying and delightful.

However, Stanford had been weak in body but not in mind. That's what he'd used against Macauley.

His heart, he'd found, was the feebler of the two.

Macauley turned to rest his bum on the iron window ledge and gazed out over the city. Why he'd built his gaming palace in the stews instead of adding another trite stop on St James's was a mystery to most. But he knew. Let society come to him. And by God, they would. Adjusting his sling on his shoulder with a slight grimace, he murmured, "Go ahead. It's excellent." He gestured with his teacup. "The whisky."

Stanford took a sip, staring at Macauley over the rim. "Ah, yours. And Tobias Streeter's. I recognize it. I've read about the success of the distillery. Congratulations."

The gears of time wound back until Macauley was a gangly lad of thirteen. Newly settled in a household of great distinction. The earl had begrudgingly allowed him to sleep in the stables, a groom's position his interpretation of recognition. Macauley had quickly come to find that his father wasn't afraid to lock lads who disappointed him in storage rooms for days with no food or water. Luckily, he had a knack for picking locks.

In any case, he'd had food, clothing, and shelter, all three at once, for the first time. He'd even been able to sneak into lessons with Stanford's tutor during his brother's summer break from Harrow. Along with a love of reading, a passing talent for math, and the ability to sell someone their own hat, Macauley had found the only person of his acquaintance who'd accepted him without malice. They had been true brothers for a bit.

That summer had been magical—until the incident.

Minor now, perhaps, but a change in life that had paved the way for him to meet Tobias Streeter a year later, a bond that existed to this day. For that, *and* his unlikely partnership with the dukes Leighton and Markham, Macauley was forever thankful.

Setting his teacup aside, he awkwardly dug a cheroot from his shirt pocket. Slipped it between his lips and breathed the scent of raw tobacco into his nostrils. He imported the very best from the Carolinas, a product that had made him wealthy. Mostly, he'd quit because of Leighton and his bleeding asthma. He'd gotten tired of the wheezy duke rubbing his chest the moment he lit one, like Macauley's greatest pleasure was killing him. "Forget about the past, why don't you, mate. I have. I only stayed on that summer for access to the library. I tore through the old earl's books like a wild dog, didn't I? When you couldn't have been bothered to read even one yourself." He chewed on the cheroot, unconsciously giving it a mock drag. "I quite liked your French tutor. Very accommodating to an inquisitive young man. The first time I saw a bare breast, though she didn't let me touch it. I still dream in the language sometimes."

"Right-o. Giselle? She did fancy you, that I recall." He hooked his thumb under his jaw and tilted his head in thought. "No, no, it was Lisette."

Macauley suppressed the urge to turn his back, order Stanford from the gaming hell. It was a desperate mental battle to keep the thin smile on his face. *Right-o.* He'd only known one person to utter that inane phrase—and he frankly didn't want to recall it right now when he felt queasy from a busted shoulder and a laudanum hangover. The weight of history settled heavily upon him, adding to his misery. "What do you *want*, Ollie?"

They both stilled when the nickname slid out, the atmosphere taking on substance. An exhalation of tender *emotion*. As charged as the air in Talbot's manor when it was coming down around him.

Stanford's lips parted, and Macauley could see he was formulating a response.

Truth or lie. Truth. Or. Lie.

Don't, Macauley silently pleaded, *don't say what you want to say.* Neither of us can take it.

Thankfully, Stanford tossed back his whisky and shrugged a shoulder. "Maybe I want to get to know this masquerade hero bloke. The man with two dukes and the newly recognized by-blow of a viscount as his closest comrades. The *Gazette* led the pack with stories since Talbot's house crisped. They interviewed one of the scullery maids you hauled out. She said you kissed her before you laid her upon the lawn like a flower petal. Then she saw stars."

"I did not bloody kiss anyone. I could barely breathe," Macauley growled, so, *so* tempted to light a cheroot for the first time in ten months, three days, and eleven or so hours. Imagining Pippa reading that rubbish lifted the hair on the back of his neck. When she shouldn't be the woman he fretted seeing a false story—and there were a damned lot of them—about his hand traveling up someone's skirt. Then he remembered she'd been sitting in his carriage while he was supposedly doing all this kissing. "Did the rags mention anyone else?"

Stanford tried to suppress his smile, but it flared with Macauley's temper. "You mean the meddlesome sprite currently driving your chef mad with questions? No, it appears the masked woman in your rig, as it was noted there was one, remains anonymous."

Macauley shoved off the ledge, his vision blacking at the edges. "You have to get rid of her. *Now.* She can't be found with me. Found here. Even by her brother. He won't understand."

Stanford ran the rim of his glass over his bottom lip and rocked back on his heels. "Carriages toppled all over the city. We nearly cracked an axle on the way here. The lanes are flooded." His lips canted, amused. "Anyway, isn't Leighton a close friend? As close as a brother, some say?"

"He's proven his loyalty time and again, mate, if that answers your question."

Stanford popped his glass to the sideboard with a bang, though his voice was soft. "There we go."

Macauley moved too quickly and wrenched his shoulder. With a groan, he braced his good hand on the wall to catch himself. "Don't," he warned when Stanford stepped forward to help. "I have it."

"I wouldn't dare. Of course, you have it. Nevertheless, your problem may be more complicated than dealing with a long-ago misplaced brother. You have an admirer. I've been fielding inquiries from your sprite for hours. In between trying to explain the rules of hazard and reminding her chaperone that she's being paid to stick by her charge's side no matter where she goes."

Macauley opened his eyes to find his brother had advanced half the distance between them but no more. *Sprite.* Jealousy lit him up inside. An attractive earl, lacking two shillings to rub together but with only a modestly seedy reputation, would make an admirable match for a duke's sister who held a dented reputation herself.

"Maybe you should get down there and work the Aspinwall magic. I'm fairly certain our father didn't leave you with overflowing coffers. An earldom is right expensive to maintain, innit? In fact, I could say, from modest research by my solicitors, that I know it is and that he didn't. Lady Philippa's brother married Helena Astley, as in Astley shipping. The *sprite's* dowry is substantial enough to strangle a donkey."

Stanford laughed, sending Macauley's blood zipping through his veins. "Holy hell, you sound like a man cornered."

Macauley blew a breath through his nose and willed away the black dots marring his vision. He needed to lie down and soon. "I'm going to say this so you understand. Slowly, if that's what it takes. Leighton's sister means nothing to me. No one, truly, means anything to me." He caught Stanford's gaze, the fire of age-old wounds stacked in his.

Stanford gave a half-shrug and crossed to the sideboard, poured another drink. "You don't have to pound home the message. You amputated me from your life like a withered limb. Which I deserved. You're done once betrayed, even if the betrayer is a lad barely out of leading strings. I'd never had family either, or someone—"

"I don't *want* a family, mate. Or your explanation. I don't believe in family." The words felt hollow, like a coin dropped down a well.

But they sounded convincing.

"You *left*," Stanford posed without turning, his voice ragged. "Left me with him. Do you know what the next eight years were like? He cut off Harrow. I was tutored at home, imprisoned for the most part. Until I was able to run away to war. *War.* The prospect of getting my head blown off was a bloody improvement over living with him. So, I purchased a commission and fled. I didn't go back to Derbyshire until after he died." He tossed back his drink. "Stanford House is a disaster, by the way. He let it rot along with his mind."

Macauley cursed beneath his breath and strode unsteadily across the room.

He was finished with this argument. Finished dreaming of an estate in Derbyshire that didn't belong to him and never would. He'd been finished for years, in fact. It was time to lose his brother again.

But for some mad reason, he couldn't leave without adding, "You gave me no choice. Our father believed I was filching him blind because you *let* him believe it. When you knew a footman was at fault. *Gutter rat,* isn't that what he shouted as they dragged me down the drive? If you recall, I was removed from the estate by the village constable. Sent to a workhouse, Ollie, where I thankfully met Tobias Streeter. Or I would be dead. There wasn't time to worry about the boy who helped send me there. I was too busy trying to *survive.*"

As Macauley reached the staircase, he glanced back to see Stanford pinch the bridge of his nose, sigh mournfully through his teeth. He looked world-weary in the solemn light of a dawning day. He knew his brother got headaches from an injury sustained in Raigad. Macauley's investigators had been extremely thorough regarding the details, although he'd read each message with his heart in his throat, his hands trembling. After India, there'd even been a period, maybe a year or so, where he'd had his men covertly retrieve the young Earl of Stanford from opium dens.

Macauley paused on the top step, his shoulder giving an unwelcome jolt that swam down his arm and through his fingers. The sling wasn't helping. Or not enough. He'd be back to laudanum and gin soon. "Are you well?"

Stanford shook his head without comment. Another sip. The flawless facsimile of a brooding aristocrat. Macauley would like to tell him that too much drink could ruin a man as easily as any drug. Easier. And some inherited the sickness. But he didn't have the privilege to say a word. *He* was the one betrayed, but he was also the one who'd never forgiven. Who'd left. "You're not the man he was, Stanford. I know... you didn't mean for it to go so badly. For me to have to leave and never return. Perhaps, someday, I thought I would."

Stanford waved his hand in a gracious gesture but didn't glance back. "Go be a hero, Macauley. Just go be a bloody hero."

Chapter Six

Where a smuggler considers his odds

Go be a hero.

He'd be a flipping hero, all right. Macauley pounded the stairwell wall on the way down with each pronouncement, which hurt like hell. One, he was going to send Pippa home. Two, send Ollie back where he'd come from. Three, find a willing chit to tup in every position he could manage with this wrecked shoulder. Four, sleep for two days. Five, open his gaming hell and take London by storm.

He liked when a woman rode him—and he very much needed to be ridden at the moment. Maybe that passingly attractive Miss Danbury whom Pippa had accidentally thrust in his path. Her molten gaze said she was willing with a capital W.

Macauley staggered toward the kitchen, hearing the laughter—when his tyrant of a chef rarely laughed—from fifty paces away. Deuced if Pippa Darlington couldn't charm her way out of a burlap sack.

Well, he was pitching her out before she could crawl into his.

Unnerved for no good reason, he lingered in the doorway, a stranger in his own space, the scent of cinnamon and nutmeg drifting over him like smoke. The teasing aroma calling to mind snug parlors and roaring hearth fires, meals surrounded by family, children racing around one's legs. The brush of a woman's body beneath silk sheets, their combined heat driving away the chill.

Things he had trained himself not to want. Not to long for.

But the world was changing. The parts of his that touched his friends were changing. Tobias, Leighton, and Markham had wives, *families*. The people he felt responsible for were growing by the hour.

He snorted softly, a grimace pulling his lips low. His friends were different. They were in *love*. Macauley was scared to stand too close for fear of catching the disease.

With Ollie back, a man whose presence generated many unwanted emotions, he felt particularly vulnerable.

His chef, Fast Fingers, now known as Pierre, was leaning his hip against the butcher's block, standing too close to Pippa, twirling a mustache as phony as his accent. Macauley had first met him years ago at the Old Bell Tavern when he worked as a bruiser guarding the back entrance, and Pierre managed the kitchen. Macauley knew for a fact the man had never left the environs of London, much less made it to France. But his food was a masterpiece, an epicurean delight despite the base manner in which he'd come to learn the trade. As long as his patrons' bellies were full and their inheritances gushing out like blood through an open vein upon his Savonnerie carpets, Macauley didn't care if Fast Fingers called himself Sir Tootles.

Trying to avoid looking at Pippa, Macauley reviewed the space he'd spent a small fortune outfitting to his chef's specifications. Of course, there was no bone-setting chaperone in sight.

As if she'd sensed his presence, Pippa glanced swiftly to the door, her hand clenching around the dough she was kneading. Her eyes were stark in the dim light radiating from the oil sconces, so green against her fair skin they appeared nearly black. She was more appealing than he wanted to admit, standing there in a too-large apron, the straps looped twice around her waist and tied in a floppy bow over her belly. Flour on her cheek, her hair stacked in an ineffectual knot at the back of her head, the flaxen strands curling around her face from the damp heat. Her breasts, quite a ripe size for her petite frame he'd unfortunately noted on previous occasions, straining against the stained cotton.

To taunt him if he required additional provocation.

Which he did not.

She's not a girl, mate, but a woman full-grown. You've been waiting even if you think you haven't. Here she is.

As they stared, his heart gave an unnecessary, revealing skip. His cock doing things it shouldn't beneath his trouser close. And he didn't have drawers on, only a thin strip of fine wool containing him. Leighton would kill him if he knew the effect his sister was having.

Why, Macauley raged in hushed desperation? *Why her?*

Perhaps innocently, perhaps not—with Pippa, one never knew—she thrust the blade in deeper, popping her thumb in her mouth and sucking off a dab of custard without once dropping her gaze as a virtuous young lady ought. "Why are you standing there glowering when you should be in bed, resting your injured shoulder? We're busy making"—she turned to Pierre Fast Fingers and gave a winsome head tilt, emitting a shy, bogus, borrowed-from-her-wallflower-routine giggle —"what is it called again?"

Pierre flushed, obviously enamored, answering one question Macauley had about him. "*Mille-feuille.*"

"*Mille-feuille.* Lovely. What does it mean?"

For all his supposed Frenchness, Pierre Fast Fingers shrugged, having no idea.

Macauley exhaled faintly and stepped into the room, the heat from the ovens embracing him if nothing else did. "Thousand sheets. *Mille,* thousand..." He stepped over a small puddle of what he hoped was water. "Oh, blast, you get it."

"His French is *very* good," Pippa snickered, her gaze dropping to her dough.

Pierre Fast Fingers glanced his way, his brow cocking. As if to ask, how can a rookery thug who could break someone's knees with a swift kick possibly speak French?

Macauley flicked his fingers toward his chef. *Move back.* It was a predatory gesture. Man-to-man, an unspoken "she's mine" when she wasn't. Pierre Fast Fingers' smile wilted like a rose. Macauley shook his head, his own smile sympathetic. *Not for you, mate.*

Not for me, either, he could have added.

While his chef turned back to his soup, or whatever smelled so delectable bubbling in a cauldron above the open hearth, Macauley halted across the block from Pippa, bowing to rest his smashed arm on the scuffed wooden edge. His attention centered on the knife lying beside her, and his heart dropped. His birthday gift. She followed his gaze, the slow slide of air from her lips audible to only the two of them. Then with her pinkie, she edged it beneath the lip of a silver serving plate and out of sight. The jewels sparkled from their hiding place, a tiny row of emeralds the color of her eyes dancing across the block.

He hoped she hadn't realized this. It wasn't appropriate, but he'd followed instinct as he'd done for much of his life.

"No smoking in zee kitchen," Pierre said and whipped his ladle through the air like a baton.

Macauley frowned. His chef having a mental breakdown days before the Lair's grand opening would be a disaster. Who the hell was smoking?

Pippa laughed and scooted an almond biscuit his way. She touched her lip, the plump, pink bottom one—and his belly bottomed out. Until he realized... *oh*...

He tossed the forgotten cheroot in a rubbish bin and grunted hoarsely at the exertion. "I don't smoke them anymore," he explained with a flare of annoyance. "Or almost never. But I like the aroma. And they're the best. Shipped weekly from the Colonies. It's soothing." What did he owe this bit of deadly female business anyway, aside from transport back to where she belonged?

She grasped a knife, not the birthday gift, thank heavens, and began cutting the dough into thin slices. "They're no longer colonies."

"It's your brother's fault, you know."

At this, she glanced up. He was sadly gratified, like a boy who'd tugged a girl's braid and gotten a response. He faked a cough that actually hurt his shoulder a little. "Just when I'm set to lay him out on the mat at Gentleman Jackson's, he coughs and pats his chest, goes all woozy duke on me."

"Woozy duke." She sputtered a laugh, the knife stilling in her hand. Her wide green-as-grass eyes hit his. *Shite.* He'd revealed something more significant than it had appeared coming out.

"You quit smoking for Roan?"

Macauley grabbed the biscuit, the taste chasing away the flavor of tobacco. The scent drifting from her skin, light and, again, close to vanilla though he couldn't recall what she'd said it was, was even tastier. He could bathe in the fragrance. "Did you make these?"

"She's talented," Pierre Fast Fingers chimed as he left the kitchen, possibly in search of the assistants he'd demanded be on-hand at all hours. "Has zee touch."

Macauley bit into the biscuit. He *bet* she had the touch.

Pippa went back to cutting strips of dough, lifting a slim shoulder in an unladylike shrug. "I like cooking. I can't do it at home unless I hide it. Roan doesn't care, of course, but the servants whisper. And there's enough talk about me as it is. Enough burden for Roan and Helena having me for a sister."

He reached clumsily for another biscuit from the platter by her elbow. It was pubescent of him to imagine, but if Pippa was marvelous with her hands, how would this measure up in other areas? Dusting crumbs from his lips, he abandoned the lewd images running rampant through his mind. His cock didn't need to get any harder. It was about as solid as the butcher's block he was jammed against. "Why?"

A fast exhalation shot out, followed by a crooked grin that weakened something inside him. "You really don't understand, do you? Women of my station aren't supposed to *cook.* We're supposed to paint pastoral scenes or read blasted poetry. Shop. Look and *be* vacant. That's why I asked about assisting with apprenticeships for your orphanage. There is no *meaning* to this life unless we fight for it. We're like bugs caught in amber, suspended, powerless. Even simple, pleasurable tasks are forbidden. Believe it or not, I actually had to prepare our meals before Roan had the duchy dumped on his back. My father..."

Her words died away, the admission fading into the sweet-scented vapor surrounding them. "We didn't always have funds for staff. Papa wasn't a capable manager of money." With skilled efficiency, she stacked the layers of dough in a neat arrangement set for baking. "Occasionally, I rebel, spend the night cooking, then before dawn, I deliver the foodstuff to

St. Mary le Bow church. I have a friend, a widowed countess, quite a charitable soul, who helps me."

Macauley swallowed the remaining biscuit, although it tasted like dust. Mercifully, his erection wilted. This damn girl. Just when he'd christened her a troublesome imp, a mindless chit the likes of which London needed not one more of, she had to go and tell him *this*. "You're delivering meals to Cheapside?"

Her mouth winged up on one side though she kept her eyes on her task. A sinister smile. A gambler's smile. "Would you rather I deliver them to Limehouse? I used to live not that far from there myself. Before Roan was gifted with his title. Don't you know anything about his past?"

"Men don't typically ask a lot of questions." Pippa Darlington was a confounding mix, an intrepid menace with a kind heart. A chit with secrets. He hadn't imagined they housed those types of creatures in the *ton*. He frowned, unsettled. He wasn't used to talking with a woman, and those he did were jaded and calculating, much like he was. The conversations were often directives in bed, and that was it.

Pippa's sincere desire to make something of her life drew him like a bee to nectar. He wanted that as well. His life to have meaning. He always had.

Nonetheless, finding common ground was not what either of them needed.

He rubbed his chest, urging away the ache. "You have to go home, Little Darlington. Today." *Before I make a monumental mistake of an undetermined variety.* "The roads must be improving. I'll have the carriage brought round. We need to get you back into Roan's townhouse before he arrives from Bath. That silly maid you and I bribed is only going to keep her mouth shut for so long. How long do megrims last anyway? She said that was going to be her excuse for your absence."

"How should I know?" She laid her wrist on her brow and mimed fainting. "Do I look like the megrim type?"

Her blatant regard, a bit cagey, noted, but female interest just the same, made him want to sneak back to his bedchamber, slide beneath the covers, and pleasure himself until he passed out. It would take longer using his left hand, which could be intriguing.

She pointed with the knife. "My word, I believe for a normal person that would be considered a smile."

He flattened his lips, hoping to hide what she might see. "You're cracked, luv."

"Admit it. You like my company."

"At best, I find you entertaining. At worst, an infuriating termagant."

Nonchalant, she went back to slicing. "Word in the Leighton Cluster is, you're afraid of marriage."

He reached to fiddle with his sling. The knot was rubbing his neck raw. "The Leighton *what?*"

Pippa laughed softly. "My sister-in-law's charming name for our odd little family. You're included, by the way. You, Tobias Streeter, Hildy, the Duke of Markham, his duchess, Georgie. And Theo. What a motley crew. When Helena and Roan were courting, although she didn't know he was courting her because he's such a dreadful romantic, she claimed we traveled in a pack."

"Like dogs," he returned, unimpressed. He grunted, not able to get the sling adjusted.

Pippa sighed and laid the knife aside. Rounded the butcher's block before he could stop her. "Let me. You're making a hash of it."

He took a sustaining breath while reminding himself: *Leighton's little sister. Reckless. Gorgeous, green-eyed, smells-like-vanilla trouble.* Do you hear that, Macauley? *Trouble.*

She circled to his back, saving him from having to drown in the splendor of her face. Dragged a step stool over from the sound of it and climbed atop. His lids fluttered when her fingertips swept the nape of his neck, her sugary breath hitting him below his right ear. He pictured a very unattractive widow who'd propositioned him last week on Bond Street and willed his body to stay within his domain.

"Are you?" she asked while retying the tattered ends of his sling.

Her skin was soft, her enticing scent dulling his senses quicker than laudanum.

He grunted, having completely lost the point of the conversation.

"Afraid of marriage."

"Resistance isn't fear, luv."

"Forever swearing off love then, according to Roan."

"His brain is pickled from passion, so I'm not sure I'd take his guidance."

"Oh, merely afraid of women then. The ones with a functioning intellect."

Only one.

Exasperated with her incessant flirting, he reached, capturing her wrist and seizing the gaze he was indeed afraid of. Her focus shifted to where he held her, her pupils bleeding black. If she dared to further engage him, he would toss her over his shoulder and carry her away like a caveman. Probably pass out from the pain in the process.

Instead, she provoked. "Do you want to tell me why you've been having me followed, Xander Macauley?"

He released her without comment. What he *wanted* was carnal in the most decadent of ways.

A strand of her silken hair danced across his jaw, and he turned, taking a stumbling step back. Goosebumps—*goosebumps*—swept his arms. If he didn't negotiate with this imp, get her out of here and soon, there was no telling what he might do. He was weak in mind and body, half-drunk on opium and *her*. He leaned in so only she could hear. "If we negotiated a business deal of sorts, what would it take to make you settle down?"

Her fingers curled into a tight fist atop the butcher's block. "Settle *down?*"

He gritted his teeth and inhaled through the pain radiating from his shoulder. "Stop investigating men for the Duchess Society settle down. Quit the wallflower rubbish settle down. Make it so a family *friend* doesn't feel the need to have you followed to keep your pretty little arse out of trouble settle down. Clear enough, innit?"

She tilted her head like she had with Pierre Fast Fingers, trailing her finger through a scattering of flour. He didn't buy her reticent routine for one *second*. "At Talbot's, during the chaos with the fire and such, your young Scot, Dash, and your coachman, Johnnie, didn't think to send for the bonesetter." She made a loopy circle with her floured fingertip, indicating his injury. "A dislocation like this, badly set..."

"I get it. I owe you."

Her lips curled in devious delight. "Yes, yes, you do."

With a genuine pang of fear, Macauley realized he wanted to lose himself in Pippa in a way he hadn't cared to lose himself before. *Ever.* Crawl between her spread legs and keep her locked in his bedchamber for *weeks*. Count each freckle on her body with his tongue. He'd rarely been affected so potently—and never with someone of her class unless it was an extremely calculated move.

"*One* favor." He held up his remaining biscuit, stabbed it in her direction. "One. Then my debt is paid. And if you renege, if I find out you've double-dealt me, Leighton will know everything quicker than you can take your next breath. Count on it."

She did the timid, finger-dragging-through-flour again, her gaze cast low. Others would tremble at his tone, but she barely twitched. "I'd prefer to term it an adventure."

"Not all adventures are good, luv."

"This one will be."

The hair on the back of his neck lifted; a gut response he should likely heed. "I'm listening. Go ahead, unbridle your pitch."

She glanced up, coyness gone. Predatory, if he had to name it. She was unfairly, infuriatingly beautiful, standing there bargaining with him. She would make someone, not him but someone, a willful, wonderful wife. "I want to come to the opening. I read about it in the *Gazette*."

"What opening?"

She gestured broadly to the space and rolled her eyes. The gaming hell.

He choked on the biscuit. "The Lair?" He slapped his good hand to the block, sending flour in a cloud around them and pain radiating down his injured arm. "No way in hell. No, as in, *never*."

"I'll stay in the gallery. I know there's one off your study that over-looks the gaming floor. Rather Juliette of your design, which I appreciate. This is the most fascinating dwelling I've ever been inside. I've searched the entire place, and this is the safest spot. It has a back staircase leading to the alley. It's perfect. I can come and go without anyone but Dash knowing. I'll bring a companion. One of the scullery maids I routinely bribe. Viviette never asks questions. I have fifty pounds stuffed beneath my mattress." She stepped closer, as eager as he'd ever seen her, and he forced himself not to back up in response. "I'll wear a disguise. I won't talk to anyone. Two hours, then I'm gone. No more investigating. No more escapades. I'll be good. I'll increase my deliveries to Cheapside. I'll even include a church in Limehouse!"

He snorted, derisive and unconvinced. And charmed. "You? Good?"

When she could see her argument wasn't working, she went in for the kill. "If you can't find it in your heart to collaborate with me, I'll tell all of society that you're this close"—she held up her index finger and thumb a hair apart—"to being listed in *Debrett's*. If by-blows of earls were listed, that is. Can you imagine the scandal rags' excitement over *that* story? And the offers you'll have to fend off? As much as a speck of blue blood will make you a more appealing bedmate to every widow and dowager countess in England. You won't be able to walk the streets without distraction."

A laugh burst from deep in his throat, though he tried to contain it. This chit had teeth. More balls than her brother, the woozy duke, and then some. And a vulnerable sweetness he found utterly, criminally appealing. "You devious little blackmailer. Blazes, I think I'm almost impressed. When I routinely conduct deals in shadowy alleys and back rooms of establishments no gentleman has ever thought to enter."

"I can come up with a suitable excuse to get out of the house that night. You'll just have to keep the Leighton Cluster out of the gallery if they're attending. Tell them a woman is up there, waiting for you. Close to the truth. With your reputation, wholly believable."

Her eyes glittered like someone had shone a light through one of those gems on her knife that should be fake but weren't. He wanted to look away, tried to look away. Looking away was the tidiest plan. The way to step out and *away* from her. "*Lud*, I know you can come up with a lie that chumps every naïve soul you encounter. Do it almost every day of the week, don't you? But this"—he scrubbed the back of his neck and worked hard to ignore how her gaze blatantly pursued the movement—"this feels like extortion. Ask around. I'm not a man who appreciates being extorted."

She flicked flour from her fingertips and watched it flutter to the floor. "Wouldn't be the first time, though, would it?"

"Actually, no. Smuggling fairly promises extortion once a year or so."

She laid her hand over his, and he jerked it away as heat swam through his body. *No drawers, mate. Remember, you're wearing no drawers, and your wedding tackle will pop right out for everyone to see.*

Pippa Darlington, if given a chance, wouldn't look away.

"No one will notice me, Macauley. I swear."

He exhaled raggedly, torn as he always was when he was within ten feet of her. She had no clue. About any of it. Life, attraction, *risk*. He was born to his role when she'd not been born to hers. She was green, true, but she had guts. He admired people with guts.

And he appreciated her desperation to experience *something*. Regrettably, this knowledge propelled him.

Why was he the only person in England who understood this untamed chit?

Deciding on at least one thing, he walked back a step, out of reach. *No. More. Touching.* "If I agree, you'll vow on every precious thing in your world that you'll stop these games you've been playing. No more toying with society, cat to their mouse. No further need for me to be rescuing you, for whatever insane reasons I have been. Possibly because no one else realizes how dangerous you are."

He held up a hand when she made to argue, his temper sparking. He had one she might not want to mess with. Not as close to the surface as her brother's but hot and ready just the same. "You don't have to marry. I'm not even compelled to think you will. If you do, the blighter you select, *cor*, I weep for the man. Your marital standing, bless me to my boots and back, is Leighton's problem. I'd also advise you to quit acting like someone you're not. It's exhausting for everyone involved."

"I'm not sure what you mean."

He grimaced. "If you're a wallflower, I'm a deuced knight."

She sent flour fluttering to the floor with a huff of laughter. "I'm not scared to marry. I simply don't want to. The wallflower subterfuge is defense against inane conversations and awkward waltzes and, heavens, I wish to avoid every pointless thing in this sister-to-a-duke farce I've found myself thrust into."

"Whatever you say, Little Darlington. We'll see who walks that plank first. My money's on you just so you know."

Her cheeks rounded, skin rosy from the stove's heat or a conversation that was mildly arousing in his opinion. "How much?" she asked after a long pause where they fought a silent battle, the air around them vibrating with awareness. Apparently, not all combat happens on a battlefield. "If we're betting."

His lips lifted against his will. He should *not* be enjoying this. "Twenty quid. That leaves thirty from your mattress stash for future bribes to terrified domestics."

She looked away, chewed on the inside of her cheek. Calculating. "Twenty pounds is a lot to me but not much to you."

He bowed his head in agreement. "True. Yet I recall when it was everything. And that, luv, makes all the difference in the world."

Bracing her hip on the butcher's block, she faced him as courageously as any man. Then adding to her adorability, she held out her hand. When only American tobacco merchants had ever offered a handshake over a deal.

"I swear to halt my secret investigations into the endlessly idiotic men of the *ton* if you, Xander Macauley, rake, rogue and smuggling scoundrel, agree to let me view the Lair's opening from the gallery upstairs. Secondly, twenty pounds will be paid by the first person to walk the matrimonial plank. Your words, not mine. That wager could be years away in payment, knowing you. Because I'm not the one who will go first."

His fingertips tingled with the yearning to touch, link his fingers through Pippa's, and tug her against his body. Tangle his hands in hair the color of sunlight and promise. She could stand on that stool again, bringing them almost nose-to-nose. He would make her moan he'd kiss her so thoroughly.

Or die trying.

And in bed, their difference in height wouldn't matter at all.

He swallowed hard, his stomach giving a little twist. "Why not ask Roan to help you find meaning in this life? Your sister-in-law, Helena? Or your tutors, the Duchess of Markham and Hildy Streeter? Anyone but me."

She shifted from one boot to the other, her rumpled skirt swishing over the scuffed planks.

"The truth, luv, no lies." He wanted it for reasons he couldn't, *wouldn't*, specify.

"I trust you," she blurted.

He blinked, his arm jerking in his sling. "Hell's teeth," he growled and rubbed his shoulder. "Trust?" He tapped his chest. "Me?"

She nodded, her lips flowing into familiar, obstinate lines. Daring him to argue when she'd given him a compliment.

Macauley hesitated, his mind working furiously, a nebulous idea swirling. "Leighton goes into every situation with fists raised, as I do. Like Tobias Streeter does. But ours is from neglect, to be blunt. We were conditioned on the streets. Your brother's temper has always surprised me, though I suppose it's the thing I like about him most." He closed in on her, and this time, *she* backed away, knocking the stool aside. "What happened to the two of you? Before this ducal muddle?"

The peril of sharing secrets shimmered like a rainy mist between them, forbidden promise sparking the air. Intimacy of a kind he'd never experienced and guessed she never had either.

Tell me, he silently appealed. *Let me in.*

Rejecting him soundly, a move he respected even as he was tempted to drag her back, Pippa turned and was gone, through the doorway and into the depths of his secluded gaming hell.

Back to a bedchamber designed for hour-long pleasures and forgotten pain.

Room number three, in case she didn't think he knew *exactly* where she'd been the entire time.

Chapter Seven

Where a determined young miss questions the various degrees of infatuation

"How do you know if you love someone? Not the brother-sister type. That it's not merely a fascination so thin it's gone by noon?" Pippa propped her chin on her fist and sighed. "Infatuation mist."

The comportment lesson, regarding suitable ways to remove oneself from a conversation with a groper, halted as if a rock had been tossed through the Duke of Markham's sparkling bay window. (The lesson was on the agenda for Theo's benefit due to a prior season's incident with a handsy earl and Pippa's ratafia ending up on his head.)

The proprietors of the Duchess Society—Georgie, the Duchess of Markham, and Hildy, wife of Tobias Streeter, former king of the underworld and Xander Macauley's closest friend—turned to Pippa with synchronized gasps of astonishment.

"Infatuation mist?" Hildy patted her chest and coughed, audibly swallowing the nibble of sponge cake she'd taken before Pippa's unexpected query.

Georgie closed her parted lips and seemed to ponder before

responding. "Are you, that is, is there someone you're finally interested in? Because you've always been rather adamant about—"

"Oh!" Pippa scooted to the edge of the settee, sloshing tea on her wrist.

She desperately wanted information, but did not, under any circumstances, wish to *disclose* information. It had been two days since her return from the gaming hell under cover of darkness and, amazingly, none were the wiser except for her corrupt maid and a suspicious majordomo.

"This question is for a friend. Lady..." She laid her teacup on the rosewood table and flicked at her sodden cuff. *A name, Pippa, any name.* Inspired, she snapped her fingers and glanced at her tutors with a winning smile. "Lady Augusta! At the musicale last month, she asked my opinion on the topic. If you recall, the baroness fainted during a break after her flute solo. She collapsed right into her husband's arms. Quite theatrical. Since I have no experience, absolutely *none*, I thought to ask you two." She chewed on her lip, fiddling with her damp sleeve. "Aside from Helena, you're the only women I know who actually love their husbands."

"I wonder who Lady Augusta could be interested in?" Hildy asked, her lips curving in what looked like delight. Pippa wasn't sure why, but Hildy and Georgie seemed to find her amusing. When she wasn't trying to amuse.

Georgie nudged Hildy's slipper and laughed faintly, shaking her head.

"Why are you laughing?" Pippa's voice sounded exactly like her brother's. Irate.

"Darling, girl." Georgie laid her hand over Pippa's, where she continued to fidget with her sleeve. Her Grace was everything a proper duchess should be. Lovely, kind, and composed. Her only misstep was marrying the wrong man the first time around. "You're going to fall in love someday. And marry. You don't have to be apprehensive about this eventuality because you're not being pressured unduly by anyone who loves you. Society's coercion, we can manage."

"Oh, no, I'm *not*. I'm not losing that bet!"

Georgie frowned, a delicate pleat forming between her brows. "What bet?"

Theo made a stumbling entrance at the perfect time. Book held open against her chest, head bowed, mouth soundlessly repeating the words. Theodosia Astley was Helena's half-sister. Now *her* sister. Aside from Roan, Pippa had never loved another human being more. She was the most intelligent girl Pippa had ever known. *And* the nicest. She rescued kittens and birds and believed in the good in everyone. Which was ridiculous because people weren't always good. Naivete that Pippa worried greatly about in a decidedly parental manner.

Pippa jacked her thumb in her sister's direction. "My bet with Theo. About which of us will marry first." Because she'd heard you should stay close to the truth when you lied, she added, "We wagered twenty pounds."

Hildy's cup hit the table with a clink. "Twenty pounds!"

Theo grinned, never, *ever*, put off by being roped into Pippa's escapades. She was astoundingly quick on her feet. "I bet on Pippa, naturally. I'm four years younger and could not care less about marriage. I'm baseborn and proud of it. No aristocratic nonsense hanging in the balance for me. If I fight for anything in this life, it will be an education. Oxford. Or Cambridge. Cambridge would suffice. Or voting rights for women. The first female MP. Of course, my dreams are too much for this world." She flounced to the chaise lounge, her book before her face in seconds. "Maybe your female *grandchildren* will be able to attend classes and cast a ballot, Your Grace. *Maybe*."

There was a collective sigh from the Duchess Society. Hildy and Georgie were also instructing Theo, and she was as tenacious as Pippa and then some. Although she looked rather sweet with her winsome smile and gentle sapphire eyes.

But looks could be deceiving.

Theo nudged aside her book and winked.

Pippa glanced down, her smile growing. Her sister was tall, almost gangly, her long legs hanging off the chaise. She had a hole in her stocking and a rip in the hem of her skirt. Yet, she'd started to fill out, curves cropping up in areas where Pippa had none. Theo was fast becoming a beauty. Vivid blue eyes and a wicked smile highlighted a charmingly crooked front tooth. Unique and enchanting, another spot of misfortune for her brother-by-marriage, the Duke of Leighton.

Pippa had tossed many a scathing look to men in the past six months whose eyes wandered, first to her, then to Theo. She would throttle anyone who touched her sister without invitation. And she wasn't agreeable like Theo, not for one lousy second. But if they wanted to see the graceless side of a girl, she would happily show them.

"What was the stimulating question that started this conversation?" Theo asked from behind one of her dreadful leather-bound volumes. Pippa squinted. *The History of England from Julias Caesar to George IV*. Ouch.

Hildy poured tea, then relaxed on the settee. She was the loveliest woman in England or close to it, her husband possibly the most handsome man. They were an eye-bleeding pair to behold. "Pippa wanted to know how one decides one is in love. Not sibling love. Not fog disappearing into the ether love. Not *poof*, here goes nothing love." She pressed her lips together until a pale ring formed around her mouth, holding back her glee. "She's asking for a friend, of course. Lady Augusta."

Thoughtfully, Theo splayed the history tome across her belly, her inquisitive, sky-blue gaze meeting Pippa's. "A three-minute kiss is one sure way to decide. At least Shakespeare thought so."

The Duchess of Markham came to her feet, her own tea hopping over the lip of her cup and dribbling on the Savonnerie rug. "That is *not* the way to tell."

Theo clicked her tongue against her teeth, drawing out the moment until it hurt. "You didn't have any three-minute kisses with His Grace before deciding? Last summer, I saw a two-minute one at your lawn party that nearly melted my slippers. The conservatory. I left before you noticed me. Heavens knows what happened after that."

Georgie fell back against the brocade cushions with a muted groan. Then pleading, she turned to her partner.

Hildy took a deliberate sip, lingering while she formulated an adequate defense. "A three-minute kiss can help one decide. True. Tobias helped me choose, certainly. Although I loved him before he ever agreed to kiss me. But a kiss has power, influence. It can make a woman forget herself. Especially the magical ones." Her gaze met Pippa's in a way that made Pippa think, *how much does she know?* "Kisses can lead to reputable mistakes not easily corrected. Those errors can take away freedoms granted by fortune. Force unions where one doesn't want them. Between people who perhaps aren't meant to be."

Theo swung her foot in a languid circle. *"'A thousand kisses buys my heart from me.'* And you know what he wrote about swords—"

Georgie clapped her hands. "Theodosia Astley, that is enough Shakespeare, please!"

Pippa rose on wobbly legs and crossed to the window. She couldn't look anyone in the eye while discussing Shakespeare's use of erotic imagery. Not with the scent of Xander Macauley a haunting, gentle sting inside her nose. Man and the raw aroma of tobacco. Bergamot, perhaps. Very light and delicious. His skin beneath her fingertips had made her burn. She'd touched him, that somewhat bogus effort to retie his sling, because the impulse was stronger than her pride.

He knew she was infatuated with him.

Infatuated enough that she couldn't hide it. Nothing misty about it.

What would his *kiss* do to her if his breath rushing past her cheek had the power to slay?

She traced a crack in the windowpane with her pinkie as an opulent vision stormed her mind. Of Macauley rising over her, his broad body blocking out the light, blocking out everything except the two of them. His weight pressing her into the feather mattress. His lips seizing hers, the kind of contact Hildy said could ruin a person.

She *wanted* to be ruined.

So far, she'd only been kissed to tedium.

By an earl, two barons, and a groom at her brother's country estate. She'd consented to each kiss, then felt lonelier than she had the moments before. Nothing like being with Macauley, no kiss on record. His hot gaze had lingered on her breasts, stuffed in that silly apron. She dusted her hand down her bodice, her corset tight suddenly. Her nipples had pebbled like this while she'd stood behind him, her hand hovering over the loops of his sling, the urge to sink her fingers into his glossy, peat-brown strands terminated only by fear. For a moment, she'd had a sense of shedding a layer and stepping into someone new. A woman who could lock Xander Macauley in a bedchamber for days and know what to do with him.

There was heat in his eyes when he stared at her if she caught the flare before he banked it. It near turned them from smoke to tarnished silver. But there were guileless parts to their interaction, too. He smiled with her more than she'd seen him smile with anyone else. It was layered, his fondness. Affection and exasperation. She'd seen Roan look at Helena that way on many occasions.

She guessed Xander Macauley wanted to *not* want her.

Pippa gave the pane a hard tap. Well, she wanted to not want him right back. Some things one would not *choose*.

She was a nuisance. A troublemaker. A firebrand.

What Macauley said about her was true. She couldn't seem to help herself. She and misfortune were fast friends. But she was loyal. Funny. She could juggle. She was a brilliant cook. And she desired to help people. She didn't crave an average life.

And she didn't want to marry a man who didn't love her.

Macauley had vowed never to marry. She'd heard Roan and Tobias Streeter whispering about him once when they'd been in the library, half in their cups, spilling out of their chairs with laughter. So not husband material—but he could be part of her adventure. An activity she included in the gaming hell visit. A two-for-one deal he wouldn't know he'd agreed to until it was too late.

He had her knife. She knew he did. She was lost without it but encouraged to imagine it tucked snugly in his trouser pocket.

"I'm afraid to ask what that smile is about."

Hildy Streeter, daughter of an earl and beloved wife of the rogue king of the Limehouse docks, settled in beside her at the window. Weak sunlight poured over her, bathing her in brilliance. Pippa longed to have her confidence and poise. "A gorgeous spring day after the storms of late, isn't it?"

Pippa braced her hip on the ledge and turned to her tutor. "You came over here to talk about the weather?"

Hildy laughed gently. "You speak your mind, Lady Philippa. For that, I admire you greatly. Although I worry about the difficulties it may bring."

"I'm listening to your instructions. The Duchess Society's. No more ratafia incidents. No more waltzes with blighters interested only in my dowry. No footsie beneath dining tables. No errant kisses in gardens. I know the one with Baron Bulette was a gross error in judgment. I'll have my marital contracts reviewed by your solicitors if I ever agree to sign one. I'm playing the wallflower with purpose. My plan is in place."

"The question about kisses..." Hildy released a pent breath. "I fear you're paying attention to the wrong information. That I've"—she glanced at Georgie, then back—"we've unwittingly shown you examples you don't need. Not yet. Marriage is complicated. Love and children can break your heart. *Or* make it whole. It's like rolling the dice, how it goes."

Children. The image of a boy with solemn, ashen eyes popped into Pippa's mind, and she lashed out, vexed with herself. Macauley would never allow himself to become a father. "True love, you mean, by examples I don't need. Reaching too high when it's a rare thing. My parents were certainly never like you and Tobias. Helena and Roan. Georgie and Markham. *Nothing.*"

Hildy wrapped the drapery's gold tassel around her finger and gave it a jerk. "Not love, passion. They are, or can be, two entirely different beasts. It's dangerous to confuse them. Which I think you're trying to figure out." Hildy dug in the pocket of her skirt and fished out a slip of folded paper. "A runner delivered this earlier for you."

Pippa's heart banged hard against her ribs before she calmed herself. Macauley would never send a note that could be intercepted. He was a professional smuggler, for pity's sake. Instead, he'd sent a spoken missive through her weak-of-moral-fiber maid, Viviette. A carriage would pick her up in the mews behind her townhouse in two days, ten p.m. sharp, and return her at midnight. The conveyance would wait ten minutes, then leave if she could not sneak away.

Wear a hood, he'd advised. *And keep your mouth shut.*

What a romantic he was.

Pippa took the note and read it without comment. "From my modiste," she murmured. "I mentioned I'd be here all day, and there's a gown."

"A gown?"

Pippa folded the foolscap and tucked it up her sleeve. "A bit of a rush."

"Is there an event this week?" Hildy released the tassel. "Tobias is attending the Devil's Lair opening since he's a partner, but other than that, I don't recall another function."

"I have a luncheon with Lady Augusta," Pippa hedged, the pointed edge of the note biting into her skin.

Hildy frowned, smelling a rat. "A new gown for a luncheon?"

Pippa shrugged. Actually, it was for Xander Macauley. Beneath her hooded cloak, she was going to dazzle.

That gown was going to secure her a three-minute kiss.

In two days and four hours, he would open the most spectacular gambling venue London had ever seen.

In exactly two days and *six* hours, he would make a massive mistake.

Macauley shrugged irritably, which sent sharp needles of pain through his shoulder. He could feel his error in reasoning straight to his bones. But even knowing this, he'd gone and made plans, sent word through that scatterbrained maid of hers, sealing the deal.

Was he mad to listen to Pippa blasted Darlington of all people? He chewed on the unlit cheroot clamped between his teeth, wishing he still smoked. Maybe he'd go out right now into the Lair's alley and light up.

He fingered the knife in his trouser pocket and scowled. What was he thinking, negotiating with that wild chit? Broken down by wicked apple-green eyes and the faint whiff of vanilla. He was pathetic, truly pathetic.

"The masquerade hero is pining," Roan declared from his spot across the room, where he'd been tasked with displaying a painting of a trio of riders galloping through Hyde Park. Macauley found the canvas hideous, actually, but the Duchess of Leighton had given it to him as a celebratory gift, so he had to hang it.

Or due to his injury, the Duke of Leighton had to hang it.

Macauley shoved off the sideboard with a grunt. "I'm not pining. And you're hanging it too low, mate. Go up two inches. Think eye level." He was ignoring the use of that ridiculous moniker. The scandal sheets could write about him all they wanted, but did his friends have to keep reminding him of it?

Roan nicked the wall with the nail to mark the spot, then lowered the painting to the floor of what would be a prime attraction of the club. Private boxing salons. Two of them. Grander than Gentleman Jackson's by a mile. Not another hell with those in the entire world. "He's pining."

Behind him, Tobias gave a muffled yawn. "What's her name, Mac?"

Macauley turned to Tobias Streeter, lounging in an armchair, lids low, arms folded over his belly. He got little sleep with all the babies in his house, currently two, but possibly more at any time the way things were going.

He met Tobias in a workhouse when they were fifteen. Macauley was recently removed from his father's home, and Tobias running from another in a long line of dismal situations after his mother's death. He wouldn't have survived without Streeter. Perhaps Street wouldn't have survived without him. Macauley had often thought they were closer than brothers, which with the arrival of his *actual* brother, sent a shaft of anguish through him. Maybe he'd given up on that relationship sooner than he should have.

"I'm not pining. I'm not in love or even in fascination. Marriage and the accompanying offspring are an obsession with you people. Don't get me caught up in that tangle. I like my life fine the way it is."

Although lately, in the dark of the night, during those lonely, barren pauses, he wished to be tangled up.

Maybe with a duke's little sister.

Which was his dirty secret.

Roan hammered the nail in with three swift blows. "How long has it been?"

Macauley adjusted his sling, trying to forget Pippa's fingertips gliding across the nape of his neck. "Been?"

"S... E... X," the Duke of Markham clarified from his spot hunkered down before a shipping crate. He'd been given the supremely critical assignment of unpacking the sparring gloves as Macauley was not a proponent of bare-knuckled fights. The room smelled of leather, chalk, and perspiration as all pugilistic arenas should. It ticked a box in his mind that said, *You're getting it right, Mac.*

Markham jammed the crowbar in a split in the wood and gave it a twist, sending the crate's top tumbling. "I get fairly irritated myself if more than a week goes by without. Of course, it never does, but I know I wouldn't like it if it did. That might be the cause of your brooding. Maybe you should make use of the sling. Women like caring for injured men. It's quite dashing, even if it limits your capabilities. Or go ahead and smoke one of those cheroots you have constantly stuck between your lips. Something to ease your wrath."

Macauley strolled to the crate and peered into it. "We're well aware you keep an active calendar with the duchess, Your Grace. How many children will this next make? Ten or thereabouts, innit?"

Markham braced the crowbar on the floor and rocked back on his heels. His smile was infectious—if one wanted to be infected, which Macauley did not. "Four, as you well know. We didn't plan on twins the one time. You talk a good game when you're quite capable with them. Amazing to us all. Anthony, Isabella, and Henry don't call you Uncle Mac because they loathe you. You should have your own someday before you're too aged to get down on the floor and play with them."

Markham had just announced to his friends that his duchess, Georgie, was expecting again later in the year. As was Helena, Roan's wife. Hence the bottle of brandy they'd torn through like a fever, which was why Street was napping in the corner, Roan was cheeky, and Markham maudlin.

All Macauley had was a slight headache and a gaming hell set to open in forty-eight hours.

"I assume because of all those infants and expectant wives, none of you are coming to the Lair's opening."

They turned in unison to glance at him, and Macauley hated two things at that moment.

One, that he'd for a split-second imagined a little girl with eyes the color of emeralds. Two, that he sounded nervous about the hell's introduction to society.

Resuming his task, Roan hung the painting, then stepped back to assess his work. "As if we'd miss it. If this venture succeeds, the return on my investment will allow me to repair the roof on the estate in Derbyshire *and* the chapel wall in Northumberland. I can't stay too late with Helena in her condition, but I'll be here to give my blessing. Ducal approval and that sort of thing. As will Markham. With all this aristocratic firepower, we may be able to lure Lord Sessoms away from White's. He's burning through his inheritance like a madman." He tilted his head and nudged the painting up a hair. "Streeter will be in attendance, too. Though a viscount's by-blow doesn't add much prestige, does it?"

"Rotter," Street whispered from his corner.

A pang of guilt danced along Macauley's spine. If Roan knew he was planning to hide his sister in the gallery and let her watch the scandalous proceedings, he would smash his fist into Macauley's face without taking a breath first.

Christ, if he knew that Pippa had spent the night in this very building after the debacle at Talbot's, he would flat out murder him. Still, he'd needed her that night, a rarity in his life. She'd made sure they called the bonesetter and helped care for him during those early hours when he'd been out of his head. Concussed and incoherent.

Hell's teeth, she'd even made *biscuits*.

He'd never had a woman fuss over him—aside from his mother so many years ago, it seemed like a dream.

Dodging that memory, Macauley dropped to his haunches and reached in the crate. Everything was awkward at the moment as it was done with his left hand. "During the event, my advice—that is, a request. Stay out of my study. The chamber off the gallery."

Roan gave the painting another bump, his grin brilliant enough to light the room. "There is a woman. I knew it! He's stashing her in his *study*. He couldn't even rescue a maid from a fire without bestowing a kiss. Macauley, there's comfort in your inability to change your ways."

Disconcerted, Macauley brought a glove to his nose and inhaled the crisp scent of leather. "There was no kiss at Talbot's. There's no woman. The space is under construction. Nails and the like. It's not ready. My books. It's, it's a disaster." He shut his mouth, stopping the flow of inane words.

The hair on his neck prickled, and Macauley turned to find Tobias's gaze centered on him. Surprising, considering his initial chosen profession—smuggling—but Macauley wasn't an adept liar. And he'd never hedged about his conquests, not with *this* group. Not once, actually.

But Pippa was... different.

Special. Although he planned never to take advantage of her uniqueness.

Later that night in Mayfair...

Hildy turned on her side, snuggling against her husband's long, lean body. The sound of carriage wheels over gravel was a distant echo. The dink of rainfall against windowpanes. The servants had retired for the night, as had their children.

Finally, the townhouse was silent.

Tobias was resting against the headboard, making notations in a hefty tome on Georgian architecture that smelled of dust, rolling the corner of the page up and back as was his habit. He was designing a set of terraces in Shoreditch and was enthralled with dormers and pediments. One of their demanding felines, Nick Bottom, was squeezed between them, his purrs a soothing vibration.

It had been one of the first things she loved about Tobias Streeter, king of the Limehouse docks. Amateur architect, smuggler, shipping magnate, whisky distiller, he was man with a curious mind and an unguarded soul. That he rescued felines, then named them after Shakespearean characters, had charmed her clothes from her body. Charm turned to love when he fibbed about his reasons for doing it. He had the kindest heart of any man she'd ever known, yet he didn't want the world to realize this. She found it all quite lovely.

"I can hear you thinking," he murmured, brushing a kiss across the crown of her head. "Out with it, Mrs. Streeter."

She paused, unsure how to address her concerns. Stalling, she traced her fingers over his belly and watched his muscles twitch. He growled low in his throat, a warning that had her pulse quickening. Maybe there would be time tonight for—

Leaning, he tilted her chin until her gaze met his. His eyes were wondrous, the lenses of his spectacles winking in the candlelight but not hiding the beauty. She'd been overjoyed when their eldest son Worth's had shifted to that exact shade of green when he was a babe. However, their youngest son, William, had sky-blue eyes like his mother. For which Tobias said he was forever grateful.

"I know what you're going to say. You want another feline. That would make three children and three furry beasts. A nice balance. I did promise you a houseful of both that I recall. I've been working on the project as hard, and I mean as *hard*, as I can."

Hildy laughed and tucked the sound into his broad shoulder, then gave him a nip that had him shifting restlessly beside her. They had two young children and a thirteen-year-old, Nigel, whom they'd adopted early in their marriage. Nigel was a delight *and* a challenge, as she was finding was the case with adolescents. She traced a figure eight on her husband's chest, the thin dusting of hair soft beneath her fingertips. Delectable. And he smelled, *oh*, like a dream. She loved that he wore only drawers to bed.

"It's Pippa. She was here today for lessons with the Duchess Society, and a messenger delivered a note from her modiste. An urgent request for a gown. When I quizzed her about the event she needed it for, I believe she lied to me." She clicked her tongue against her teeth, thinking back to the cunning expression on Pippa's face. "*Definitely* lied to me."

Tobias closed his book, placing it on the bedside table. His spectacles were next, atop the digest, then he brought her in tight against his body. "She indeed lied to you, Hildy girl."

Hildy flinched, startling Nick Bottom, who leaped to the floor with a hoarse *meow*. "How do you know?"

"Because Macauley lied to me today, too. Despite being a canny bounder, that's a rare move for him."

Hildy collapsed to her back, grabbed a pillow, and pressed it over her face. "I feel woozy. This is more than the Duchess Society, more than Georgie and I can handle. I knew Pippa stared at Macauley too often at Markham's dinner party last month. Her gaze fixed on him every time I looked her way. I pleaded with her, find anyone, *anyone* else! I warned her about the dangers of such a man. That ridiculous wallflower routine, all the while she's smitten with that bounder. But did she listen? No, she has to go and invent a hopeless infatuation with—"

"I'm not sure it's hopeless."

Tossing the pillow aside, Hildy scrambled to a sit. "*What?*"

"Breathe, darling. In and out, slowly." Tobias pulled her into his arms and pressed a muffled laugh into her hair.

How could he find this amusing? The most recalcitrant woman the Duchess Society had ever worked with, the impulsive, headstrong sister of their dear friend, was circling the ruination drain like a frothy bubble.

Tobias drew a soothing ring on her arm with his thumb, distracted. She knew from experience he was trying to solve a riddle. The man loved riddles. "I don't think there's anything to find out. Not yet. He's attracted, she's attracted, we suspect. It happens every day. At every ball, musicale, or lawn party. Across the aisle at church. Mostly when people don't, in fact, *want* it to happen. Look at us. We fought our fascination for weeks, and where did that get us but nearly breaking my drafting table from our antics. The good news is, he can hide his feelings, even if she can't. No one is better at hiding his emotions than Xander Macauley. But this..."

He whistled between his teeth, searching for words. "I have a gut feeling there's more. Something real between them. Like he's revealed one of those secrets he keeps bottled up, which astounds me to even imagine. He's never told me much about his past, actually. But the look on his face today was interesting. Telling."

"That slip of a girl will never tame the likes of Xander Macauley, Toby."

Tobias gave Hildy a squeeze and another kiss, this on her temple. "What I'm contemplating between them, my darling, is more dangerous than a mere tup behind closed doors. True intimacy lies down the path of shared confidences if that has happened."

"He's too old for her," Hildy murmured, realizing she sounded petulant.

Tobias's lips brushed her cheek, the corner of her mouth, her chin. "Maybe he's exactly what she needs. A dose of wisdom to tame her bold impetuosity. She'd be enough to keep him busy, that's for sure. Mac likes to stay busy."

"Busy in bed." Hildy sighed raggedly, her shoulders slumping. "I bet she drops the wallflower routine like a heated brick. Instead, introduces some silly ploy to gain his attention. I understand the games women play, even if I rarely played them."

Tobias rolled her beneath him and settled between her splayed thighs. She nearly let out a purr as loud as Nick Bottom's. "Oh, you played them. Besides, do you honestly think either of those brash devils would be suited to an ordinary person? This could be a match made in hell but a marvelous match just the same."

Hildy threaded her hand through his hair and brought his mouth to hers. The kiss was languid, children-asleep, bodies-awakening perfection. "Roan will kill him when he finds out," she whispered and nibbled on his bottom lip.

Groaning, Tobias grabbed the hem of her nightdress and skimmed it to her waist. "Someday, someone is going to bed and wed Lady Philippa. Likely in that order. Why not an honorable man who would protect her with his life?" His hand roamed between her thighs, fingers circling. "Roan will accept this if the intention is good. Macauley is, after all, the best of men. The very best."

"I'm interested in *this* man. The one atop me." Hildy wiggled her hips, thought leaving her as he slid a finger deep, his gaze narrowing in concentration.

She loved that look.

It meant *she* had become Tobias Streeter's riddle to solve.

Chapter Eight

Where a smuggler takes a dangerous bet

The night of the opening, Macauley could feel Pippa's gaze burning through layers of linen and superfine, roasting his skin.

Arousing, troubling awareness.

Visceral and problematic.

He had to stop himself from searching the gallery for her. Dash had alerted him the moment she'd arrived. He'd taken the precaution of situating a guard who usually handled the distillery's night shift outside his study door to ensure two things.

That no one got in.

And no one got *out*.

He didn't believe Pippa would stay put for one minute if she didn't have to. Not with the enticements surrounding her. This crush where half of London's elite had decided to show. Temptation of every variety. Sight, sound, taste, as he'd planned. The air scented with a mélange of decadence. Brandy, wine, roasted duck, peppered venison, sweetbreads, and citrus tarts. Tables abounded with food and drink. The click of dice and crystal glasses married with the laughter of couples who would soon settle into a room upstairs for a fleeting interlude. Perhaps chamber number three even.

Although Macauley had briefly entertained the absurd idea of closing that space off, keeping it... pristine.

Because Pippa bloody Darlington had slept there.

Macauley grimaced and curled his fingers around the pair of dice in his fist. He was alone in this battle as the Leighton Cluster was long gone, hurrying back to their squalling babies and raging love affairs. They'd done the ducal posturing as Markham had promised, then left him alone in a mass of ravenous society waste while *she* lingered upstairs.

Not the typical chit awaiting him, clothes in disarray, thighs spread in anticipation.

His heart stuttered for a telling second. His cock doing something wildly unsettling beneath the finest clothing money could buy.

He *hoped* he wouldn't find her like that when he finally made his way to his study.

He was a strong man. Resolute and determined. But a naked Pippa, golden strands spread over his desk or that settee he'd jammed in the corner so she'd have a comfortable place to sit, creamy skin bathed in candlelight, those feral eyes glowing with eagerness, was probably more than he could handle and win.

And he liked to *win*.

Macauley rolled the dice across an empty stretch of baize as he passed a hazard table and bestowed a tight smile that said, *Welcome, but don't come any closer.*

He wanted to make money, not friends. Not with this set. Two dukes in his circle were enough, thank you very much.

Slipping his pocket watch from his waistcoat fob, he noted that it was fifteen minutes before midnight. Signaling to Dash, who stood by the roulette wheel, he let his factotum know he'd be back shortly.

On his way to the staircase leading to the first floor, Macauley's gaze seized on a woman across the gaming hall, mask in place, her identity protected, silken hair flowing down her back in a wanton style she'd never employ in a ballroom. Lady Wnydem-Blanche if he had his guess. Recently widowed from an earl twice her age and enjoying her newfound freedom. Her smile was savage, her regard indiscriminate, sweeping him from head to toe before focusing on his improvised sling. Tonight, a black silk cravat. He'd figured if he must don one, at least he could make it tasteful.

Women seemed to like the accessory for some bizarre reason. Lord Niedermeyer's mistress whispered about taking it off and tying her wrists with it.

Of course, the entire conversation made him think of tying *Pippa's* wrists together. Which possibly proved how demented he was becoming.

Macauley took the stairs to his study at a jog, the pain in his shoulder reduced to a dull ache. The sconces flickered as he passed them, tossing shadowed silhouettes across the Axminster runner. The oak banisters gleamed, highlighting walls covered in imported Italian silk exquisite enough for bloody Mayfair. There wasn't an auctioneer in London, not *one* he hadn't negotiated with for something housed in this place. A complete and utter gut from studs to rooftop. He'd turned a rotting warehouse in the middle of Limehouse into a destination.

Where he would now rule from the rookery, the only place he'd ever belonged.

Unaccountably jittery, Macauley halted before the door. Released the guard with a nod of his head. Pressed his palm to the beveled walnut and sought to gather his thoughts. Then shifting from foot to foot, he tugged his watch free and consulted it. A Bainbridge, the most accurate timepiece in the world.

Thirteen minutes to midnight.

Thirteen minutes of torture. Dusky candlelight, two glasses of gin swirling through his head torture. The muscles in his belly tensed. The news arriving rapid-fire from his brain and other regions of his body wasn't good.

He'd begun to dream of her.

Frothy bursts of sensual mist that left him hard and aching when he woke to cool sheets and unmet promises. Time was creeping up on him. Or perhaps it was his damned friends. They were marrying and having babes faster than he could keep up. So, it was only natural he felt left out, lonely on occasion. When he designed his life, he'd known that fantasies of love and romance weren't a part of the plan. Survival. Success. *Control*. He'd found that anything he attached significance to —his mother, and for a time, the Earl of Stanford—disappeared like a vapor, taking his heart with it.

Sex was one thing. A wholly *necessary* thing.

Dreams where he experienced an odd burst of happiness, another.

He'd even tried kissing another woman to rouse his interest in someone unrelated to a duke. Miss Danbury, who'd tracked him down at the distillery yesterday afternoon. Feeling cornered, he'd given in. However, he wasn't a dupe, and he'd put exertion into the act, expecting to be consumed. Or at least slightly titillated. Instead, Pippa's face had popped into his mind right when it was getting good. He'd sent the chit home, unspent passion spilling across her lovely face and frustration across his.

He blamed his lack of desire on his recent injury.

Improbably out of sorts and vexed at Pippa *and* himself, Macauley opened the door without knocking and before he had a firm introductory conversation in hand.

She was standing at the gallery's balustrade, a hooded woolen cloak covering her slender body as she'd promised. She could have been any woman—when she was only one. *The* one. Her scent had arrived to capture the space, unrelentingly apprehending it. He shut the door and leaned against it, watching her turn to him with a feeling of predestination.

Letting the curtain fall from her fingers, shielding them from the view of the crush on the gaming floor below, she stepped into the safety of the room. Two steps, no more, then she slid the spencer from her shoulders and hung it on the peg by his desk.

He recorded the performance in helpless fascination.

Her smile when it met his was as cunning as Lady Wnydem-Blanche's, though less practiced. An innocent edge that sent his temperature soaring.

This is what he got for trusting a defiant hellion, he thought while he waited for his heart to start beating again.

Although she'd stuck to the bargain for the most part.

The gown was a vision. A fantasy. Tempting him, her game, he could see. Frothy layers the color of smoke, a shadowy blue-gray affair not far off from the shade of his eyes. Silk tulle and chiffon organza if he wasn't mistaken. Since he imported both every day, he wasn't. An impossible amount of fabric, a dazzling scattering of beads winking in the candlelight. A subtle spark with each shift of her body.

He controlled the brutal urge to rip the delicate silk from her body by pressing his good hand against the door until his knuckles cracked.

Did he like the gown or not?

Was he going to say she looked lovely? Was he even going to blink?

Pippa forced herself not to fidget. Or beg the bounder for a compliment. *Be a lady for once, will you?* Smoothing her hand down her bodice, she experienced a minute bloom of satisfaction when his gaze followed the gesture.

Xander Macauley always had to win.

Well, *she* wanted to win, too.

She shook out her skirt, the beads lining the hem scattering prisms across his costly carpet. She could wait him out. He'd no idea the patience she could employ when she wanted something.

The horse hadn't crossed the finish line, but she believed she wanted *him*.

He sighed and shoved off the door. "If I admit it's the most gorgeous creation I've ever laid sight on, will this satisfy you?"

She scowled, her fingers clenching around a fistful of organza that would have Roan expiring when he received the bill. "You're a barbarian."

Macauley laughed, a real laugh, shallow groves shooting from the corners of his eyes. Drawing her attention to the injury on his temple, now little more than a rosy-red mark. His skin had regained its healthy bronze, his jaw covered with a stubbled fringe she yearned to brush her fingertips over. The tips of his nut-brown strands were appealingly scorched.

He looked like a modern-day pirate.

An impossibly handsome ogre.

But he'd laughed.

Making a man laugh was a good thing, wasn't it?

Instead of giving her so much as another side-glance, he crossed to his desk and began to rifle through a box she'd already investigated. A recent delivery, Hatchards Piccadilly was stamped in bold black ink on the label. The man did have a keen appreciation for books. And they were, anywhere she'd seen them, abused from handling.

He certainly knew how to crack a leather spine.

She picked at a loose bead on her gown, wondering how to get him to reveal more of himself before he dispatched her back to Mayfair. "You like reading, then? Books seem to be everywhere."

He shuffled through the stack, making indiscriminate noises as he glimpsed the titles. "Let's merely say I recall a time when I couldn't afford them. I was forced to steal, which did add a deuced spot of fun now that I think on it."

She couldn't imagine this man having to filch anything. In formal black attire, even down to the cravat being employed as a cavalier sling, he looked like he owned half of London and could bring the other half to its knees with a flick of his hand. The elegance he concealed glistened like sunlight around him, now that she knew to look for it.

She'd watched him all night, this effort consuming her even more than the scents and sounds from the gaming hell. The clank of dice, conversation, laughter. So many aromas she couldn't place them. Food, wine, perfume. The air was crackling, alive. Everything she'd wanted from her adventure. Well, almost everything.

She'd seen things he wouldn't appreciate. Wouldn't like.

He held himself apart. She recognized the inclination. He belonged to this world, confident, calm, yet he didn't. And he didn't belong in hers. She'd never have guessed that Xander Macauley didn't know quite where he fit, either.

And, *oh*, he was a joy to behold.

She liked the way he moved. At this very moment, his long fingers curled around a book he brought to his nose and sniffed like he would a glass of wine. His gaze trapped hers over the spine, and the quiver in her belly was visceral, a caress.

"About your chaperone, luv," he murmured, "that was part of the deal."

Pippa nodded to the brocade settee improbably shoved in a far corner. And the elderly woman perched upon it, knitting manchettes with single-minded focus.

His dark brow rose, his expression inscrutable. "That is *not* the maid I bribed at Talbot's. She of questionable moral integrity. My favorite kind of female, by the by."

Pippa chewed on the inside of her cheek. *Shocking.* "This is her nanna."

"Her *nanna*?"

"Viviette could not attend this evening, so she sent her nanna in her stead."

"Is Nanna deaf?"

Pippa laughed. "Goodness, no. She just doesn't speak English."

Macauley threw out a sentence in French. Something about light and time. Pippa's heart sank to her tummy. *Lud,* was he a captivating rascal. Nanna glanced up, shrugged in incomprehension, and returned to her knitting.

Pippa gave her skirt another flip. "Italian, I think."

Macauley braced the book on the desk and leaned over it. A hair's breadth closer. Unfortunately, not close enough. "You brought a chaperone who can't speak English to keep your reputation from sinking into the pits of hell should you be caught in a gambling den with me? Ridiculous plan, innit?"

Viviette's nanna must have understood *something* they said. Or she'd noticed the heat blistering the air around her.

With a whispered batch of advice in a language Pippa didn't understand, Nanna dug in her patchwork satchel, then rose creakily to her feet. In her hand, she held two knitting needles. Waving Pippa back, she placed one needle on the floor and gestured: *don't step past this.* Going to Macauley, she shoved him closer to the door and did the same. Then, old-country etiquette in place, she retreated to her spot on the settee.

Macauley glanced at the needle grazing his polished boot with the most perplexed expression Pippa had ever seen on his face, his book clutched limply in his hand.

Her amusement was unplanned—but there was no way she could hold it in.

He glanced up, his own smile growing. "I feel chastised."

Pippa poked her finger in the middle of her cheek. "Mercy, you have a dimple."

He scrubbed hard at his jaw. "I bloody do not." Sulking, he jammed the book under his injured arm and extracted a gorgeous timepiece from his waistcoat.

Theo's whispered advice—*a three-minute kiss*—roared through her mind. With a tight breath, Pippa scrambled to fill the void before he made her leave. Cinderella returning to her staid life. Although she supposed she wasn't getting a kiss with a nanna around. "You won't be able to ride anytime soon with that shoulder."

He pocketed the watch, his eyes going a smoky, knowing gray. He'd spotted her ploy. "I swim in the Serpentine. At night. During the seasons I can stand it. Streeter and I used to as boys, the finest bath available to two rookery rats. Although he was scared to go in the dark. Still is, poor bloke. Riding I can live without for a bit. Swimming, I'll miss."

Images flooded her mind of his nearly naked body cutting through the murky waters of the Serpentine. Her throat went bone-dry, no acceptable response coming to her.

His mouth hitched on one side, his gaze shimmering like hot ash. "There are other things I do with that hand. It's a challenge, but I'm trying. Mostly every night lately. And some mornings."

Pippa palmed her belly, urging her pulse to calm. She knew enough about men to understand what he was crudely implying. She could shock him. She touched herself, too. However, her hunger was heartbreaking because she'd never, *ever* pictured anyone but Macauley climbing atop her and sliding inside.

He'd not once claimed he pictured *her*.

Nudging the knitting needle with his boot, he retrieved the book from his armpit and flipped through the pages like what he was saying mattered for naught. "What Nanna doesn't understand, *you* don't understand, is that I don't have to touch you to light your wick. You don't have to touch me to light mine."

Pippa hummed huskily as her body ignited. *Adventure number two,* she realized from the depths of her mind.

Macauley continued, his gaze centered on the page. He seemed unmoved. Encounters of this type possibly happened to him every single day. "Have you been kissed, Little Darlington?"

"Yes," she whispered, walking backward until she hit the gallery column. His penetrating expression, though indefinable, made her breath catch.

"*Who?*"

She shook her head. *It doesn't matter. It wasn't you.*

"I would kiss you like a man starved, luv. Press you against the nearest wall and make your vision disintegrate. Memorize each curve, imprint the feel of you upon my fingertips. I would find every vulnerable point of surrender and use it against you." While her blood pulsed in her ears, he returned to his book, a text she suspected he was not actually reading. "There would be no half measures. I don't believe in them. I'd keep us busy until our legs could no longer support us. Our lungs run dry. Our minds empty. Deafening bliss."

Her terse sigh circled the space. "Why are you telling me this?"

He stilled, murmuring something she couldn't catch. His eyes, when they met hers, were filled with thunderous emotion. Confusion, exasperation, impatience. "Because you trust me, so-called, and I want you to understand you shouldn't. I'm trying to warn you, honor among thieves, without alerting your companion, of course. Although any lock on any door is easily picked if I want a woman enough to get into the room. I'm an honorable man in this arena, but I'm still a man."

Pippa thumbed at a bead on her gown, her hand trembling. "Theo said a three-minute kiss would be enough to show me what I need to know. The ones before were seconds and, frankly, didn't tell me anything."

He closed the book with a snap. "I'm not going to do that, luv. Showing you what's what isn't my responsibility."

"Is someone waiting in your bedchamber?" The thought was like a dagger to the heart, but she had to ask. "Is that it?"

The knock on the door interrupted whatever he'd been planning to say. The glower on his face meant he'd been about to say something.

"*Wait.*" She hopped over the knitting needle, invading his space. "Did you read the gossip column in the *Gazette* today?"

Macauley's fingers clenched around the spine of the book. "I *didn't* kiss that scullery maid at Talbot's. Blind rubbish that story."

"It's not you. It's the Earl of Stanford."

Macauley flinched, then muttered a pained groan following it. "What did it say?"

"There was trouble, a brawl, at White's. He was ejected." Pippa reached for him, but the glance he released was savage, so she tucked her hand back by her side. "I spoke with him, a little, during your convalescence. He's searching, Macauley. After the war, that horrible childhood, an earldom saddled with debt. If you could find room in your heart to forgive him for his transgressions, give him a position in your organization—"

From across the room, Nanna squeaked as Macauley made an awkward grab for Pippa, grasping her elbow and giving her a gentle but convincing shake. His book tumbled to the floor. "You dare more than any person I've ever known, Pippa Darlington. When I'll thank you for keeping your bloody opinions to yourself."

Pippa knocked his hand away. Being half in love with the scoundrel didn't mean she would tolerate his temper tantrum. "My family has been created from circumstance and fate. Helena and Theo. The Leighton Cluster. As yours has been. But family *born* matters. Blood matters. Only forgiveness is going to bring either of you peace."

Kicking the book aside, Macauley gave the doorknob a vicious twist, allowing Dash to enter the room.

He took one look at his employer's face and clicked his tongue against his teeth. "Aye, it's the gown. I told ya, boss. Grand enough for a palpitation of the heart. Don't go so hard on yourself, you ken?"

Nanna retrieved Pippa's spencer and tossed it clumsily across her shoulders. Then she gave her charge a none-too-subtle shove toward the door with another snatch of unidentified advice trailing along behind it.

Pippa held out her hand to stay her duenna. She wouldn't allow Macauley to boot her out without some minor recompense. "I'd like my knife back, please."

Exhaling irritably but without a word of dispute, he tunneled his hand in his trouser pocket, withdrew the knife, and slapped it into hers. The metal was warm; she closed her fingers around it to retain his heat.

"Baron Marbury's doxie shoved a card up her sleeve. Queen of spades. If you check, I'm certain you'll find it. You can see a lot from the gallery." Furious for no good reason when he'd upheld his part of the deal, Pippa yanked her hood over her head and sailed from the room without looking back.

Although she could feel the sting of his gaze until she hit the lower-level landing.

The alley was deserted, the carriage waiting, door held open by a man who looked like he could crack bricks with his teeth. He and Dash conversed before the hulking beast assisted her and Viviette's nanna into the conveyance.

Dash offered no more information when she quizzed him on the ride along cobbled lanes, the fetid scent of coal smoke and roasted meat a primal whisper through the open window.

It was not meant to be.

Her adventure had turned out to be only a minor ripple on the pond of her life.

PART TWO

ENCHANTMENT

Chapter Nine

Where a wallflower decides to bloom

Engagement Fete, Dalton House
One month, three days, and twenty-two hours later
(If one were counting, which one was.)

Like a bit of lint on her sleeve, Pippa plucked the wallflower routine free.

Because her sister had suggested, in her academic way, that making a man jealous was a straightforward endeavor. Then Theo discussed biology, chemistry, and inclinations the weaker sex—*men*—couldn't help experiencing due to raging hormones and varying brain matter.

Although Theo ended the conversation by saying making a man jealous was the "oldest trick in the book," which sounded rapacious but, truthfully, the way Pippa preferred to handle things. Pippa couldn't possibly attract a man's biological interest if she continued to bleed into the wallpaper. She couldn't be perfectly honest, either.

Therefore on this night, during the celebration of Sir Reginald Norcross and Lady Sarah Dalton's betrothal, Pippa decided to step from the shadows. As the Duchess Society's latest probable cata-strophe but a high-profile one, Hildy and Georgie had requested she attend. Though they didn't need her. The society was doing almost as well as Macauley's gaming hell, their triumph in introducing two people with no solid prospects who'd fallen in fast and furious love gripping London like a fever.

Love after the signing of marital agreements protecting Lady Sarah's future and the future of her children in a binding trust, of course. According to the Duchess of Markham, the unromantic yet necessary part of the transaction.

Norcross, a former soldier who managed security for Macauley's distillery, was ecstatic. Lady Sarah's smile when she gazed at him was bright enough to light a thousand candles. That he'd once loosely courted Helena, Roan's wife, was a topic no one discussed.

Standing by the refreshment table, Pippa sipped from a glass of ratafia she wished to dump on someone's head simply to erase the monotony of the evening.

No one in the ballroom would be unduly surprised if she had a second go.

Certainly not Xander Macauley. Running into him was the only reason, aside from a ducal summons, she'd agreed to attend.

He stood across the ballroom, leaning nonchalantly against a pilaster, his brooding gaze prowling the space. He looked like he knew better, and she bet he did. Brutality mixed with refinement the *ton* was puzzled and intrigued by.

She knew the reasoning behind the mix. It branded her soul, this shared understanding.

Which made her the most foolish of women because he could not care less.

Pippa hadn't seen him since the night at the Devil's Lair. Not so much as one sighting in Roan's study or across a crowded avenue. No dinner parties with the Leighton Cluster. Except for an unmarked box arriving a day later with the bonnet she'd left behind, there'd been no word from him. No attempt to approach her this evening, either.

Proving how much her ridiculous adventure had meant to him.

Although he'd not been featured in the scandal sheets of late, which was slightly mollifying.

She lifted her gaze, inviting attention for the first time in a year or more. Smiling when she didn't feel like it, the dance card attached to her wrist with a satin ribbon searing her skin. She understood it would be filled tonight from the admiring glances thrown her way.

When no man in London could compare to the one she wanted.

She glanced back at Macauley, vexed that he'd not once glanced at her.

He'd dressed to slay. A wolf in superfine, no effort to conceal his rough edges. Attired in black down to the silk cravat again serving as a sling, an accessory more than one bold chit had felt the need to trace her fingers over. Perhaps he'd worn it to keep from having to dance. A breeze from the terrace doors rolled across the assemblage. Pippa watched somewhat hungrily as Macauley's hair danced, glinting in the light cast from the chandelier he stood beneath. Ignoring social dictates, he'd declined to wear a hat.

As if he sensed her regard, his gaze, finally, *finally*, caught hers.

And there it was. The reason he'd avoided her.

Recognition. *Heat.* A hearth fire roaring through her veins.

He didn't react, the bounder. Simply lifted his flute to his lips and studied her over the rim as he drank. Then with a sluggish blink, he looked away.

There was nothing special about her this evening to interest him.

Her hair was wound into a severe knot at the back of her head. Her gown the same one she'd worn to the gaming hell, mainly because Roan and Helena had assumed it'd been reserved for this event. She even had a smudge of ink on the hem she couldn't get out. Her skin was flushed from the crush surrounding her, tendrils escaping her chignon to curl damply around her face. She felt pathetic and looked worse.

This was not her realm. Only the one she was expected to *inhabit*.

"The masquerade hero," Lady Burton-Chelis murmured as she and Countess Annesley shouldered in beside Pippa at the dessert table. "How I would like to take a bite of that tart. I've tried, but he must have a new mistress. Never gives me the time of day."

Countess Annesley sniffed and reached for a lemon scone. Everyone knew she had a close association with her cousin, Frederick. A cousin-lover *and* an earl-husband were enough to satisfy. "He was only invited because of his friendship with His Graces, the dukes, Markham and Leighton. And his working relationship with Norcross in that distillery. I don't know why ruffians appeal to you. Men of trade, darling, are never the men you want to engage. They have callouses on their fingers, I can guarantee."

Lady Burton-Chelis licked crumbs from her lips with a positively lethal purr. "Sounds divine. Just *look* at him. I wonder what he could do with that sling and a bedpost? Only Tobias Streeter comes close, and everyone knows that's hopeless. He actually loves his wife."

"Frederick, my dear cousin, has visited Mr. Macauley's horrid establishment twice this week." Countess Annesley chewed irritably and reached for another scone. Rosemary this time. "Instead of visits to me. I'm rather put out."

"Maybe I'll ask him to dance. Forward, I know. Nevertheless, be a coup, wouldn't it? He's never been known to take the floor, not once. I bet he dances like he—"

Linking her arm through Pippa's, Theo yanked her away before she heard the rest of Lady Burton-Chelis' diatribe.

"Ignorant clodpates," Pippa seethed as Theo dragged her along the ballroom's perimeter.

Theo grabbed Pippa's glass and settled it behind a potted fern. "Remember the ratafia incident and the trouble it brought you. The Duchess of Markham made me come to fetch you. Since Helena is expecting any day and Roan couldn't attend, she's being a watchful parent. Now that you've decided you're not a wallflower, no one wants to let you out of their sight. When I have all the freedom in the world. Bookish girls have all the luck."

"Where are you taking me?"

Theo yawned behind her book, weaving in and out of societal clusters. "To the suitable gentleman settled by the drink cart. Duchess Society orders. Between us, if you're going to make him jealous, you'd best start now. Xander Macauley isn't known for lingering in ballrooms."

Pippa halted so suddenly that a matron of some age and notoriety stumbled into her.

Theo turned to face her as the crowd flowed around them like water rushing around a boulder. Her smile was tender. And knowing. "It's not absurd that you're attracted to him. You're alike, you two. I don't know why no one else sees it. Two stunning, surly, defiant beasts. Chained by standards they disregard most days. Unobtainable in some mysterious way that only makes people want them more. Faultless intellectual sense to me, your connection. If I were to write a love hypothesis, you would be my test subjects."

Pippa kept herself from spinning to look at him, Theo's words making her heart skip a beat. She'd not suspected anyone thought she and Macauley made *sense*. Goodness, love had never factored into any acknowledged equation.

"Did I tell you he likes to read as much as you do?"

Theo nodded. This information was not part of her love hypothesis. "A man who likes to read is rare."

Pippa seized a flute from a passing footman and gulped champagne. *Oh*, the things Pippa could tell her. Macauley was kind, the last thing he'd want anyone to know. The night of Talbot's fire, he'd defied expectation. Instead of running to Roan, protecting a treasured friendship, he'd chosen to protect *her*. He was intelligent, thoughtful. Loyal. After repeated requests for information, Dash had told her that every person employed at the Devil's Lair had been born inside the Limehouse district. Macauley was making a concerted effort to funnel money *back* into the stews. Going so far as bringing the *ton* to him. Funds to improve the streets once the aristocracy saw how much faster they could get to their destination if they supported the creation of better roadways.

He had grand plans.

Pippa's fingers clenched around the flute. So did she. She would have to go slowly. Secure his friendship. Then, all bets were off.

He wanted her as much as she wanted him. His pupils expanded, flooding his smoky eyes. He fidgeted when the man could stand down a Greek god. He'd had her followed, which meant *something*.

It wouldn't be misleading if he desired her, too.

"*Gads*, the expression on your face is terrifying. Here I stand, fearing for a man most in London are deathly afraid of."

Pippa deposited her glass on a footman's tray and glanced over her shoulder because she could no longer deny the impulse. Macauley was in the same spot, negligent stance against the pilaster unchanged.

Only now, he had company.

Lady Bergeron. Whom it was rumored he'd had a tryst with. Her hand was on his wrist, the injured arm, fingers traveling deliberately up the crease in his sling while she said something that made his lips tilt in a modest smile.

Pippa palmed her belly to halt the tremor working its way from her knees.

He's not yours, Pippa.

But he could be. With a bit of tenacious perseverance.

Theo gave her a shove that had Pippa turning away from the vapid scene. "*Go.* Bump into Lord Bilbrough. He's been staring at you all night. Tell him how agile his mare looked at Epsom. Bat your eyelashes. Oh, and act stupid. Men have no use for clever women."

It was quite easy. Giggles when she wasn't a giggler. Inane comments about a horse race she'd paid no attention to. Phony compliments and idle chatter.

Suddenly, Lady Philippa Darlington was no longer a wallflower.

Her dance card filled up while her heart remained empty.

He'd imbibed one glass of champagne too many.

His shoulder was aching like the devil.

Lady Bergeron was becoming a nuisance.

Macauley decided on these facts as he escaped to the terrace for a supposed smoke. He'd even stuck a cheroot between his lips to validate his excuse. Unfortunately, Eloise had followed him, confident their affair would continue.

How to tell her nicely it was not?

Macauley glanced through the French doors to the slice of ballroom visible through the gap, the vision making him pause, former-lover-rejection forgotten. Pippa. In that layered confection that had nearly choked him when he'd first seen it. Bilbrough hovering. Making a play without so much as one improper gesture.

When the asinine coxcomb should absolutely make a play.

Macauley had encouraged Pippa to drop the wallflower act. Now that she had, men were responding. *Appropriate* men behaving appropriately.

Macauley was the unsuitable who didn't belong.

Although he'd jammed himself in her world somehow, between two dukes and a viscount's by-blow. He smiled and dragged the toe of his boot along the marble flagstones. Wouldn't Street bust a gut if he found out Macauley was an *earl's* by-blow? A frigging step up on that ridiculous blue-blooded chart they seemed to keep. But that was his secret for *life*.

His, Pippa's, and Ollie's.

"You're fretting," Eloise said in a faintly fretting tone herself. "Why don't we leave? My coach is on Curzon." She gave his sling a tug, her lips pursing as if she were blowing out a candle. "I'll be careful with you, darling. *Very* careful."

Macauley took a moment. Pulled the night in like a fierce breath.

A torchlit garden. The fragrance of hydrangea blooming somewhere behind him. An orchestra's prep notes as they sought to begin a new set. Laughter. Crystal clinking. The splash of a fountain he'd bet even money had been in this family since the Middle Ages.

The ribald aroma of roses lifted from Eloise's skin when he preferred vanilla.

Lady Bergeron looked magnificent in the scattered moonlight. His type, as it were. Not a trace of guiltlessness. Bosom swelling, eyes glittering, the color lost to his memory already.

Yet, she was no longer for him.

His expression must have registered because she took a step back in a durable representation of gallantry. "There's someone else."

He didn't argue. Only wiggled his cheroot free and leaned in to kiss her cheek.

That's when Pippa and Bilbrough spilled out of the ballroom with a group of revelers who'd apparently decided gadding about on the lawn was the next big thing.

He should have let her go off with that cream puff in buff breeches who would surely try to steal a kiss beside the medieval fountain and then apologize for it.

But he didn't.

Because Pippa had a hold. He *knew* she liked him, and he couldn't help but use it to his advantage when he feared he liked her back. So when her gaze collided with his over his former lover's shoulder, he changed his life by mouthing one word: *help*.

Her reaction was laughable. And goddamned adorable.

She nearly tripped over her skirts.

Headstrong chit that she was, she made her way to him. Leisurely, like he hadn't asked for salvation, Bilbrough trailing behind, a stray hound. Her smile was fake, her laugh as well. He studied each during her stroll across the terrace.

Macauley both hated and *loved* that he knew this with certainty about her.

Halting before him, where he'd made sure to have no part of his body touching Eloise's, Pippa's smile spiraled into something close to a glower. "Macauley."

He bowed his head just enough to signal indifference. "Darlington."

The creampuff stepped in with a distasteful sneer. "Sir, you're addressing someone above your station."

Macauley spun the cheroot in his hand in a token display of disinterest while heat lit his skin. "You'd best remove him before I feel the need to," he whispered for Pippa alone.

"Markham's looking for you," she blurted, giving the dance card splashed with black ink a spin on her wrist. "Some, um, something to do with the distillery and—"

"The oak vats being delivered from Bruichladdich. A transport issue. I'll find him. Or better yet, you take me to him for efficiency's sake." He snagged her sleeve as he passed, uncaring—for the first time in his life—if he showed his hand.

He simply, selfishly desired her focus to land entirely on *him*.

Instead of heading inside the terrace doors, he took the long way around until they stood in a fragrant side garden surrounded by shrubs and a lone cedar that looked as ancient as the fountain. They weren't back in the ballroom at all but close enough to a side door should they want to return or have an excuse for having planned to. Muted light from chandeliers inside the house washed over them.

And moonlight. Plenty of that, too. The faint stirrings of the orchestra. It was an entire romantic package. A sense of intimacy, as if they were the only two people in the world.

What the fuck am I doing?

Pippa yanked her sleeve away. He was not wearing gloves, and her skin sizzled across his. "I believe you left your paramour on the terrace."

His temper ignited, a flash fire in his belly. "That's my life, luv. Maybe trot on back to yours, how about it?"

She gave her dance card another whirl. "You *asked* me to help, you crooked dealer. Don't deny it after I'm made a proper fool of myself!"

He wanted to refute the accusation. Instead, he tapped his temple with his finger. Hard. "I must be cracked. That's the only explanation. A couple of days of laudanum and you, and my brain is cooked."

A twinkle shimmered in her eyes. Fearsome and frightening. Turning them sea-green and weakening something substantial inside him. As if he needed *that*. She reached, then halted the move, propping her hand on her hip. "You cut your hair."

Shrugging, he dragged his fingers through the recently shorn strands. "The ends were scorched. I've got a valet person now. It's absurd, but Street said once you employ one, you can't live without them. *He* cut it. Spivey Dalton. He's a former longshoreman, so not proper or anything according to your set, but he's quite a handy mate to have around. Very capable with a pistol, even better with a knife."

"Your valet carries a pistol?"

He frowned. "Doesn't everyone's?"

When she let it show, her genuine smile was a glorious thing to behold. She was bloody gorgeous standing there in that stunning frock made to be ripped away with one's *teeth*. Her cheeks rosy, her lips moist where she'd wet them with a splash of champagne he wanted to lick off.

And her eyes, they were more than windows to her soul.

They reeled him in, brought him closer than he wished to be.

Powerful negotiators for a man who liked to bargain.

Jamming his cheroot between his lips, Macauley considered lighting it. A tiny puff to calm his nerves. When he was *never* unnerved. "Nice gown," he said after their silence had started to hurt. Not knowing what to say but not wanting her to sprint back inside, either.

She trailed her hand down her bodice, a charming move that looked unrehearsed. "I *had* to wear it again. Roan thought it was for this event, and what was I to say?"

"That you bought it to wear to a gaming den's opening?"

She gasped and tilted her head, searching his gaze. "You didn't tell him, did you?"

He shook his head. *No.* She had a scattering of freckles on her cheeks. The bridge of her nose. He touched one with the tip of his cheroot. "Cassiopeia."

Her lips parted, but no sound came out.

He scrubbed at the back of his neck and made an unnecessary adjustment to his sling, stalling. "Your freckles. Cassiopeia. The constellation. You know, the Greek goddess who created havoc by boasting she was more beautiful than the sea nymphs. Kingdom-ravaging havoc. Sound like anyone you know?"

She fiddled with her dance card again until he sighed and grabbed her wrist. Then skillfully with one hand, he thought, he untied the ribbon and let the card fall to the flagstones.

Pippa watched it slip away without complaint. "You like books and astronomy. Quite a feat for, what did you call yourself, a rookery tough? If I didn't know better, I'd guess you're pulling my trick on society. Playing a role you're not."

"I like books and astronomy. Chemistry. Latin." It was the first time he'd admitted this to anyone outside of Ollie years upon years ago. Maybe Tobias Streeter a bit. Because it didn't match the persona he'd created for himself. Hulking brutes from the slums didn't *read*. Lie in bed on lonely nights conjugating *regere* after they'd pleasured themselves. He was the brawn behind his businesses, not the brains.

Brawn kept people at a distance. With his broad body and fierce demeanor, it was the easiest sell.

"What if you truly met someone? Or tried to?" he asked without considering it first. The orchestra had begun playing. Some lilting tune that made the evening even more celestial. He was keeping her here, wasting her time *and* his when she should be parading around a ballroom securing her future.

"Lord Bilbrough, you mean?"

His lips flattened. He yanked the cheroot from his mouth and threw it to the flagstones. "Sure, why not? *Debrett's*, page ninety-nine. Although he made a fast exit the moment anyone bigger invaded his space. Not sure he's a keeper, luv. Feeble horses are never a sound bet."

"He thought you were going to punch him. Our only saving grace is your close friendship with my brother. Protecting the little sister and all that nonsense."

Macauley rubbed his knuckles over his jaw. "He thought right."

"Wiping the floor with every posh nob in London, as you call them, doesn't solve anything."

"But it *feels* good. That's the plan, innit?"

"Your plan, I suppose." Pippa flipped her skirts, her face getting a look.

She was scheming. Macauley experienced an answering spark of excitement. *Hell's teeth*, this unruly chit was trouble.

"He pulled me out here because he can't dance. Bilbrough. Now, I'm missing my chance to waltz"—she nodded to the ballroom—"as that's what they're playing. I believe Lord Delacroix was on my card for this set. Here I am with you instead."

She was as subtle as a sledgehammer. "I was only given one summer of gentility, luv. Grooms, even bastards of the master, weren't provided dance lessons. I was lucky they allowed me access to the library. Regrettably, I have no skill in this arena."

"Take my hand." She stuck it out, wiggled her fingers when he didn't immediately comply. "We'll go slowly, tuck your injured arm between us. All you need to do is memorize the steps. Pick up the rhythm."

He studied her hand with a spiraling sense of dread. "No."

He didn't like dancing. He wasn't even entirely sure he liked *her*.

She huffed and grabbed his left hand and settled it on her hip. His fingers clenched around the gentle curve, a tide of sensation rushing through him, hardening parts he'd rather she *not* know this farce of hers was influencing. "Step forward with your left foot. Right foot sideways to the right. Left foot to the right."

She placed her hand on his upper arm, the other on his hip, her scent overriding the floral fog surrounding them. "This isn't perfect hand placement, but I don't want to jolt your shoulder. Let me lead."

"Like you don't insist upon it at all times," he returned heatedly. Though he tried the steps she'd suggested, cautiously, feeling foolish but also wanting to bloody please her.

"This coming from the Limehouse Prince. That's a new one."

He stared intently at his feet. "I *hate* that moniker. Please stop."

"Too bad because it fits." She guided him through a series of moves. Two gradual rotations until he began to gather the sequence. "Step back with your right foot, sideways to the left, then bring your right next to your left. It's quite straightforward. People who dance poorly have poor *rhythm*. From your wealth of surreptitious activities, I have a feeling your rhythm is excellent."

When he could without stumbling or stepping on her toes—and not a moment before—he brought his gaze up, meeting her eyes. For all her might, she was a petite fluff of a female. Macauley towered over her, making him feel graceless and formidable in confusing surges. His hand flexed again around her hip. She wanted to tangle with him about subjects they should never discuss. "I've never gotten any complaints."

She hummed a response, her lids fluttering when their movement began to clumsily match the music. His heart kicked, a vision of him sliding inside her, her moan ricocheting off the walls, storming his mind. He wondered what he would have to do to make her scream. His fingertips burned where he touched her. An imprint as indelible as ink. His shoulder was throbbing, but he wasn't about to stop this wonder of a first dance on a darkened terrace in the middle of Mayfair.

Not if his life depended upon it.

He understood why the waltz was considered hazardous. Thighs brushing, breath mating. It was the closest one could come to having sex while clothed.

"Look at me," he whispered, his senses rioting. He was close to doing something, although he wasn't sure what.

Her lashes lifted, her gaze seizing his. She lost count at his look, lost her step. He caught her, bringing her closer.

This was glorious. Horrendous. Bewildering. He'd never desired anyone so fiercely—and so fiercely against his will.

They slowed to a halt in a triangle of light spilling from a bay window, the music from the ballroom having ceased moments before. While his pulse hammered, and he tried to unravel what was happening to him, Macauley absurdly took time to count the freckles on her nose. Seven. Record the burst of gold at the edge of her pupils. The lock of hair that had come loose from her chignon. A mocking gust of wind took the flaxen strand and slapped it across his jaw. His cock strained against superfine until he feared his shaft would pop his buttons.

"What do you think?" she asked, her voice ragged.

He exhaled softly. "It feels strangely intimate."

"Macauley," she whispered, her breathy plea sealing the deal. Her hand crept from his shoulder to the nape of his neck. Negotiating.

"If I admit I want to kiss you, somewhat desperately, will you trot back into the ballroom and forget we ever talked about this?"

She shook her head, unwilling to let him go. Paying him back for calling to her on the terrace, a time he'd been unwilling to let *her* go.

"Roan will kill me if he finds out."

"He won't."

He grunted. "Find out or kill me?"

"Either." She laughed and rolled her bottom lip between her teeth, destroying his resolve in one second. "Or."

"It's attraction, luv. It doesn't mean anything."

Why did he sound like he was trying to convince them both?

She placed her hand over his mouth. "Stop talking." Then she trailed her thumb over his jaw, the caress sending his blood blasting through his veins.

He brought her closer until she bumped his chest, his injured arm.

His shoulder had stopped being an issue at some point. This, *she*, was more potent than opium. He was in no pain. Or only the pleasurable kind.

He was going to do it. He was going to kiss the stuffing out of this girl. She'd more than asked for it.

"Three minutes, innit? Your time limit for the perfect kiss." If he'd had the ability, he would have dragged his Bainbridge from his fob pocket. This was only for her blasted adventure and no more.

She glanced around hurriedly, spotting whatever she sought as her smile went leagues wide. Sliding her hand down his arm, she linked her fingers with his and pulled him along the side of the house. He hadn't held hands with a woman in ages, forever mayhap, and he lit up where she touched him.

She stopped before a set of stairs leading to a domestics' entrance. Chipped, not-to-be-used-by-guests steps. She hopped up on the bottom one, then turned, bringing them near to eye level. "I can barely reach you without assistance. And for this, I need to pay attention." She wound her arms around his neck cautiously, still thinking of his shoulder while he was imagining how quickly he could tear her damned gown off her body.

She was slight yet perfectly curvaceous in the right spots. She smelled of promise and yearning, at least to him. Her longing traveled through him like a shot of whisky, leaving a scorching path behind it.

But the way she was looking at him, her arms gathered around him in a loose hug. He almost laughed, knowing she wouldn't appreciate it. She thought this was going to be *sweet*. Like something she'd read in a novel or seen in Vauxhall behind a hedge. An embrace set to calm her frustration, not create more.

She had no idea what this could do to them.

He cradled her face, tilting her lips into view, into reach.

Here goes smashing her naïve dream to bits.

And me putting myself on the path to ruin.

Chapter Ten

Where a curious woman learns how long three minutes truly is

He delayed, hand gently cupping her jaw, indecision written in the depths of his bottomless silver eyes. Pippa didn't want him to think. She wanted Xander Macauley, king of the underworld, tyrant, lothario, scoundrel, for *once* concerning her, to simply *do*.

Kiss her like he had every widow, actress, and opera singer in London.

Hence, having no plan and less experience, Pippa went on instinct. She slipped her hand into the hair at the nape of his neck, silky, over-long abundance, and brought his mouth to hers.

The last thing she witnessed was his dark lashes sweeping low.

Perhaps it was the months of yearning, awareness bouncing between them like a ball. The dreams she'd had of touching him. The moments she'd observed him across a dinner table or striding down a crowded boulevard while thinking, *yes, him*, that let them dissolve into each other so seamlessly.

Two becoming one.

Her lips parted at his invitation, then he sipped. His tongue grazed hers. Lightly, then with more urgency. Inviting her to play. He asked before diving deeper, silent consideration. Held back even. She could feel the tremors shaking his broad shoulders, his muscular arms.

For a time, he let her lead as he had in the waltz. But as the heat between them fired higher, her fingernails scored his scalp, her rasping murmurs escalated, sounding out her pleasure. Losing patience, his hand skated down her side, curved around her hip and fit her against his hard body. She bloomed like a rose, petals wide. The rush was remarkable, a sweeping jolt traveling from her toes to her fingertips. When they couldn't get close enough, with an oath, he wrenched his arm from the sling and let the silk drop to the flagstones. Slanted her head for better access.

His long body bowing over hers, his arm hanging by his side, only sparse layers of clothing standing between them. His thigh tucked between hers, steadying her in the most carnal of ways.

The kiss spiraled. Moist heat. Tongues dancing. Her senses overwhelmed. The milled soap he'd used during his bath filled her nostrils. His heart beating rapidly against her breast. From hip to chest, coupled in a way she'd only imagined. He was strapping where she was soft, muscles flexing, chest heaving.

He wasn't indifferent, passionless. He was alive, willing, *eager*.

The man beneath the gruff exterior roared into the picture, into her life.

Into her heart.

A thrum of pleasure, a pulsing pressure, situated between her thighs. She wiggled against him, tunneling her hand deeper into his hair. *More.* She whispered the appeal, the vibration where their lips joined adding to the delight. Another moment, then they caught each other's rhythm fully, smoother than their waltz, turning what she'd planned as a simple encounter on its head.

Her breath backed up in her lungs. For the first time in her life, she felt faint.

Halting the kiss before she tumbled off the step, she dragged her mouth across his jaw. Nibbled on a spot beneath his ear that had him blowing out a ragged exhalation. Grabbing his shoulders, she clung to support herself.

"Wait," he murmured against her throat, pressing his lips to the beating pulse. "Hold on." His voice was tattered, thready, and deep. His hand rose to circle her ribs, halting at the curve of her breast. Her nipple pebbled, begging for his attention. *There.*

"No waiting. No thinking. I have at least another"—she settled her mouth atop his, searching for the connection she'd broken—"minute left."

"Did he kiss you?" he asked, moving a hairsbreadth away, dodging her. His eyes were stormy skies. Tarnished silver. Desire and indignation were an intoxicating mix. "Did he try?"

She blinked him into focus. Kiss? *Bilbrough?*

Macauley cursed and seemed to come apart at the seams. Before she could take another breath, he caught her around the waist, lifting her up the remaining steps. Until her back hit the door, his body closing in to secure the fit. Hairpins scattered as his fingers dove into her hair, tilting her head at his direction. Opening her wholly to his assault. His fingertips tattooed his need on her skin. Devastating her—until she lost herself.

To his passion. His fury.

The kiss was his from that moment. Pippa gladly surrendered.

His skill and her adoration were dangerous partners. The rising urgency was fraught with risk. They could be seen. Someone opening the door at her back, where they'd tumble in. Any number of dreadful possibilities.

Possibilities to drive him away forever.

Or deliver him to her in a way he'd hate her for.

Nonetheless, it was too late. Rational thought had died an honest death. There wasn't space for anything beyond sensation.

She understood now how people were ruined, how they *enjoyed* their demise.

This was magical. His mouth played over hers, his tongue engaging her in sly practices that transformed her body and mind. His thumb traced the round lower swell of her breast, teasing her. Then with a murmured command, an urgent appeal she missed in the asking, he let her slide down his body until her feet hit the step.

She experienced everything, *everything* he was made of on the way there.

His shaft was stiff and wedged quite brilliantly against her hip. She reached, thinking only to touch.

"*No*, Pip," he ground out, catching her hand. "That's too far."

The sounds of the night threaded into her awareness. The cadence of their furious breaths batting each other's cheek. Their combined scent, heat-blended, mingled with the aroma of decadence drifting from the house. A fragrance she would never in her lifetime forget.

He pressed his forehead to hers, his skin moist, not allowing an inch of space for her to maneuver. It was bliss. She was where she wanted to be—her body bonded to his.

She drew a lazy circle on his upper back and smiled against his collar when he stretched into the caress. "I hate to tell you this, but I had thirty seconds left."

In response, he seized her lips in a disordered final siege, temper crisping the edges. His loss of control had made him angry, she could see. She fisted her hand in his shirt and pulled him slightly off-balance, hoping to imprint this kiss on his memory for all time. They were passionately furious in a way she hadn't expected was a part of this game.

He stepped back suddenly, tearing himself away. His injured arm cradled loosely at his hip. The expression on his face was nothing short of thunderous.

He wasn't going to touch her again this evening, that was evident.

She forced herself to breathe. Only so she could breathe him in.

"Splendid," he whispered and spun away from her, yanking his hand through his hair. Tipping his head back, he stared long and hard at the sky. A bit like he was seeking answers to questions no one had asked.

He was shaken. So was she. Her rapture was immediate.

"Macauley, look at me."

He lifted his hand in a dismissing motion. *A moment, please.*

It was too late if he thought to wait until his masculine "problem" went away. She'd felt how hard he'd gotten. Even if he hadn't allowed her to touch him... *touch* him.

Too far, he'd said.

Well, she was not going to forget about it. Even if he wished her to. She *owned* his reaction.

The only piece of him she would ever own.

"Stop whatever damned plotting you're doing back there."

"I find you..." She twisted her hands together, wondering where to go with this. How to tell him. "It's not the kissing. Or not only kissing. Like it is for a man. The physical piece. I find you interesting. Intelligent and..."

Ingenious. Courageous. Kind.

Sighing dejectedly, he turned to face her. He appeared slightly dumbfounded, which was gratifying. The sounds of the orchestra fluttered past as the musicians began another set. Sir Roger de Coverley. The last dance of the evening.

A lonely boy who'd never been taught to dance wouldn't know that.

They stood, staring, words lost. Passion an indescribable shackle linking them and tugging hard. He was heartbreakingly handsome, moonlight pulling amber glints from his tousled hair. Silver eyes shimmering. Jaw flexing in indecision.

Of course, she wanted him now more than ever.

He'd been right to warn her.

While she watched, his face closed. Boundaries in place. She'd lost him.

"I'll find Theo and send her to you. Make excuses with the Leighton Cluster should any be required. Stay put. Right *here*. Not one move elsewhere. If a servant comes to the door, tell them you felt faint in the ballroom and stepped out for air."

"But—"

He cut her off, gesturing to her hair, her body. "You look ravished, Darlington. More than a trace. I'm sorry, I lost control. You need assistance I can't give. Sneaking into Roan's carriage is your soundest option. I'm gathering, of all people, your sister somehow knows about us."

Us.

Most women would take his dismissal as a failure—but there was an *us* where there had never been before. No woman in London could claim an *us* with this man.

His lips tightened. A light rain had begun to fall, and she stepped beneath the eave to protect what was left of her sad presentation. "Don't fixate on any one pronoun I'm using, luv."

Oh, he was clever, her rookery scoundrel.

"Wipe that grin off your face, Pippa. This is a *disaster*. A flawed adventure in every sense."

He flattened his arm to his belly, his shoulder obviously paining him. His breath churned from his lungs, little rips of air that made her want to press her mouth to his again. *Lud*, could the man kiss. "We have dinner next week at your brother's. Helena's birthday, innit? Remember? I plan every engagement with you like I'm entering battle, so I do. You have to hide the way you're looking at me right now. And I have to hide this." He motioned to the raging erection tenting his trousers.

Gazing at his physical reaction because she couldn't look away from *that*, she licked her lips, her belly constricting when he reached to brush his hand blindly across his mouth.

"Stop it," he growled.

"I don't see the problem. It was one kiss. Maybe not even three minutes."

Oh, but it was a problem. A looming, spectacular one.

"You see, luv, I can't spend time with you after this and not want you. That's trouble for me." He circled his finger around his temple. "This kiss muddled the entire deal in my head, somehow. I feel a bit like I do after I've been swindled."

Her temper sparked, and she shoved away from the door. "Because you snap your fingers, and they come running. There are no consequences when you go in with such a solid plan not to have any. You're used to getting any woman you want, then sending them away like the washwoman with your dirty trousers. Complications never enter the picture. It's by your supervision, the whole experience! Sorry I didn't follow along."

"I don't want any bloody woman, I want *you*."

Her heart lifted, almost bringing her slippers off the flagstones. "Then *take* me."

He swore and jabbed his finger practically in her face. "Stay. *Put*. I'll send Theo out to retrieve you. Devise a plan to get you home safely while ensuring the way is clear with your Duchess Society chums. Dash is here. He can escort you. He's trustworthy and, better yet, purchasable. Five pounds in his pocket, and he'll never speak of this incident again. All you need, all *I* need, is London's wittiest matchmakers finding out about a ruinous, never-to-be-repeated fiasco with one of their own."

"They aren't matchmakers," she called to his retreating back. "You arrogant oaf."

Crossing the terrace with a ground-eating stride, he halted, dropped to his knee, and snatched up her crumpled dance card. Then he was gone.

Leaving her to catalog his splendor.

He had the longest legs of any man of her acquaintance. Lean yet nicely formed in his finely fitted trousers. Broad shoulders. A trim waist. A tight, round bum. A dimple. He had a dimple; she'd almost forgotten! A stunning smile when he let it rip. And he smelled utterly divine.

Also, she could not deny—the man kissed like a god.

His kiss, *blazes*... she was destroyed. No wonder women chased him down the street. Her previous efforts were sad, sad, sad in comparison.

Pippa whistled a feeble breath and slumped against the door.

Tipping her head, she gazed at the sky, searching where Macauley had been moments ago. A burst of stars glistened like diamonds in black velvet. Cassiopeia was somewhere up there. Pippa touched her cheek, her freckles now her most beloved feature.

She wrapped her arms around herself and grinned, knowing her rookery rogue would be livid should he see so much as a flicker of joy cross her face.

She couldn't have stopped smiling had someone held a pistol to her head.

Kissing Xander Macauley had been the si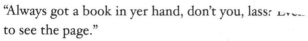
of her life.

Now, she merely had to figure out how to

⁂

"Always got a book in yer hand, don't you, lass? ~~~~~~
to see the page."

Startled from her musing, Theo glanced up from her perch atop the stone wall circling Leighton House's garden to find Xander Macauley's pet project leaning carelessly against the veranda's balustrade, a rosy-tipped cheroot dangling from his lips.

"Am I intruding?" he asked when he knew he was. "I have a spot of time before the guv picks me up round the corner, on Albemarle. Since I had to escort ye fine ladies home, mostly to save your unruly sister from further disaster. The chit has a certain penchant. Nae the first of her fixes I've been involved with if the truth be crawling from my throat and into the night."

Theo started to argue, although he was right about Pippa, so why bother? She was, however, unwilling to tell this uncouth scamp that this was her favorite spot on the entire estate. Her *private* spot. Lest he expect to find her here again. The grandest garden in London, a lush arrangement of primrose, mallow, delphinium, and peony rumored to have been designed by Capability Brown. She pruned the shrubs and brought fresh blooms into the house herself, even though Roan had many servants to do those things for him.

She also didn't mention that he should call her Miss Theodosia. Or that his being alone with her was a risk to her reputation. The lout. Which was laughable because no man would be tempted to take advantage of Theodosia Astley. Besides, she couldn't rudely dismiss the lad when he'd helped her earlier this evening. Helped Pippa, actually. He'd spirited her sister from the engagement ball, escorting her home without anyone in the *ton* or, heaven forbid, the Duchess Society, knowing she'd been kissed to within an inch of her life by the most infamous blackguard in London.

eo was correct in her assessment, her love hypothesis still in
sting stages.

Dash strolled over when she failed to object. More a swagger, actually. Ridiculous when he hadn't done enough in his brief life to earn the
right to swagger.

He gestured to her book with the glowing tip of his cheroot,
resting his hip on the balustrade a few paces to her left. "I reckon it's
good, then. The way you're hugging it so."

She dropped the novel to her lap, title down, reluctant to let him
see that tonight's selection was rather lurid. Nothing academic by any
measure. Theo enjoyed a rousing love story as much as she liked a
stimulating text on chemical processes. Mostly because she suspected
she'd never have a love story of her own. Therefore, it was fitting to
read about someone else's. She shrugged and ran her thumb along a
crease in the spine. "It's passable."

He hummed a vague reply and threw a calculating glance around
the garden. "This is quite the posh plot. I dinna think I've ever seen a
garden as grand. Nae outside Glasgow, anyways. The botanical garden
there is a bonnie sight to behold."

She understood his reaction. Some days, she could hardly believe
she'd landed in this lush world herself. In a few short steps, her half-
sister Helena's marriage had chucked Theo from the rookery to Mayfair.
Then she was introduced to darling Pippa, the sister of her heart, who
she would do *anything* for, even lie through her teeth about perilous
adventures with men likely to break her sister's heart. "Capability
Brown is rumored to have designed it in 1790," Theo finally murmured
when it appeared the young Scot expected her to say something.

He turned to her, his smile close to irresistible. His eyes were a
pale, moonlit blue, shining with humor at something she hadn't meant
to be funny. This often happened as the things she found humorous,
no one else seemed to. His hair was a heavy fall over his brow, black as
tar, not a hint of any other color. He tilted his head, his amusement
growing at her inspection. He had a crooked scar on his chin that she
wondered how he'd gotten.

Theo glanced shyly to her book when she indeed couldn't see the words in the wash of hazy light unless the text was pressed practically to her face. She wasn't taken in by the aristocratic charms dangled before her so often of late, so why be entranced by this? Men, who couldn't *wait* to tell her about their titles and the number of estates attached to each, seemed around every corner now. The stories had started to repeat themselves in dismal glory.

How many times they'd met King George or been invited to Carlton House. Grievances about attending class at Cambridge or Oxford, discussions that infuriated her because she would never be allowed to study at either, and these featherbrains didn't appreciate the opportunity. Men were only flitting about because her dowry was big enough to raise shipwrecks from the sea, according to Helena. Plus, her brother-in-law *was* a peer of the realm. The highest, a duke squatting right beneath a prince.

Theo had status she'd never wanted nor knew what to do with.

She was plain and bookish, and a hundred luxurious gowns made by the costliest modiste in the city wasn't going to change that. Or a duke for a brother. Or a pocketful of blunt. She often thought to tell them— Helena, Hildy, Georgie, Pippa, Roan—but she didn't want to disappoint.

She glanced at him again, intrigued despite herself. Silence was hard to maintain comfortably.

This was ridiculous to consider. Dash Campbell wasn't attracted to her. Or cultured enough should he have been. Roan had "standards" regarding the gents who would someday court her. This scoundrel, a pair of dice in his hand every time she saw him, would never make the list. But he *was* interesting. She'd heard Roan and Helena whispering about him being the shrewdest card sharp in England. Maybe even a pickpocket before being plucked from the stews. If he kept his bridle clipped to Xander Macauley's, he'd be wealthy as Croesus in a few years.

According to Dash, he was going to own his own gaming hell and would burn through the *ton* like a flash fire. She had no doubt he'd someday rule the city.

Hop in and out of every bed, too, if he chose.

Because if his lilting voice wasn't enough to entice, there *was* the matter of his face.

Not that Theo cared about such things—if she ever fell in love, the man would be a noteworthy academic with a predictably unappealing countenance—but Dash Campbell was blindingly good-looking. The kind of splendor that halted people, men *and* women, on the street. Full, stumbling stops. She'd seen it happen more than once. A hazard to her way of thinking rather than a boon. Bringing attention to oneself no matter the circumstance.

She would have hated being that beautiful.

He knocked his hair out of his eyes and took a long pull on his cheroot, his patience for their companionable silence over. "Maybe ye could help me. A wee project I'm undertaking."

She scooted to the edge of the wall and hooked her slippered foot on a jutting stone. "Me?"

"Aye. In the writing of my book."

Theo blinked, as stunned by those six words as any she'd ever heard. "Your book?"

Dash skimmed his gaze her way, the trace of vulnerability mixed with devilry tugging curiously at her heartstrings. "Marked cards, reflectors, holdouts, manipulations. I ken them all. Collusion. Conspiracy. I have a chapter name for each already thought out. Breakdowns of the major games. Hazard, poker, roulette. Faro, even. Ways to spot tells. Or put the doings to your own use should that be your gambit. Nae a topic I've missed."

Theo brought her book to her mouth and laughed into pages that smelled faintly of mildew. "You want to write a book teaching people how to *cheat?*"

He rounded on her, his hip coming off the balustrade. "I'd sell more copies in one month than that Austen chit does in a year. Do ye ken how many men in this loathsome city are losing what piddling blunt they have nightly? Desperate to find a way to stop the bleeding? I used to hold lessons in the back of my flat in Glasgow, then in Shoreditch. More demand in each than I could keep up with. Every nob in town sailed through my battered doorway, yearning to ken what I ken. How do ye think I met Macauley? He was there, as was every gambling proprietor in England. My book would be solid information from a professional."

"Solid information from a professional," she repeated, charmed to her toes.

He blew out a furious breath and tossed his cheroot to the ground where he promptly stomped on it. A tantrum from a man she'd never seen the least flustered. "Forget I asked, Lady Theodosia."

"I'm a miss, not a lady." When he went to stalk from the garden, genuinely insulted by her reaction, Theo scrambled up, grabbing his sleeve to halt him.

He gazed down at her, his teeth a white flash as his lips parted on a fractious sigh. A man in defense of his dream. She documented this like she would a lab experiment. No one understood grand plans better than Theo Astley.

He was tall and lean, on the side of gangly. A body in debate over progressing from lad to man. His jaw was covered in a faint dusting of jet stubble, patchy in spots. His clothing was informal but high quality, thanks to Macauley, she guessed. He smelled of a spicy masculine fragrance that was subtly enticing. She didn't have enough experience with such things to even imagine what it was.

The most intriguing piece? He fairly vibrated with emotion. Sentiments flew across his face like rubbish in a gust while they stared, making her wonder, *what is he about* for the only time in her eighteen years. People mostly ignored her, and she them.

She released his sleeve when it occurred to her that neither of them was wearing gloves, and his skin was hot against hers. A strange feeling seeped into her belly, weakening her knees. She swallowed hard against the temptation to sweep his hair from his jaw. "Can you read?"

His shoulders went back, a fighting stance. "Nae very good, I suppose."

Life was a puzzle. Dash Campbell, rookery pickpocket and renowned card sharp, a young man with perhaps the most exquisite face in England, had presented a challenge Theo couldn't have turned down for the world. "I'll help you. Reading first. Writing after. One requires the other."

He glowered, little plackets settling beside his lush mouth. His eyes were clear enough to dive into. He really was unjustly attractive. "Canna I dictate it to ye? Less time involved. I'm a busy man, what with the gaming hell and keeping blokes from swindling the Lair and all."

"Do you plan to work for Macauley forever?"

He rocked from one boot to the other, his gaze narrowing. Trying to figure out her game. What he would never understand was, she didn't *have* a game. What she presented was what she *was*.

"If you plan to open your own business at some point, Mr. Campbell, even manage the accounts for your publishing venture, you'll need to read well. *And* write well. Math would be a useful subject to add to the list."

His grin broke through his skepticism. "I'm *brilliant* with numbers, lass. I can count cards like no one you've ever seen in your wee life. Then, add in my noggin like a whirlwind."

"You can do this arithmetic on paper, then?"

He glared and wiped his fist beneath his nose, looking finally more boy than man. "I can pay ye. My reserves are growing like a weed shooting right through the cobbles. Regular monies from Macauley, every Friday without delay. I dinna think he's a bloke to miss a payment."

Theo laughed, utterly, unexpectedly enchanted. "Oh, no, *no*. You misunderstand. I wish to *be* a teacher. But life is a very thorny predicament and working at any position is not easily attainable where I've landed." She shrugged, her hand going out as if to shoo a fly. When it was her dream she was flicking away. "You'll be my first, and maybe only, student. I have texts. Loads of them. Materials. We can use the blue parlor—"

The kiss was soft. Tender. Barely there before it was over.

He didn't touch her anywhere else, only his lips grazing hers. His sweet scent filled her nose, her heart thumping hard, then gone.

All gone.

Theo blinked to find Dash pulling away, his lids sweeping up to reveal eyes gone blue as ice. "Why did you do that?"

He nodded to the book she clutched, forgotten. "Ye looked so lost for a wee second there, I wanted to snap ye out of it. Someday, your fine fella will come. Flesh and blood. *Blue* blood, I expect your clan is planning for. With only Theodosia Astley in his sights. He willna be tucked up inside some dusty pages. Dinna worry about that." Dash strolled three paces, then threw the full force of his charm over his shoulder. "But I thank ye for the lessons. I accept. Then I'll owe ye. And someday, lass, that owing will be worth something."

Theo watched him stroll from the garden.

She bet it would.

Chapter Eleven

Where a scoundrel who doesn't believe in love questions love

T he raucous sights and scents of the Devil's Lair were comforting.

Macauley liked that he couldn't *quite* catch a stray thought with so much going on around him. The sound of dice bouncing across baize, the cries of the croupiers, the inebriated laughter of his patrons. His mind was occupied. There was no time to dwell on kisses given— and wholly *received*—on a moonlit terrace two days ago.

He equated this ease with turmoil to his upbringing in the slums. A constant cacophony, never a moment's quiet. All night. Every night. Aromas from the varied existences being played out on the streets, flowing uninvited into whatever tiny abode he'd managed to secure for himself. A time when he'd been unafraid of anything. An angry bastard.

There was strength in being fearless.

Although he only knew one fearless person anymore. A woman who *should* be frightened down to her gorgeous toes of the mess she'd stepped into on that terrace.

"What a spectacle," Tobias Streeter murmured as he settled in beside Macauley in the gallery's narrow alcove, his gaze sweeping the gaming floor below. "More than you'd planned even, am I right, Mac? Bigger crush tonight than last and the one before it. I think the chap in the crimson cape is a prince from the continent. He's lost well over a thousand pounds this eve already. And there, the nob with the elegant walking stick. An MP, isn't he? Pays to have friends in high places."

He leaned his hip on the balustrade and spun a pound chip between his fingers. "I'll make my investment back fast enough to buy another distillery. That one I'm looking at in Scotland. Near Oban. You're in if I decide to sign the papers, right? I've got your young Scot investigating some of the particulars since it's his area of the world, so to speak. The deal will go smoother if a native is involved."

Macauley brought his tumbler to his lips, the whisky, his and Tobias's from distillery number one, flowing smooth as silk down his throat. "The lad is busy enough with his duties here, but yes to both. I'm in, Street. Dash is at your ready should you need him. He understands the brogue where you and I have trouble. Lad's got a fine mind, which I've heard rumor he's preparing to sharpen like a blade against a stack of books. Word in the family is Theodosia Astley wishes to teach the urchin, heaven help us." He balanced his glass on the railing, an argument brewing between a boozy baron and the mistress of an earl's second son capturing his attention. If they so much as touched each other, unless they were planning to employ one of his chambers upstairs, he would pitch them into the alley himself. Bloodshed was sure to calm his mood. "Anyway, when have I not been in, mate? My role, innit? Partners till death does us in."

"Markham and Leighton have agreed as well. I think we should put something regal on this label to honor their friendship. What do you think about, 'two dukes blessed this brew'?"

Macauley laughed, though it rang hollow. Tobias was the by-blow of a viscount, acknowledged only weeks before his father's death—and he'd never considered himself to be part of society. Too, being half Romani didn't garner the *ton's* favor. Although he'd gotten the jump on society by marrying Hildegard Templeton, the daughter of an earl. So his ties were binding, whether he liked it or not. Where Macauley's were hidden, known to only three people in the world.

Tobias gestured to Macauley's shoulder. "Still in the sling?"

Macauley tossed back his remaining whisky. His discomfort was a reminder of his foolishness. "I overexerted myself. Activity too soon." Kisses and waltzes. The waltz honestly more emotionally conflicting than the bloody kiss.

He'd kissed plenty of women but never danced with one.

What a mistake *that* had been.

Tobias pinched back a grin. "I begin to see the picture. I heard Lady Bergeron was quite persistent at Norcross's engagement bash. Smashed your shoulder with horizontal refreshment, did she?"

Macauley spun his empty glass in a circle on the rail. "You see for shite. I cut Eloise off. Kindly, I hope. I wish her nothing but the best." He shrugged, exhaled carefully, feeling foolish. "I sent round the usual."

"Tiara?"

Macauley snorted. "That was *your* parting gift, mate. How many of those did you stick atop some chit's teary-eyed head? Famous for 'em. The Streeter farewell. I think I bought a couple for you in crisis. I go for simpler pieces."

Tobias slid a pair of spectacles from his coat pocket and adjusted the curved arms behind each ear. They were all wearing them these days. "It's been so long. Now it's just Hildy and the babies. Those cursed cats. Another, a mouthy calico, has started hanging around the kitchen door. I know I'm going to end up with three in the house. Hildy has been dropping hints. Given him a name. Reginald. Reggie for short. Once they have a name, they never leave. I don't know how I got here, but I'm grateful every day that I did." He flipped the gaming chip between his hands, a contented man in his prime. "I haven't visited that jeweler since I got married. Not even walked past his shop, that I can recall. Hildy doesn't care for baubles. She's more a kind act over gifts girl."

"The proprietor weeps at the loss of profit."

"You could make it up to him."

Macauley gave the railing a tap with his glass. "I use a bloke on Sackville."

"So, who will it be now that Lady Bergeron has been dispatched?"

Macauley made a snap decision. "I'm taking a break."

The chip slipped from Tobias's hand and bounced off the Axminster rug, coming to rest by Macauley's boot. "Taking a break as in..." Tobias circled his hand in the air, speechless.

"No women, Street. Only business. Work clears the mind. Isn't that a saying?" Macauley glowered at the dumbstruck expression sitting like a toad on his friend's face. "I know you won't understand, mate, cracking lovebird that you are. Can't live without Hildy, I get it. Soul mates or some such, innit? Made for each other. Well, that is *not* happening to me. I can go it alone for a bit. Might enjoy it, even."

Tobias laughed so raucously a crowd gathered around the faro table looked up, searching for the sound. "You, my friend, are deluded about the irrefutable benefits of finding the right woman. The *only* woman when you find her. But a man must conduct lots of experiments to find her. I can see you're still in the midst of your research."

Macauley jammed his hand in his trouser pocket to confirm Pippa's dance card was still there. Which, of course, it was. Crumbled from repeated handling.

Talk about a cracking lovebird.

I find you interesting. Intelligent.

When in his *life* had a woman cared about his mind?

A gnawing ache settled in his chest. Pippa wasn't an experiment. She was a friend he'd made the mistake of kissing. Or perhaps the mistake had been in expecting the kiss to be meaningless. Typically, it was. A path to pleasure only.

He'd never cared to dawdle long on that path.

When he'd pressed her up against the door, he'd had no notion but to go on kissing her until the end of time. Until they expired on the spot. A romantic, moonlit garden in the middle of Mayfair. The setting infuriated him it was so maudlin.

The only reasoning he could find for his absurd reaction was the fact that she'd made him dance. Something about the waltz screwed with a man's head.

Then she'd opened like a blossom and invited him in.

What was a half-starved bloke to do but *take*?

"What is that coxcomb doing here?"

Macauley grasped the railing and leaned out. The Earl of Stanford stood in the shadowed entrance, his hands fists by his side, looking like he was debating whether to run back into the street. He swiped his hair from his brow just as he had as a boy. Macauley's heart gave a twist, similar to the one it had given when Pippa looped her arms around his neck. His brother standing there utterly uncertain of his welcome was more than Macauley could take.

"He's not, actually. A coxcomb, I mean. He's merely young and searching." Macauley crossed to the staircase leading to the main floor. "I wanted to talk to him about investing in one of our businesses. He has a medieval estate to support, and I assume his father left him unprepared financially." Pippa's words resounded through his mind. *If you could find room in your heart to forgive him, give him a position in your organization.*

He hadn't had the chance to tell her he'd heeded her advice. Or was about to.

Tobias was right behind him, their footfalls a dull echo along the carpeted hallway and down the stairs. "Another of your rescue missions? Nothing like taking a lost soul under your wing. Scottish foundlings and opium-addled earls. Workhouse orphans. Who's next?"

Macauley refrained from comment, realizing the state his brother was in as he began to weave his way through the *vingt-et-un* tables. An incredibly foxed Viscount Trotsky had insulted Stanford in a way a less distressed man would have shrugged off. However, when rage was close to the surface, any slight could make it blow, no matter how insignificant.

Macauley had been there himself a time or two.

Trotsky threw a punch before Macauley or the patrols posted in each corner could thwart the scuffle. A solid blow that connected smartly with Stanford's jaw, sending his head back with a crack. His brother went to his knee but only for a moment before he dragged Trotsky to the floor, his arm going around the viscount's neck in a vicious grip. A soldier's response to an attack. Lethal and mindless.

Evidently, Macauley's urge to wipe the floor with the viscount meant he still loved his little brother.

Tobias got there first, able to sprint without an injured shoulder, taking hold of Stanford's arm and yanking him off the viscount. Stanford turned, eyes filled with fury, arm cocked.

"*Ollie!*" Macauley shouted before he could stop himself. His guards were sliding to a halt beside the melee, ready to take punitive action first, question their reasoning second. They were stevedores who'd been looking to leave the docks behind. Brutes, all told. Well-paid and ruthless, as Macauley required.

Tobias, too, would take no abuse. Like all rookery boys, he fought dirty when the need called for it.

Stanford blinked, his breath rushing forth in a hiss. Yanking his arm from Tobias's hold, he hung his head, his chest heaving.

Macauley signaled to Dash, who'd come running from his office on the ground floor when one of the guards rang a bell signaling trouble. *Divert the crowd while I take care of this.*

Tobias caught Macauley's sleeve when he tried to shove past him. "*Ollie?* Who is this person to you?"

"Later," he whispered and devised a fast plan for getting Stanford out of there before the prattling started.

Yet, as he glanced around the gaming floor, fascinated gazes glued to the scene, he realized the questions about his past were only beginning.

"That was damned stupid," Macauley snapped as he climbed in the carriage he kept parked behind the Devil's Lair for emergencies. With a gaming hell, there seemed to be one every night. He banged on the roof and fell against the squabs as the conveyance jerked into motion. His shoulder gave an indelicate shout of protest that he ignored. "I can see now that you were going to get into it with someone. I suppose I should be happy it wasn't me. Or Streeter, who wouldn't have taken it well. At least you picked an intoxicated toff to assault."

Stanford was sprawled in the far corner of the seat across from Macauley, his gaze focused on the city bits they passed. Flickers from the carriage lamp danced across his clenched jaw, his pale cheeks. For the first time, Macauley saw pieces of himself in his brother's face.

"You were the one who used the bloody nickname. I haven't been called Ollie since"—he flicked his hand, flippant—"well, since you left. Father preferred Oliver. Actually, he preferred when I was in another wing of the house entirely."

Macauley yanked a flask from his pocket. Then remembered his brother's addictions and shoved it back with a snarl. "I was removed from the estate by force. There was no *leaving* about it. No explanation from the heir in residence who knew the truth, either. That his lowly half-brother was in fact *not* a thief."

Stanford dropped his head to the cushion, his eyes closing. "I'm finished paying for my mistake, Xander. For the past. I paid *every* day after you were dragged away. Then in India, on every battlefield. I tried to apologize, repair our relationship. I don't have more to give. I am depleted."

Macauley's belly knotted at his brother's emotionless tone. This was a fork in the road he'd not expected. He was either going to help Stanford or be forced to watch him sink beneath the waves. "Tomorrow. My warehouse on Narrow Street. Ten o'clock and not one minute later. I mean it, boyo."

Stanford raised his head. "You're going to, that is, you mean to..." He rose from his slump, his lips parting in confusion. "*Why?*"

Macauley fiddled with his sling, unable to stare into eyes precisely like his own while negotiating a man's future, his *life*. "It's your legacy, the earldom. Not mine. Someday, you'll have to own it. I honestly want no part. But I *am* a part of you and you, me. Until that time, until you're ready, I have businesses, multiple, where I require able minds. I have enough strong backs. I'm running myself ragged trying to be everywhere at once. Distilleries, the shipping enterprise, the gaming hell. Now Roan has some grand idea to invest in railways. I have a few personal projects, one involving the workhouse Streeter and I occupied for a time. An orphanage in Tower Hamlets I'm funding. I can't trust many people in this world."

He shrugged, utterly uncomfortable with this conversation. "Oh, and wear gear suitable for a brawl. We're heading to Gentleman Jackson's after the warehouse. You're going to pound that aggression out or have someone pound it out of you. With rules in place, so no one breaks your pretty face."

Stanford's jaw worked as he struggled to speak. "You want me to be your business partner?"

"What it sounded like, innit?"

"Right-o," Stanford whispered and sat back, his voice cracking. "You need men you can trust."

"You can join the Cluster, too. What the hell. Two dukes and an earl will make us the toast of London."

"Cluster?"

Macauley smiled but turned his head to keep it private, thinking of Pippa for some befuddling reason.

She'd be happy about this extended olive branch. He just knew it.

Chapter Twelve

Where a couple find themselves in a tight space

Pippa had to stop herself from staring as Macauley, Streeter, Markham, and Roan discussed their agenda for an urgent meeting with a dock agent on the morrow. Macauley's deep voice rolled through her like a slug of brandy, warming her in a drove of secret nooks and crannies. He was the leader of their odd little group in some respects. A fact he seemed charmingly unaware of.

Unfortunately, he was situated two seats down from her at the enormous dining table. And on the same deuced side. Her only way to watch him was in the oval mirror hanging on the opposite wall.

He was without the sling this evening and dressed in his customary black. His valet, Spivey something or the other, had had another go at his hair. It was shorter than she'd ever seen it, exposing his jaw and brow for her inspection. The mahogany strands twisted quite adorably at the edges, more curl as the day progressed. His skin was pale at his hairline where the sun hadn't had a chance to strike it yet. He looked young and was smiling like an invisible weight had been lifted from his shoulders.

Although *she* had nothing to do with his happiness because for most of Helena's birthday fete, he'd avoided her altogether.

As she roasted beneath silk and muslin, her body melted at the mere sight of him.

Their kiss had kindled a blaze inside her. For days it remained lit, unable to be extinguished. She'd tried. Books, watercolors, a night of cooking and food delivery to the church. Walks in the garden with Theo. Rides along Rotten Row. Shopping on Bond, which she loathed. A musicale. The opera. She'd finally given up. Let Macauley stay wedged like a splinter in her brain. Her unsuccessful efforts left her with the unassailable notion that another kiss was in order. To help her forget the first. Or perhaps to prove it hadn't been as incredible as it had seemed. She'd had two glasses of champagne that night and been fairly floating in her slippers.

Pippa propped her chin in her fist, running through ways to get him alone, wishing she had a quill and paper to jot down her ideas.

The discussion turned to the standards for this group. Babies. Teething. Leading strings. Nappies. Skinned knees. First words. Wet nurses. Governesses. Helena was due any day but had decided to hold the party anyway, against Roan's better judgment, saying she couldn't miss her own birthday celebration. So talk then fell to names and what color eyes they hoped the babe would have. How the siblings were going to respond to a new brother or sister.

Pippa took a sip of wine and held back a yawn.

"I believe Pippa has an admirer," Roan popped in as if they'd been discussing her, which they had not. His words were bracketed by laughter.

Conversation halted like someone discharged a pistol. From the corner of her eye, Pippa saw Macauley's fingers clench around the vaulted stem of his glass. In the mirror, she noted his fading smile.

"Lord Bilbrough sent flowers. Roses," Roan continued, unaware that two people in the room had been startled into immobility. "He sent a note round asking about having us for tea next week."

Pippa swallowed a curse that would only land her in more trouble if uttered. Her brother, the woozy duke, thought his wife's birthday celebration was the appropriate time to bring up his sister's love life.

Theo kicked her under the table. Pippa lifted her gaze from the perusal of her plate, realizing someone had asked a question.

Helena smiled from her place at the head of the table. Roan was incredibly progressive and had given his duchess the seat of honor. "I asked if you like him, Pippa darling. Lord Bilbrough. If you do, it will be a first. With your word, we'll have the Duchess Society begin investigating him. I don't think he has a mistress. But he could be riddled with debt. They sometimes hide that fact until the agreements are signed. It would be good to know."

Pippa glanced across the table at Theo, who had a diabolical grin on her face. She was cheerful as a puppy lately because she finally had a student in Dash Campbell.

"He's nice." She drew a circle on the starched white tablecloth, then snatched her hand away when she realized she'd begun writing the letter M. "Very agreeable."

Hildy's sigh drifted down the table. "That means no."

Roan grunted and took a gulp of wine. "Ah, well, he's a horrid rider. Tumbled from his mount in Hyde Park last month. And he's an even worse pugilist. Lost a match with Baron Mercer-Dresden, and he's as round as he is tall. Couldn't welcome that lack of athletic skill into the fold. Forget I mentioned it, although the roses were a decent touch. This conversation completed means more time to discuss my latest fossil."

"Hold up, maybe she does like him. Or could. Don't strike the clumsy bloke from the list just yet. Not everyone rides well." Macauley settled his glass by his plate. Where he'd moments ago drained his remaining wine. "Tea might be a reasonable way to give the chap another go. Passing fair, innit? Only so many men will have the courage to try with this one."

Markham clapped his hands, his steady consumption of wine this evening bound to give him a dreadful headache tomorrow. "Look at Macauley, giving advice about matters of the heart. I never thought to see it myself."

Pippa leaned over the table, catching Macauley's gaze. Silver met sapphire. For the first time this evening, he wasn't smiling. "Mind your business, will you? I can handle my own."

He lifted a dark brow as if to say, *are you sure about that?*

"*Pippa.*" Roan gestured to Macauley, to his sister, then between like he was tying them together with string. "We're all friends here. Play nice in the supper room. She doesn't mean it."

She threw down her linen napkin. "Oh, yes, I do!"

Macauley smoothed a wrinkle from the tablecloth in a move meant to show how undisturbed he was to discuss this topic. "Return to my statement about the scarcity of men willing to step into the lion's den."

Everyone in the room looked on with pity. Only Tobias Streeter and Theo seemed amused. And Hildy troubled, tiny grooves radiating from her eyes, the ones she got when she was worried.

While Macauley appeared incensed beneath his bland smile for no explanation she could deduce.

Fine. "I'll have tea with Bilbrough. And send a note to Lord Samuelson. He asked me to go riding in Hyde Park. Has a high-perch phaeton he wants to show off. Maybe that will get me more flowers. A foyer full of them. And a proposal, a dozen proposals even!" Thoroughly put out, she refolded her napkin in her lap and tried to ignore Theo's gust of laughter. "Although I don't care a lick for roses."

Her birthday knife seemed to heat in her boot. Xander Macauley, dirty devil, would never give a gift so mundane as *flowers*.

Pippa leaned out for at least the fourth time, catching his gaze. Astonishingly, he didn't look away. *Happy?* she mouthed.

No one in the room noticed, but his lips took on a hard edge.

Something only *she*, the woman who knew him almost better than he knew himself, would notice.

Macauley wasn't good at apologies.

He stalked three paces, then turned. Paced back until the tip of his Wellington bumped the door. He'd completed ninety-nine in a span of, oh, a good ten minutes. The linen closet was narrow, hence three steps taking him across it, and it smelled comfortingly of starch and linseed oil. The door was cracked enough for him to see anyone who should pass. The oil lamp he'd purloined from a parlor emitted golden light from the tall cabinet he'd set it on.

Most of the Leighton Cluster had left. After jam tartlets and rum cake. The opening of gifts. More wine. Languid, friends-forever conversation, though he'd shared none with Pippa. They'd treated each other like combative cats, distant but aware. When her silence began to chafe, he'd made his excuses, early morning at the gaming hell, accounts to review, etcetera, then snuck into Roan's linen closet.

Which proved how cracked he was becoming.

He knew, and it didn't matter *how* he knew, Pippa traveled this corridor to her bedchamber.

Sighing, he rested his brow on a pillowy pile of towels, the fragrance of lemon drifting cozily into his nose. Slipping his arm from his sling, his shoulder gave only a modest twinge. He wasn't looking for a repeat of the terrace adventure, even if his body lay in silent wait for her touch.

He'd embarrassed her. Been rather cruel, which was not his way.

So here he stood, hiding actually, in pure masculine vacillation. Her dance card in his pocket, which he'd been planning to return but had not.

He wasn't going to let her go to bed without apologizing. Thinking their kiss had meant nothing, although he would not tell her it had. He'd turned a corner with Stanford. Entered a partnership and a reluctant reclaimed brotherhood. He'd sworn off women for the moment. No opera singers, no actresses, no widows. No light-skirts, no demimondes. His plan was solid. He was going to focus on friendship, family, and business. Lamentably, Pippa was caught somewhere between the first two.

She mattered. Her brother mattered.

And that was that.

He heard the light tread, the hair on the nape of his neck rising in response. Peeking through the crack, he saw his senses were correct in their assessment.

As she passed, he whistled once, very softly.

Later, he would laugh about her flummoxed expression when she realized who stood in the darkened entrance to the linen closet. Damned if it didn't feel good to get one over on her.

She braced her forearm on the doorframe, her smile a feline mix of confidence and charm. He loved that she seemed to like him so much, although he'd no idea why she did.

"You really couldn't leave without kissing me goodnight, could you?"

He nudged the door wide, gestured. *Get in here.*

She glanced over her shoulder to view a deserted hallway—he'd already checked, they were safe for the moment. Courageous chit that she was, she followed him inside.

He kicked the door shut and leaned against it, making no effort, absolutely none, to touch her. Though his fingertips had begun to tingle, her scent, that faint trace of vanilla, put his body at attention. "This isn't about a kiss. This is about an apology."

Pippa's lips parted, a sigh he wanted to catch with his own slipping free. "An apology. From Xander Macauley? The Limehouse Prince?" Patting her chest, she bumped back against the shelf of linens.

He didn't need a reason to drop his gaze to her breasts. But there they were, straining against her bodice, inviting his tongue and his teeth. His hand curving around the plump mound and squeezing would have made him very happy.

"I feel faint."

"Little Darlington, you've never been faint in your life."

She hesitated, caught in indecision. As was he. He wished he didn't want her. Wished the Duke of Leighton wasn't one of his closest friends. Wished the reasons to stay away from her were convincing enough to stop him. But he wasn't sure they were. His self-control was eroding with each second he remained in her presence.

The lamplight bounced across her eyes, a swirl of gold and green that had his blood heating, his heart setting out on an uneven rhythm. "You really want me to have tea with Bilbrough?"

He shook his head. He, in fact, did not.

"Then why put me in this situation with your contemptuous comments? Helena is penning a note to Samuelson in the morning, placing me in his new phaeton by mid-day. You arrogant toad! Wasn't it enough that I quit playing the wallflower and brought this attention on myself?"

He shoved off the door and took two deadly steps to get to her. Braced his forearm on the shelf above her head, forcing her to tip it back to meet his gaze. Trapping her. Hell's teeth, she was beautiful. Her hair, the color of lost sunrises, escaped its confinement to curl around her jaw. Lips plump and moist. Petite and slender, the top of her head barely hitting his chest.

He had a brutal urge to toss her over his shoulder and be off to the nearest bedchamber. Protect, soothe, *ravage*. A confounding mix. She made him feel things no other woman ever had. She made him feel *everything*—when he didn't want to feel everything.

"Do you remember what I had inscribed on your knife? Samuelson and that milquetoast Bilbrough are the types you're supposed to navigate the waters with, luv. Not me. I suppose I'm trying to remind you. Remind both of us. Some of the things I've lived through, I can't forget. Those things change a man forever. You need someone with a blank slate."

"I don't want a blank slate," she murmured. Then she did what he couldn't and touched him. Trailing her finger down the arched line of his lapel. His skin lit beneath wool and linen. "It's going to eventually happen with someone, my next kiss. Why not with you?"

He leaned in until there was only a feather-space between them. Cupped her jaw, losing patience with this flirtation. His cock was painfully erect, his heart hammering, his blood high. "I have callouses on my hands, scars on my body. I'm not for you, Pip. I don't play in half measures, remember?"

"I want your hands on me." She dragged his from her face to her breast to show him, flattening his palm over her hardening nipple. Sick with desire, he watched her face, her pupils, as he stroked the peaked bud with his thumb. Her lids fluttered, her moan echoing in the chamber.

That's when he made the decision. One more kiss. What could one more kiss do that the first, devastating in its intensity, had not?

Immediately, he went against his pledge. Instead of starting with a kiss, he began to make love to her in that airless space smelling of linseed and starch. Who, indeed, was he fooling? His mouth skimmed her neck, the delicate curve of her shoulder. As he licked and nipped her fragrant skin, he went to work below. Down her ribs, her waist, cupping her bottom and bringing her into him. Her head fell back in surrender, her hands gripping his shoulders to steady herself.

He wedged his thigh between hers and urged her to use him.

He seized her lips, an onslaught. Control diminishing, they quickly slipped into a sensual rhythm. Tongues mating, frantic breaths permeating the room. She knew how to manage him, a bit. She'd paid attention, as she said she would. What he liked. What *affected* him. Slanting her head to bring him deeper. Scraping his scalp with her nails, tugging on his hair. Her hums vibrating against his lips and making him dizzy where he stood.

Following a blind impulse, he grabbed her skirt, wadded the silken material in his fist, drawing it to her waist. The kiss was enough, truly, without him adding this. The feel of her dewy thighs beneath his fingertips, heat rising from her core as he grazed his knuckles across it. Her illicit scent soared high to slay him.

He should stop, but he wasn't going to.

She rolled her head to the side, breaking contact, her throaty plea ringing through him. "I can't... help me. I'm on fire."

He studied her, the moment ripe with precognition. "Pippa," he finally said, his voice as hoarse as after Talbot's blaze. "Look at me."

She blinked, her eyes darker than the emeralds in her knife. As murky as he'd ever seen them. Her lips were swollen, her cheeks rosy. She needed to be naked. He needed to be inside her. He needed them to come in gasping, lung-shaking shudders.

This would have to suffice.

"I can take care of you. This frustration you're feeling. Do you want that?"

She licked her lips, nodded. *Yes.* "Until I..."

"Until you find your release. Until the world slips away. There'll only be me. And you. But you have to come back to the present, return to your bedchamber once we're done. Understood? We can't go any further. This is too far already. Only, I can't help myself."

"*Us,*" she breathed, her eyes closing.

Through the bountiful layers society demanded a woman wear, he tunneled through them, finding the slit in her drawers. The fleece of soft curls. Moist invitation. Although he realized in the back of his mind that she'd not vowed to forget this. Run back to her bedchamber like he'd asked.

He ignored the warning, taking her under, his mouth capturing hers. His only motivation the quest to pleasure her.

He slid the tip of his ring finger inside her, parting the velvet folds. *Christ*, she was tight. Wet. Slicking his skin, his entry eased. The gentle tug and pull as he stroked was more elegant than their waltz. He curved his other arm under her bottom and lifted, his finger still buried inside her. Angling so he could thrust, driving deeper.

Her head dropped back, her cry rushing forth.

"There," he whispered against her jaw, his chest swelling with each ragged breath. He ground his cock against her hip. He was going to come himself if he didn't marshal it. Like a lad in the schoolroom. "When you're alone, lie back on your bed, spread your legs, and slide your finger inside. Curl it. Like this. Stroke slowly, then faster."

He worked her precisely as he instructed, teasing, then backing off when she started meeting his movement with her own. A sensual bump and grind. "When you're ready, the delight too intense, touch yourself here, luv." He thumbed her swollen nub, circled, circled again. "Until you find the exact spot, the pleasurable rhythm. Your body will unleash its secrets."

He kept at it until he found it himself. She liked the circle, then a hard press.

Pippa buried her face in his chest, no longer able to maintain their kiss. Gave a faint sniff, smelling him like she had his jacket two years ago, the first time he'd realized she might want him as much as he wanted her. She arched her back, helplessly caught in his hold, her slippered feet digging into the back of his thighs. Her words were meaningless and mostly unintelligible. This was madness, but it was also incredible. He'd never wanted someone this desperately in his entire, lonely life.

Ideas stormed his mind as he brought her close to her peak.

If he hoisted her a little higher, wrapped her legs around his waist, he could fuck her against this shelf and bring them *both* relief. And possibly a mountain of towels and sheets down upon them. He could lay her on the floor, drape her legs over his shoulders and let her crest with his tongue buried inside her. He'd seen a small chair in the corner. Big enough to hold him. With her on his lap, her thighs spilling wide.

He closed his eyes to the fantasies, illumination sparking behind his lids. His pulse raced down his spine, drawing his balls tight in his drawers.

She didn't hesitate to take what he offered in full measure, as he'd vowed. She was courageous, his girl. Suddenly, he wanted to stop playing. He wanted her to come—and come so hard she'd never forget this, forget him. He placed his lips by her ear and whispered every obscene thought he'd had about her. How he would take her, make her *his*, make her orgasm a thousand times. Kiss, lick, bite, stroke, thrust.

His tactics weren't honorable. He surprised himself with the raw display.

But she *liked* it. Whispered replies, her words muffled in his shirt-front. Groans and pleas, promises and faint threats, until it hit her.

Rapture.

Her cry spilled across his chest. Filling the room with the scent and sound of them. She shuddered, shaking, her breath tattered. He didn't relent, not until she wiggled away. *Too sensitive.*

He rested his brow on her shoulder, his hand slick to his wrist, coated with her release. After a moment, he let her skirt fall to her ankles and smoothed his hand up her spine to cradle her head against him, unwilling to let her go. Her shudders were subsiding, her whispery sighs dying. Then entirely without purpose, he tipped her chin and seized her lips. He wanted to drown in her. Sink them both to the bottom of the sea.

"I saw angels," she whispered. "The most incredible sensation of my life."

He smiled, burying his nose in her glorious, tangled hair. It smelled faintly of citrus, inviting his fascination. "Should be devils you're seeing, shouldn't it? Like the one holding you."

She snuggled deeper into his embrace, a perfect fit if he would only allow himself to admit it. "I want the rest. What we saw in Talbots' garden."

He pulled back enough to gaze at her, hunger lingering hotly in her eyes and burning up his. "That's not going to happen, Pip. I can't go back, then."

She shook her head, her frown familiar. Stubborn, intractable female. "What does that even *mean*?"

"It means I've overstepped the bounds entirely. Risked your reputation and a valued friendship with your brother. You're going to run up to your bedchamber and forget this happened. Except for the lessons. You can use those for the rest of your life." Which made him despondent *and* elated. Every time she crested, he wanted his face, his fingers, his *words* to be the impetus behind it. He wanted to imprint his touch on her as she'd imprinted hers on him.

Which was bloody selfish of him, all told.

He moved away while he could, stumbling back awkwardly, praying she didn't notice. "Don't be vexed. I made love to you. If you'd only realize, I did. In a way." He yanked his hand through his hair and glanced anywhere but at her. Towels of every color, stacks of linens, that silly chair he'd imagined taking her on. She wasn't giving an inch, her gaze intent when he looked back. "This moved us up a step, a *hundred* steps, above a mere kiss, Little Darlington. Your juices are clinging to my skin rather maddeningly as we stand here debating the situation."

Unable to stop himself, he lifted his hand to his nose and brought her unique fragrance into his being. He wanted to *taste* her, drink her in. Even in the muted lamp's glow, her shock was evident, followed by a serving of good old female satisfaction.

"It isn't sweet, this kind of thing. Or romantic. Passion. *Real* passion. Yearning. Longing. It's messy and..." He tapped his chest, unable to suitably frame his feelings. "The desire I feel for you is more than I've experienced with anyone. I'm perplexed, quite frankly. Ridiculous, innit? I'm being truthful, so you know. Consider it my second apology of the evening. I'm also not touching you again."

"What about you?"

He backed up another step, his boot hitting the door. "What about me?"

She gestured to the front of his trousers. His shaft was currently stiff enough to split wood; a physicality he couldn't hide.

He glanced away. Sighed. Dug in his coat pocket, extracting a cheroot he wasn't going to light. Slipping it between his lips to keep himself from kissing her again, he stayed there a moment to absorb how tender his skin was. Shaking his head, he chuckled at his absurdity. "I don't know why I'm so graphic with you when you're untried. I think it's the bold way you look at me. Every bit of your hunger is there for the taking. Confidence I've not seen in many women, even ones in the oldest of professions. It's bloody tempting, I have to say. Enticing as all hell."

He worked the cheroot from side to side, then murmured, "I'll stroke myself, my fingers wrapped around my cock. Not too hard, from crown to tip. If I think about this, tonight, about you, the taste of you on my lips, the scent of you on my skin, I'll last a minute, maybe less. In fact"—he flexed his hand at his side, fingers wide—"I'm going to refrain from washing this hand until I climb into bed in an hour or so. That should do it. I won't go to sleep without my release, don't worry, luv. The promise of you staining me. You'll take your part, even if it's only in my dreams."

Pippa took a fast step forward. "Do it now, where I can watch."

He'd not been rendered speechless in years. His mouth opened, the cheroot tumbling out.

Maybe someday, he almost said. Mad as a hatter, he was. This chit had brought him low. He'd never touched himself, not to completion, in front of anyone.

Unexpectedly, it was his greatest wish.

He turned, opened the door a hair, and peeked through the crack. Thankfully, the hallway was empty. Glancing over his shoulder, he found Pippa in the same spot, delightfully disheveled, fury in repose. She did *not* like when she didn't get her way.

"Say you were looking for linen for a spill if a servant sees you tumbling out of here. Give me five minutes. Then go."

Her hands rolled into fists at her hip. "I can make up my own lies, Xander Macauley."

He was already in the hallway when he heard her reply. Sticking his head back in the closet, he winked. When the last thing he wanted to do was leave her. "Don't I know it, luv, don't I know it."

Macauley didn't make it to his bed.

His cock was painfully erect and refused to subside no matter what horror he visualized. He had a fifteen-minute jaunt across London in the dark of the night, alone in a carriage. What better way to occupy his time than recalling the feel of Pippa's core tightening around him when she came? Her ragged sighs filling his ears. Tremors rocking her slim body. The scent of her clinging to his skin.

Willing, eager, curious Pippa. Open to anything he suggested.

His fantasy brought to life.

When had fantasy *ever* matched reality?

He unbuttoned his trousers, worked at his drawers and pulled himself free. Dropping his head to the velvet squab, he closed his eyes and remembered everything that had happened in that linen closet. He stroked exactly as he'd described, crown to tip, slowly, then with more urgency. Paused only once to lift his hand to his nose and breathe her in.

Her pleasure was his, her heat, her moisture. Her *release*. His hips lifted near the end, her name ripped from his throat. He shuddered as she had, long and hard. Satisfyingly depleted.

His breathing frayed, he yanked a handkerchief from his pocket and cleaned himself up. *Christ.* He was a bloody boy around her, spilling in his trousers.

He stared out the window at the passing night, pondering her offer. She'd made one, of course. Blatantly and with fewer words than any proposition to date. *Do it now, where I can watch.* The most sexual request of his life, coming from the virginal sister of one of his closest friends, amused him when it shouldn't. Caught him not only in his nether regions but in his heart—in a manner that felt mildly disastrous.

His carriage coming to a halt behind the gaming hell, visions of Pippa Darlington clouding his mind, Macauley realized he might not be strong enough to resist her.

Pippa closed the door to her bedchamber and leaned against it. The room had been prepared, the crackle of burning logs in the hearth calming her ire. She brought the strip of cloth to her nose and inhaled deeply, his scent stealing through her like a fever.

Macauley had left his sling on the closet floor. Somehow, it had become tangled about her ankle during their adventure, a silken chain.

His words came back to her. Perhaps as he'd planned, her body fired like the hearth across the room. *Lie back on your bed and slide your finger inside when you're alone. When you're ready to explode, touch yourself here.*

She'd fantasized about him touching her, making her feel... *things.* Now that she knew, in part, what lovemaking could be, she could prescribe no words to the experience. It wasn't as if ladies of her circle discussed such happenings.

Her body felt *different.* Invaded in the most wondrous of ways. Altered.

Forever and irretrievably altered.

His fingers trailing over her, sliding inside without a hint of resistance. As if it was meant to be. His groans ringing in her ear, lush, filthy suggestions. His long shaft pressed to her hip, brazen want surging through them.

She'd dreamed of him and not truly known. It was why he'd begged off, pleaded with her to let him be. Forget their attraction. He understood that passion would complicate their relationship beyond reason.

He was right.

Now, her hunger was a beast, her need unyielding. He'd pushed her over the edge, into a pond of pleasure. Her body was no longer her own, and she was happy with the offering. Giggling, she crossed the chamber with a skipping stride and flopped face down on the bed. She wasn't fibbing when she said she'd seen angels. *Coming*, as he'd so crudely called it, was *magical*. The feral promise shimmering in his silver gaze assured her there was more.

She wanted his body atop hers. Wanted the messy, sweaty, hungry *all*.

She wanted his love. His children. His future.

Rolling to her back, she threw her arms wide, his silk cravat caught in her fist. He would drop like he'd taken a left hook to the head if she told him.

Dear heaven, Roan would have one of his rare asthmatic episodes.

Therefore, she would plan accordingly. One step at a time. It wasn't scheming if Macauley wanted her. Helping a man see the correct path, choose the right *woman* wasn't devious. It would take every one of the skills the Duchess Society had worked for two years to impart. Patience. Determination. Self-confidence.

With a slender amount of cunning. She couldn't change who she was *entirely*.

She would jam her way into his life as elegantly as possible.

Until she was so entrenched, he couldn't possibly live without her.

Chapter Thirteen

Where friends try to nudge a love affair along

Macauley loved the distillery almost as much as the gaming hell. He found himself going there when he was troubled of late. It was peaceful. He'd gotten quite good at the chemistry side of things, after long nights of reading texts he'd later found were the same used in Oxford's classes.

The smell of fermentation hit him when he walked in the door. Pungent, malty, slightly stale. He'd always thought the unique flavor of their brew derived from the scent. They owned each other.

He was walking with his head down, lost in thought, and didn't see his partner until he'd practically stumbled across him. Tobias Streeter was laid out on the floor, beneath one of their brand-new copper stills. "Hand me that rag on the table, will you?" he asked Macauley, not startled by the unexpected arrival.

Macauley grabbed the rag and thrust it into Tobias's fist. "Is there a problem?"

Tobias grunted and ran the cloth along the seams of the still, brought it back to his nose, and sniffed. "I thought we might have a leak. I'm a little unnerved going away from oak in part. On the other hand, I'm sure this thing will last forever." He hoisted himself to his feet, brushing his hands down his front. He was dressed for brewing in tattered trousers and an untucked linen shirt. His cat, Nick Bottom, a lazy, orange beast who preferred to be where Streeter was, sat licking his privates two paces away.

Macauley found a spindle chair and threw himself into it. He didn't care what, he was not attaching himself to a woman *or* a feline. He simply wasn't. Pippa didn't even seem to particularly like cats. "The best soup is made in the oldest pots. But copper, maybe it's the future. We're being clever, using both. Very distinct flavors from each."

Tobias grabbed a folio and quill from atop a crate, then took a turn about the still, making notes. "You sound cranky."

Macauley propped his chin on his fist and slumped low in the chair. "I'm not cranky, mate."

Tobias scribbled without reply, his averted gaze allowing Macauley the freedom to introduce certain topics that were needling him this morn. Like this one, for instance. Twelve hours ago, he'd been kissing the breath from the Duke of Leighton's sister. A rather intense experience considering no coitus had been involved. He could still picture the slip of silk wrapped around her ankle. Brilliant he'd seen *that* before sneaking from the linen closet. No wonder he'd not been able to make it home. Orgasm by carriage.

Blast, if he started imagining what he could do with his missing cravat and the obstinate chit who likely had it stuffed down her bodice, his cock would *not* play fair.

That was all he needed with his friend looking on.

"I can hear you brooding." Tobias jotted another note on the page. "Out with it. Who is she?"

"I'm giving up women. Like I said. Celibacy doesn't exactly bring clarity. Give me time to work through it, mate."

Tobias stilled. Lifted his head. "I thought you were kidding. A bad reaction from having to pay off another mistress. Like a nasty rash. You forget about it once you're cured and dive back in."

He rolled his thumb over his lips, thinking of Pippa. Nasty rash, indeed. "Since when do I kid?"

"Does your sulk involve the Earl of Stanford? Are you ready to talk about it?"

Macauley cast his gaze to the ceiling and the tangle of exposed pipes painted bright crimson. The mix of steel and glass in the warehouse was stunning. Tobias had picked a prime spot for the distillery, their second, then made it almost as flavorful as the whisky they produced. An abandoned shipping warehouse in need of an architect's eye to bring out the beauty. Which insanely, for a boy from the rookery, Tobias was. Self-taught and, for the past year or two, in great demand.

To hell with it. This secret was dying a swift death anyway. "He's my brother. Well, half. Sorry to tell you, but you're not the only byblow in town."

The folio slipped from Tobias's hands to the floor.

"You saw his eyes. Don't tell me you didn't consider it, Street. No two so alike."

Tobias blinked, stunned. "I need a drink."

Macauley gestured to the dwelling. "You're in the right place, then. We make the finest."

Tobias stalked to the crates in the corner serving as a mock sideboard. Pouring, he glanced over his shoulder, his gaze hot. "I'm trying not to take this personally. Tolerance I employ with my children and my felines. And often, my beloved wife. I've known you since we were lads, and I'm just finding out your father was an earl? That's where you were the summer before the workhouse. You were the angriest boy I'd ever met. There were rumors I recall hearing. Fantastical ones of you being housed in a lord's home. Rumors I didn't believe until now."

Macauley scrubbed his eyes, exhausted by the past two weeks' events. "Not so fantastical, innit? Both of us footnotes in *Debrett's* should they start a bastard's page. Maybe I'll petition them to."

Tobias threw back his drink. "Would have been helpful for me to know back then."

"My situation isn't like yours. The earl was never going to acknowledge me. He gave me a position in his stable and nothing more. I would have died before acknowledging him. Thrown myself in front of a carriage first. Your father was a bad dream. Mine was a *nightmare*. A nightmare I left Stanford to deal with. Though it was partly his doing, the reason I was escorted so nicely to the workhouse. But he was a scared boy, and as you said, I was a damned angry one. I was stronger, mostly because I'd had to be. I guess I've come to see I made mistakes, too. Left my only family out in the cold. War doesn't seem to have helped him figure anything out. So, I suppose I'm going to try."

Tobias knocked his glass against the crate twice, treading lightly. Which he was excellent at, hence his negotiating the contracts that required a delicate touch. Macauley entered into discussions with a mallet. "Now you're going to protect him. When do *you* ask for help, Mac? Or expect it? As your friend, that's my concern."

"Stanford's more burden than brother at the moment, fair enough. But that won't last forever. I remember climbing out of the pit. Who better to help him do the same? A title doesn't make a man or a life."

Tobias debated pouring another drink, glanced back, rubbed his chin with his shoulder, his reluctance evident. Vacillation was rare for the former rogue king of the Limehouse docks. "A woman could be a godsend. Someone to support you. Someone to *listen*. I say this with all sincerity. Not because I have a houseful of cats, children, and a wife I love beyond reason. Maybe it's time to let her in."

Macauley's heart hammered, his pulse ringing in his ears. His friend sounded sure of something. "Her?"

"Pippa."

Macauley's boots hit the floor as he straightened from his careless slump. "Does Leighton know?"

Tobias rested his bum on the crate as if his legs were no longer going to support him. "Holy hellfire. Hildy was right."

"*Hildy?*" Macauley dropped his head to his hands and whispered through his fingers, "It isn't what you think." *Not yet.* But it might be if he didn't get over his infatuation. Soon.

"I think Lady Philippa Darlington has a perceptible attraction to you. And that you seem to, maybe, perhaps, on a fragile day, suffer from the same affliction for her."

Macauley launched himself from the chair and took an aimless sojourn around the room. Past three oak barrels they'd purchased from a distributor in Dublin, stepping over a stray pile of copper tubing.

"She's a pest. Dogged as any woman I've ever met. Like a rampant disease, I can't seem to cure myself of the chit."

"Attraction can be bedeviling. I remember it well. Hit me so hard I felt like I'd been knocked off my feet. Almost from the first, too. You must know that it's never the one you'd point yourself toward." Tobias shrugged, advice complete. As if Macauley's future could be decided by a kiss. Pleasure. Obsession. "Then before you know it, you can't imagine life without her. End of story."

Macauley yanked a length of twine from a stool he passed and snapped it between his hands. His shoulder gave a pained shout he chose to ignore. "She's too young."

"She's a grown woman, Mac. A spirited one at that. It'll take a courageous bloke to tame her. I don't know any in the *ton* I'd suggest. A mature, settled, equally tenacious man sounds like a suitable fit for the girl to me."

Macauley tossed the twine aside, his temper soaring when he noted the amused compassion on his friend's face. He wanted to tell Tobias he was mad, losing what was left of his mind. *Confused.* But he couldn't quite squeeze the lie out. "I'm not settled, mate," is what he came up with.

"You are. It's fascinating you can't see it. You have a fashionable terrace, two if we count the Devil's Lair flat. An estate in Hampshire would be a marvelous place to raise children. You're one of the most successful men in London. One of the wealthiest. You're giving back to your community. The workhouse, the orphanage. You and I never forgot where we came from. But the key trick? You're compassionate. Protective of your family. Honorable, even for an oft-time smuggler. Pippa could do much worse, my friend."

"It isn't like that. Anyway, this discussion is pointless because Leighton would never agree."

Tobias smiled, his head tilting like a hound's. "If you felt strongly enough for her and she for you, he'd be relieved. Guiding the girl is a tricky undertaking. If my daughter is as defiant, they better make space for me at Bedlam."

Macauley strode to the sideboard and knocked Tobias aside. "I kissed someone else."

Tobias's lips pressed to hide his smile. "Did it help?"

Macauley tossed back a shot. "No." However, the whisky burning a path down his throat was.

"There you have it."

Macauley snorted. "I don't have it, but the rest of you *definitely* do."

"At some point, you need to be honest with yourself. Or watch her marry someone else. Sooner or later, that *will* happen. Beautiful, clever women who also happen to be a duke's sister only remain on the block so long."

The notion of Pippa in another man's bed gripped Macauley's heart and gave it an agonizing squeeze. He would choke the nob before they finished their vows, forget about getting Pippa to a bedchamber. "How did you know with Hildy? That it wasn't merely attraction? I've had that happen. Demented one day, caring less the next. Over and over since I was thirteen."

"Because I liked her."

Macauley lowered his glass to the crate, his brow pulling tight. "Like?"

Tobias dusted the toe of his Wellington across the scuffed planks, suddenly, remarkably bashful. "I liked the sound of her voice. She has these absurdly charming dimples. I laughed when I was with her. Then I thought about her the entire time I wasn't. She was caustic at times, fast on her feet. She didn't put up with my tomfoolery. She saved herself from a kidnapping attempt by talking her abductor out of it. I mean, desire was there, eating a hole in my belly, but I wanted toast and tea over a breakfast table even more than I wanted the rest."

Macauley dug a cheroot from his pocket and slipped it between his lips. "You know I prefer coffee."

Tobias laughed beneath his breath. "One must find out these things for themselves."

That's precisely what Macauley was going to do.

The Duke of Leighton's equipage was parked outside the workhouse when Macauley arrived later that afternoon. The sidewalk was swarming with people, the street with carts, horses, hacks. The scent of burning coal and charred meat hung heavily in the air, a smell that typically comforted him.

But he only felt furious. Because he knew damned well there was no duke inside that carriage.

Bounding from his conveyance before it came to a full stop, he stalked over and pounded on the lacquered door, right above Leighton's bloody family crest. Pippa thought to arrive in the stews with a coach displaying her family name for any thief to witness. Her audacity knew no bounds.

Before the coachman could scramble from his perch, Pippa opened the door a crack. Her smile held traces of their kiss. Secretively sensual, knowing. Because she now *knew*. At least a little. Macauley punched a breath past his lips, ignoring his steadily rising pulse. The coachman skidded to a halt beside him, a hulking bloke by the name of Winston that Leighton brought whenever he visited the rougher sections. She'd at least thought to include someone who could possibly protect her.

"I have it, mate," Macauley said and waved the lad away. Winston nodded and backed up, bewildered. Who wouldn't be if their job was to haul this recalcitrant chit all over London?

Macauley leaned into the carriage, observing the easily influenced Viviette sitting calmly in the corner. No nanna on this run. "How much did she pay you?"

Viviette grinned, recognizing him from the Talbot debacle. She had a gap between her two front teeth he could shove his finger in. "Five shillings, with the promise of another two should we arrive back no one the wiser. I'm saving the bits for a new hat. These bonus earnings are starting to pile up." The maid ticked her chin toward the coachman's seat. "Winston refused her monetary persuasion, morals and all, but reckoned he had to escort her anyway. 'Gel's bound for trouble,' he said. But he promised not to tell His Grace. He's kindhearted that way. Says his sister is a wild one, too. He's caring, he is."

"You're charging too little for your services." Stepping back, Macauley slammed the door and gave Winston terse instructions to return Lady Philippa home. He jammed a half crown in the lad's hand.

"Don't let her out of your sight. And keep this quiet. For that, you have my thanks."

He was halfway up the cracked steps leading to the workhouse, dodging bodies, grasping fingers, requests for offerings, before he turned back. *Damn her.*

He was at the carriage in ten paces, knocking on the door. More gently this time.

She opened it slowly, her smile beauteous. "Yes?"

He leaned his shoulder on the doorframe. He wasn't going to touch her even if he wanted to more than he wanted to live to be a hundred. "What are you doing here?"

She scooted to the edge of the squab, cutting Viviette's view of the proceedings. "Oh, *my.*" She sighed longingly and patted her chest, a marvelous place his gaze refused to go. "You're going to take the time to ask? Instead of slamming the carriage door in my face?"

"*Pippa,*" he snapped, patience bleeding out like water from a cracked pot.

"I have a proposal."

"Another one?"

Her brow shot high. Did she not think she'd thrown out two or three rather cheeky ones to date? *Truly?*

Glancing at a somber sky that looked set to release a deluge at any moment, he defied the urge to tuck the lock of hair clinging to her cheek behind her ear. He absolutely *loved* her hair. Had fantasized about the flaxen strands spread across his sheets for longer than he should have. A spill of moonlight.

Maybe he wasn't such an awful person for desiring her. Tobias was right. Pippa Darlington wasn't a girl. She was a woman grown. She knew what she wanted.

And she apparently wanted *him.*

She reached, grabbing his wrist before he could close the door again. Which he honestly hadn't been preparing to do. He glanced down, her ungloved fingers slim and perfectly lovely. She'd raked her nails across his scalp and back when she'd come. Need burst through his body at the remembrance. At her touch.

Christ, he had it bad.

162

"I have positions in Roan's household I can offer. Two." Her eyes shone as green as the newest blades of grass in spring. "A scullery maid and an apprentice to our gardener, who is hoping to pension next year. For the young men and women you said were too old for the orphanage and ready to seek employment."

His heart thumped once, hard. Saving these communities was very important to him. A vital goal in his life. Anyone playing on those feelings would be forever struck from his list of friends or partners. Without a thought, struck.

Pippa wasn't playing. Her expression radiated sincerity. She was searching for her purpose as valiantly as Stanford was searching for his. Why *he* had to guide them both, he wasn't sure of. Although leaving them to figure it out alone wasn't an option he'd consider.

He stepped out of reach. Jerked his head toward the workhouse. "You're not going in there. It's foul and unpleasant. Unsafe. Leighton would rather find you in my bed than there."

Her lips parted, her breath hissing out.

Why had he admitted *that*?

"I can stay," she whispered.

"You're not staying. Get that out of your gorgeous head. I could be hours yet, and these streets get mean after dark. I have business to conduct, and you're not conducting it with me."

"But my offer. The two positions. In a duke's household, no less." Her cheeks fired, obstinacy he'd seen before. "A benevolent employer who pays proper wages. You can't possibly turn me down." Before he could disagree, she forged ahead. "I have plans to court every society hag in town. With assistance from Hildy and Georgie, I've scheduled three teas next week. A marchioness, an MP's wife, and a dowager viscountess. Excruciating but worth it. I'll find every vacancy in every household in this city if you give me enough time. And I plan to keep the conversation open for the future."

"They'll need training, Little Darlington. Anyone coming from this life has no idea how to live in yours."

Her mouth cocked up on one side. She knew she had him. "The Duchess Society is going to help me. Hildy has been looking to expand. This is their philanthropic portion, according to her. She has bequests from a few grand dames, and we plan to publicize our plans with the others. Do you know how many fat cats in this city need somewhere to stuff their pin money?"

He dipped his head, charmed and amused. He recalled Tobias's words. *She made me laugh.* "Fine," he said, deciding. About everything.

She clapped her hands. "Excellent. You'll need to send me their names. And let me know when we can meet. I'll arrange the rest from there. Hildy would like to start training next week."

He glanced over his shoulder in time to see his solicitor climbing the workhouse steps. "I have to go. I'm late for my meeting."

Pippa sat back against the velvet squabs, pleased but not entirely. She'd wanted more. Time. Answers. A slice of him. However, she knew better than to ask. Not now. The girl was learning.

He closed the door, then left it open, just enough. So, she was left staring into his eyes, and he into hers. "Leave your balcony door unlocked tonight, luv."

Her shock was palpable. Delicious. Sending a jolt through him, all points of pleasure somehow ending up at his cock.

"But, that is, I mean... I'm on the first story."

He rolled his eyes. "*Please.* I can manage. It'll be late. Once the gaming hell is under control."

Her mouth formed an O, her sigh escaping.

He reached then, helpless. Grazed his thumb across her bottom lip. Her lids fluttered—and he wanted to crawl inside the carriage, tumble her atop the seat, and lose himself.

Stepping back, he closed the door and gestured to Winston. *Go. Before I kiss her in full view of half of the rookery.*

But he wasn't waiting much longer.

Chapter Fourteen

Where a ravenous couple engage in naughty antics

Pippa spilled wine during dinner. Dropped her fork on the floor. Twice. Made several inane comments that proved she wasn't listening to the conversation. Smeared butter on her sleeve. Madness. To the point that Helena asked if she was ill. Theo smiled the entire time, muttering not a peep. Roan looked, as usual for her brother, confused.

She was not ill; she felt *wonderful*.

Pippa did a little dance around her moonlit bedchamber.

He was coming to her. Xander Macauley. Without her having to chase him about London like a love-starved idiot. Bribing servants and making a veritable ninny of herself. Dropping her key down her bodice to keep him from leaving her bedchamber type of antics she'd imagined doing. He was coming. To *her*. And maybe *in* her.

She smiled a secret smile, wicked and delighted.

She'd prepared. Told her maid not to disturb her as she had a blinding megrim and was going to bed early and sleeping late. Left her balcony door not only unlocked but open to the man and the acrid city stench. Brought cheese, bread, and wine from the kitchen and placed them near the hearth. Like a picnic. A chess set, too, in the event he wanted to play.

Maybe he simply wanted to talk. About business and her assistance with the workhouse. The new staff she was bringing into Roan's household.

Although he'd hit her in the carriage with a scorching glance that hadn't spoken of conversation.

She spun in a circle, her joy overflowing.

"You really have no idea what you're getting yourself into, luv."

She turned, gasping, her step unsteady. He stood in the open French doors, the velvet drapes fluttering about him. Dressed in black, looking sinister and gorgeous. Like something out of a novel. Or a dream. Then he was there, cradling her face in his broad palms and bringing her lips greedily to his. Stepping between her thighs and pressing her back against the bedpost, devouring her.

It was decided.

He'd not come for conversation.

He kissed like a man possessed. Starving, even irate. His tongue tangling with hers, creating a battle from a mere kiss. She bounced up on her toes, giving all she could. He groaned, his hand sweeping to her breast, cupping, thumbing her nipple through layers she wanted *gone*. Her skin lit, goosebumps erupting.

"Help me," she whispered against his lips as she struggled to slide his coat off his shoulders. Laughing wickedly, he shrugged and let it fall to the floor. He heeded her plea, unfastening his waistcoat buttons until the garment hung loose on his chest. She pressed her nose to his shirt and breathed unevenly. He smelled of tobacco and moss, something woodsy and horribly masculine. Tantalizing. Edible.

With a tattered sigh, she sent his waistcoat to the floor, then slid his braces off, leaving them dangling at his hip. "Take off your shirt."

His gaze, roving to her feet and back, was smoky gray, as penetrating as London's vaporous fog. She wiggled her toes. She was not wearing slippers. His dimple sparked when he noticed, his lips folding in to hide his smile. "Take off your gown."

She lifted her hair and turned. "I'll need assistance."

"You have it." He stepped in, his arm curling around her waist, pulling her back against his broad chest, his mouth falling to her neck. Sucking, biting. Her response was frenzied, echoing in the tranquil chamber. His touch was magical. His fingers dexterous, *experienced*, which she didn't want to think about.

While he feasted on her, he freed her inhibitions and her clothing. Ties on her gown, laces on her stays. He kicked her petticoat out of the way after she shimmied from it. Her hairpins scattered on the Aubusson rug, his hand fisting in the strands and bringing them to his nose. Her drawers tossed somewhere behind her, leaving her in a chemise, garters, and stockings. She turned in the circle of his arms, her breath catching at the ravenous expression on his face.

"You had *this* on under your gown? Before, at all those rubbish dinner parties Leighton loves to hold? Celebration for a new fossil he's acquired? I'd have climbed over the bloody table to get to you if I'd known." Lifting her chemise to her waist, he trailed his finger underneath her garter, pausing to circle each tiny rosette, mesmerized to see she wore impractical garments beneath practical ones. Feminine bits of whimsy, according to her modiste.

French-inspired, Macauley-approved.

"You'd imagined stiff, white cotton, I suppose?" This ensemble was pink. The garters and stockings were as dark as rose petals, the chemise the delicate shade of the inside of a conch shell.

His groan rushed forth, his finger drawing delicious circles on her thigh. "I don't know what I imagined, luv. Not undergarments fit for a light-skirt. Or a queen. I may never recover, but I thank you from the bottom of my bruised heart."

She gestured to him, nervous but undaunted. "Now you."

He loosened the knot of his cravat, slipped it from his neck, stared at the strip of silk for a long moment, then tossed it atop the bed. He pulled his shirt over his head, grimacing slightly as he rotated his injured shoulder. His body was a marvel. Lean hips, flat tummy. His chest covered with a fine dusting a shade darker than the hair on his head. He was all muscle—with a smattering of scars. She wanted to know every story behind each, told while she trailed her lips over him.

He was stunning.

She was curious.

For one, about the bulge pressing insistently against the front of his trousers.

He stroked his hand over the hard ridge. "If you continue to stare at me like that, I'll arrive before we get to the good part. Parts, actually. Many." He pulled his bottom lip between his teeth and unfastened his close, his fingers casually working the bone buttons, putting on a show. "Do you know, I didn't make it back the other night? After touching you in that linen closet, I completed before I arrived home." He stepped from his trousers and rolled his drawers free, tossing both aside until he stood naked before her. "Like a lad with his first taste."

He'd touched himself in his *carriage*?

Before she could comment on this or the challenge to fit *that* inside *her*, he took her hand and placed it over his shaft. His skin was hot. And he was harder than she'd imagined.

"I'm going to push myself inside you so deeply you'll never forget what we feel like. The enchantment of us."

Dazed, she wrapped her fingers around him, instinctively stroking from base to tip, brushing her thumb over the rounded head. She had no clue what she was doing, but he seemed to like it. He shifted his hips, tipped his head back. He was moist, a drop of dew coating his skin. Groaning unevenly, he captured her lips, fisted his hand in her hair, and slanted her head to deepen the contact.

"I love your hair," he murmured against her mouth as he positioned her back against the bedpost. "The scent of lemon, how silky it feels. I'd bathe in the strands if I could. Drown in them. But there are better things even to drown in." Dropping to his knees before her, he flicked the hem of her chemise. "Time for this to go." He gazed up at her, his eyes shining in the shaft of moonlight spilling in the window. "*If* you're ready for it to go."

She peeled it from her body without another thought.

In response, he rocked back on his heels. "*Cor*, Pip, as I live and die, you're the most dazzling chit I've ever laid eyes on. I must be dreaming." Leaning in, he nipped her thigh, scoring the delicate skin with his teeth, and released a scalding breath that fluttered across her. "Are you certain? There's no going back from this, I promise you. For either of us."

"Macauley." She waited until his gaze found hers. "I've always been certain."

With deliberate intensity, he unsnapped her garters and slid her stockings down her legs, pausing to caress each bit of skin he exposed. By the time they hit the floor next to her, she was a quivering mess.

Parting the flushed folds of her sex, he settled his mouth there. He gave her a moment to steady herself against the bedpost, then he nudged his finger inside. Mercilessly, he matched the pace in a clever rhythm that left her gasping. She arched against him, the pleasure unimagined. Rocking her hips, her hands tangled in his hair, gripping for purchase.

"Remember when I told you to touch yourself here," he breathed, teasing her swollen nub with a flick of his tongue. Then he sucked hard, nearly bringing her to her knees. "*This* little wonder"—he flicked again—"is the key to your pleasure."

She hummed, unable to form a coherent reply. He wasn't letting her think, unyielding in his quest to devastate her. She shuddered, her head going back. *Close.* She was close to capturing that extraordinary feeling from before. Skin tingling, sparks erupting behind her lids. Sensation, waves and waves of sensation. Tugging on his hair, she gasped, pleading without words for deliverance.

He stroked, inserted another finger, going faster. Harder. "You're so wet. I'm wild for you, Pip. I want to make you shatter into a thousand pieces, like a vase smashed against marble. Then lie with you for a week, a month, never leaving this bedchamber." He moved his mouth to fully cover her peak, and her vision blurred. When he didn't get *exactly* what he wanted, he lifted her leg over his shoulder, spreading her wide. His stubble burned her skin in brilliant contrast. "There, that's it," he murmured and dove in. "What I've dreamed of doing. What I long to do until you dissolve. A puddle on the floor."

It was hard to internalize what was happening. His lips, his *tongue*, pressing inside her. His fingers joined in. Everywhere at once, circling, stroking, pressing. Like before, but better. *More.* She glanced down to see his head stationed between her thighs. Seeking her release, she followed his movement with halting ones of her own, watching until it was too much. Closing her eyes, she cried out, beginning to fall from the highest height, her bliss expelled into the night. Serrated sounds unlike any she'd ever made echoed off her bedchamber walls.

He whispered his delight. How she tasted. *Ambrosia*. How responsive she was. *Remarkable*. His passion for her. *Enormous*.

She moaned, shaking, tremors racing down her spine to settle between her spread thighs. "I need—"

"Not yet." He teased, slowing when she started to pulse and slide over. His words swirled like mist, his touch dulling her mind to anything but him. "I'll bring you another, stronger this one, in less than three minutes. The length of time for the perfect kiss." He drove his finger deep, sending white sparks before her eyes. "If not, you win."

She panted and arched against his mouth. "Win what?"

He laughed, his breath skating across her skin. "Me."

The combination—his fingers, tongue, voice, and scent of them mingling with the aroma of the city pouring in the window—pushed her over the edge in waves. In less than one minute, she was destroyed. She started to tumble, clutching the post to steady herself. "I can't stand anymore," she said against the hand she'd brought to her lips, her leg dropping from his shoulder. "Fainting from pleasure up here."

He took a lingering lick, drawing out her release.

"I can't, Macauley," she whispered, wilting where she stood.

He picked her up in his arms with a satisfied groan, kissing her gently. He tasted of *her*, and she should be repelled, but it was beautiful. He held her tenderly, like she was precious. She'd never imagined Xander Macauley, rookery overlord, formidable smuggler, ingenious gamester, could be like this. She tensed, hating anyone who'd ever known this part of him.

"Stop thinking." He dragged his lips across her throat as he laid her on the bed, then he rolled over her like a wave. Bracing his forearm by her head, he held back. When she *wanted* his weight.

Dragging her hand down his back, she grasped his hip, pulling him to her. Opening her legs and allowing him to settle between them. His eyes glittered, shadowy magnificence. His cheeks were flushed, his skin moist. He looked like he was burning up from the inside out. "It's never been like this. I've never wanted anyone this madly. Been blind with desire. *Never.* Put them out of your mind. I have. For this night, there's only us, Pip. To me, it feels like it's always been us."

He caught her lips in a kiss, rolling her under in seconds. Until they were twisting atop the bed, tangling the sheets about their legs. Sighing, begging, demanding. His hunger drove hers higher when she'd believed she was fulfilled from what he'd done on his knees before her.

He muttered something wicked in French and bent low, drawing her nipple between his teeth. Tormenting one, then the other, cupping, squeezing. Lost, she wedged her hand between their bodies, circled his shaft and brought it to her entrance. "Now, Xander, *now.*"

He released her nipple, his sigh shooting across her breast. "Wait. Too fast."

She bumped her hips into his. *Now.*

He snaked his hand down her body, his breaths staggered. "You're one brash piece, luv. Good that I love it." His voice was frayed, his hands trembling.

She decided to make it worse. After all, he'd teased her. Drawing his mouth back to hers, she kissed him ruthlessly. Trailed her lips along his jaw, biting. Whispering things she wanted him to do to her. Her hands everywhere she could get them. His back, shoulders, hips. His firm, round bottom.

All the while, he worked below, moving his shaft into place. Fumbling a little, she was pleased to note. "Look at me, Pip."

She did, struck anew by the blaze in his eyes. There could be nothing more beautiful in the world, not to her. "You own me," he whispered hoarsely. "In this moment, I am yours."

Then he kissed her as he pumped his hips, his cock sliding inside. He lifted her leg high on his hip, allowing a gentle entry. The pressure was...

She blew out a breath and arched into him, breaking the kiss.

"Too much, luv?"

She blinked to find him watching her, his pupils spilling black into his eyes. He looked starved, wild. "No, *never,*" she whispered as he thrust deeper. There were no words for what it was to be joined with him.

The pain increased, a hard pinch that left her gasping. He whispered soothing words and slowed his cadence, his arm coming around to draw her close. Then when she let him know he could, lifting her hips, seeking, he began again.

His strokes lengthened. Deep, steady, sure.

The comprehension circled, surprising when she'd known. Xander Macauley was *filling* her. Inching his shaft into her in long, delicious thrusts that were making her lose her mind. He eased until their hips bumped. Then he growled and dropped his brow to her shoulder. "Don't move for a moment, Pip."

She arched, unable to stop herself. "Why?"

He took her skin between his teeth and sucked, the sensitive spot between her shoulder and her neck, marking her. "Because I'll come before you do. And that's not happening in this bed. Not tonight."

"Again? Me?"

He lifted his head, his smile radiant. Her conceited rogue in full glory. "Oh, yeah, luv. Oh, yeah."

Palming her hip, he guided her rhythm until it matched his. She visualized the intrusion, then looked to confirm. Watched his long body curve over hers. Hips dipping, thrusting with increasing speed. She could see he was losing himself, losing control.

And she loved it.

Her skin tingled, the urgent vibration starting at her toes and sweeping north. She strained, arching to get closer to him, her hand grasping his shoulder, his back, his hip. The sounds ringing in the room were raw, the slap and grind of bodies in motion. Shuddering, he reached between them and touched her. Circling her crested nub, as he'd learned she liked.

He wanted her to arrive before he did.

She appreciated his diligence.

Sensation spread until she was mislaid. Her nerve-endings sparked. Her nose filled with his scent, her mouth his taste. Their passion became synchronized. Every shift of his body was brought back around by hers. It was a dance more elegant than their waltz. More intimate than anything she'd ever thought possible. They kissed carelessly as his thrusts increased, meaningless bits of nonsense whispered to the night. Long, hard, deep strokes. She was pinned to the bed beneath him.

Astonishing, primal *greed*.

Pressing her cheek to the mattress, she watched his hand flex, fingers spreading atop the snarled bedding as he moved in her. His knuckles paling as he gripped the counterpane. A simple gesture—but his ardent response to their lovemaking pushed her off the cliff. She splintered in mindless spasms, the air replete with her bliss. Rising to meet his thrusts, she cried out until she was breathless, boneless. A wasted puddle in silk sheets.

He brought her close and trembled, his release arriving quickly. Groaning raggedly, he pulled out at the last moment. She'd heard it whispered this was a man's way to protect his lover. Without a plan, she grasped his shaft and stroked him to closure. Messy, dazzling closure, as he'd promised long ago.

"Pip, *luv*." His hand fisted in the counterpane, his head hanging low. A bead of sweat rolled lazily down his temple, right over the scar he'd gotten the night he rescued her. "You don't have to do that." He swallowed with a throaty click. "But oh, *God*, your touch is... leagues better than my own."

She smiled into his shoulder, gave it a nip that he growled and twisted into. "You're not going without me, darling. Not tonight, not in this bed."

Chapter Fifteen

Where a couple negotiate a compromise

Macauley was amused by her impromptu picnic. The dimple that only appeared when he flashed an authentic smile emerged, much to her delight. Entertained or not by her efforts as she served him her meager bounty, he accepted the foodstuff with evident gratitude.

They'd worked up an appetite.

They sat across from each other on a woolen throw spread before the hearth, a chessboard situated between them. Feet close to touching but not. The pungent aroma in the room spoke of their activities a mere hour ago. Joining, passion. She wanted to bottle the scent.

Macauley tilted his head in concentration, unaware of her risqué thoughts, drawing his bottom lip between his teeth. He'd never looked young to her before. Strong and confident, arrogant at times, but never young. Like now. Impossibly so. He wore only drawers and had a dazzling burst of firelight skipping across his chest and belly. His index finger rested on his pawn as if he wasn't sure about moving it. His gaze flicked her way, seeking a tell, but she kept her expression composed. This wasn't her first aggressive chess match.

In the semi-nude with her lover, *yes*, but other than that...

Oh, he made a bad move. Pawn to d5. She laughed softly, utterly charmed by how terrible he was at the game. It wasn't even reasonably possible to let him win because he was so dreadful.

Her adorable smuggler realized his dismal situation, his smile growing. She admired that he could laugh at himself when so few men could. He flicked his pawn aside with a muttered oath and grabbed a hunk of bread, chewing purposefully while he studied her. She'd have loved to know what he was thinking, but she'd learned she got more from Xander Macauley if she let him come to *her*.

She'd donned his shirt when they rose from the bed, the length of sleek linen hitting her mid-thigh. *After* he'd cleaned her with tender consideration, that is. The sweetest thing anyone had ever done for her. She took a sip of wine, holding back her grin. His gaze kept creeping to her exposed skin, although he'd yet to make a comment.

"You're too rigid."

He coughed and straightened from where he rested against the settee. "Excuse me?"

She gestured to the chessboard with her glass. "I think three steps ahead and react quickly while you agonize." She nudged her knight into place. "About the moves. Every single one. Instead of going with the decision, then not worrying."

His chest muscles rippled as he reached for her birthday knife, cutting a thin slice of cheese. His skin gleamed in the amber light, calling her hands. Her lips. Her teeth. She wanted to take another bite of him as the first had tasted so divine.

"If it were up to you, everyone would make decisions without a hint of deliberation. Disaster around every corner? Brilliant, let's run right in." His lids were settled at half-mast, a sated, drowsy lion lounging across from her. Crumbs were clinging to his lip, and his hair was in feral disarray. Contented in a way she hadn't seen before. She held on to her jealousy by a meager scrap of control because she believed what he'd said earlier about this being, if not exceptional, at least different. "I didn't grow up with the freedom to make mistakes, luv."

"I didn't either, actually."

Something in her tone alerted him. He stilled, placing the knife on the plate. "Your father?"

She fiddled with the cuff of his shirt, rolled it up and back before sliding her gaze back to him. "You can't ever tell Roan. He would lose any feeling he had for our father if he knew. He'd feel like he *should* have known. Should have stopped it."

Macauley's eyes flared, his fingers curling around the rook he'd decided to make an ill-advised advance with. "He hit you?"

Pippa shrugged, those few incidents, maybe five, roaring past like a putrid gust. Only one had bruised her badly enough to force her to hide for a few days. "Roan got the worst of it. I was a minor concern in every way. Trust me."

"I would kill him if he still lived. Gut him with your birthday knife, in fact."

Pippa beamed, pleased beyond reason. Absurd, but there you had it. "I would kill yours, too."

Macauley winked, but she could tell there was more behind his expression. He winked when he wanted to hide things. "He was inherently killable."

Scooting the chessboard aside, she leaned in before he could move and grazed her fingertip across the scar snaking across his ribs. A wicked one, the worst of the lot. He sighed, his lids quivering in a way that held her captive. He was like a stray dog she'd invited into the kitchen, cautious and thoroughly distrustful of her attention. His vulnerability twisted her heart into knots. "What's this one?"

"A scuffle Street and I were involved in. By the Limehouse docks. I was fifteen."

"Fifteen." She recalled how sheltered, even with her father being what he was, she'd been in comparison at that age.

He lifted his glass to his lips and issued his warning against the rim. "When I said my upbringing was rough, luv, I meant a harrowing kind of existence. At least for a time. Except for that summer with Ollie, my person for a bit. My family. Then it went to shite again."

Fury tunneled through her. She knew what he was thinking.

He slapped his rook to the board. "Ah, hell, what's *that* look for?"

"You think we're different. Too different."

"We are, Pip."

She started to argue, but he waved it away, his own temper firing. "You have terrible judgment concerning me. I don't know why you don't see me for who I really am. How bad I would be for you. My business is dangerous, my contacts netherworld. You'd be cut off from society completely should you choose me. Shunned."

"I don't care about society. *You* would never hurt me. That's what I see. A kind, intelligent, generous man who created a kingdom with his bare hands."

He stretched his legs out, his toes brushing her calf. Her fingers trembled around the glass's stem as she wondered if this was an invitation to touch him. "Not knowingly. But I eventually hurt everyone. Ask the Earl of Stanford."

"He hurt *you*."

Macauley sighed and yanked his hand through his hair, leaving the mahogany strands in worse shape. He tossed back his wine. "We hurt each other."

"Now?"

He hesitated, then seemed to give in. "I followed your advice."

She rocked forward, giggling in delight. "I *knew* I was right!"

His eyes, as gray as midnight fog, narrowed. "Overconfident much?"

"It was solid advice."

He fiddled with his glass, ran his thumb across a crimson thread in the throw. "He's going to help with a few of the businesses. His mind is sharp, his desire to contribute genuine. You *were* right. He needs a purpose. I can't shun his overtures any longer." He shrugged, embarrassed to share his life with her. "Rather, I don't want to. I think he needs me. And maybe, I need him."

"What about *my* overtures?"

His gaze made a languid circle of the chamber. Finally, he tapped his shoulder, the uninjured one. "Like the teeth marks I saw in the mirror above your vanity? An overture, innit, to mark a man?"

"I was provoked. Next time, I'll be more careful with your person."

He hesitated, sending her heart plummeting.

"We didn't completely destroy the bed. The sheet is clinging feebly to one corner of the mattress. Still, I don't know"—she gestured unconvincingly to his shaft, which had begun to tent his drawers—"if you could again. This soon."

He stared into the fire for a minute, maybe two, then his gaze sliced to her. "We don't need a deuced bed. And I can. If it's not too soon for you."

Setting her glass aside, she crawled across to him. Threw her leg over his body and situated herself cheerfully on his lap. Astride, like she preferred to ride when she was in the country.

"This is dangerous," he whispered, but he wrapped his hands around her waist to secure the fit. "In this house. In your bedchamber. You weren't exactly quiet the first time."

She pressed her mouth to his, patient. When he parted his lips, she slanted her head and used every trick he'd shown her. Did everything they both liked. Tongues touching, tangling. Hands roving. Bodies grinding. Until they were gasping.

Until she made him forget to say no.

"I'll come to the gaming hell. I loved it there. Too, I want to learn hazard. What better place? We'll have the next picnic atop one of the tables. It's the most beautiful space I've ever seen."

"*You're* beautiful." His hand swept her body, pausing to palm her breast, gently tweak her nipple. His shaft swelled against her folds, demanding. "Hazard is much easier to figure than chess, luv."

She wiggled, searching for relief. He closed his eyes and palmed the nape of her neck, drawing her lips to his. A jolt of raw lust muscled its way home when he groaned deeply, rocking against her. They shifted, breathless, excited beyond measure.

"You kept the cravat," she murmured against his mouth. "Right there beside us in the bed."

He unbuttoned his shirt, one sensual tug and pull at a time, his fingers caressing the skin he exposed. When he could have ripped the garment from her. But this tormented her more. Xander Macauley loved to torment. "I thought about tying you up."

"*Yes.*"

He shook his head and spread the linen wide, his lips going to her nipple and sucking. Her moan seemed to inspire him, his hold on her tightening. His teeth getting involved. "My bed at the gaming hell is better. Ball-shaped finials will hold the knot. And before you ask," he murmured against the side of her breast, "I've never had anyone in that chamber. Just you."

She sank her fingers into his snarled strands and held him as he suckled, the tremors starting. Between her thighs. At the base of her spine. Her toes. Her mind was losing coherence. He moved from one breast to the other, then rolled her over before the fire, knocking her thighs apart with his knee and anchoring his hips between them. The chess pieces rolled across the floor.

"I want to taste you," she whispered, her voice thick. "Down there. Show me."

He left her long enough to remove his drawers, then came back in a fury, seizing her lips, sliding a finger inside her. Tenderly, letting her get used to him again. She was ready, new and old dew, and he slipped right in. She dropped her head back, hips lifting, sighing through her teeth.

"If you put your mouth there, Pip, I'll last ten seconds."

"Someday, then. Say it."

He positioned his shaft and thrust, a lengthy, deliberate glide. In seconds, they found their style, their unique rhythm. The carnal *us* they'd talked about.

"Someday," he whispered into the shell of her ear, his lips and tongue following, sending her pulse soaring. The feeling of fullness was as remarkable as she remembered. His body spread her wide, allowing her to blossom. Locking her legs around his, she rocked against him with increasing momentum. Grinding, then pumping, his hard thrusts moved them off the throw and to the cool, planked floor.

Gasping, they clutched each other in passionate desperation. The firelight threw tawny shadows across their moist skin, moans and cries circling the chamber. There was no coherent discussion, only animalistic mating.

Pippa was wild for him. Savage. Changed. Reborn. Finally, in his arms, the woman she *wanted* to be. Her true self.

Macauley reached, cupping her bottom and lifting her into his thrusts. Brutal, incredible desire. His fingers tunneled through her hair as his body trembled. "Too soon," he whispered in her ear and rolled them to the side without breaking contact. Looping her leg over his lean hip, he channeled them into a steady tempo. One where he could ease the movement when he was close.

It was a molten mix from then on. A languid, base-to-tip glide, jolting parts of her the first encounter had not. A different angle presented different pleasures. And easier access.

His hand was there, circling her peaked nub, swollen from their encounter. Mindless pleasure rolled through her. Her lids slipped low with the demand to keep her release at bay. If she watched him, his eyes as dazed and dark as a blustery sky, his hair damp and sticking to his fevered brow, his forearms flexing as he thrust, she wouldn't make it another minute.

"Don't do that, luv," he breathed against her neck, her shoulder. "Let it go. Come with me. I'm nearly there."

Pippa opened her eyes to find Macauley's fixed on her. They glowed with emotion, things she couldn't define. The intimacy, their bodies joined, their gazes intertwined, reverberated through her like a spring rain shower. Bringing a feeling so *overwhelming*, she bowed her head into his chest to hide from it.

"I'm here," he said and seized her lips, not allowing her to retreat. "Share it with me. Share everything with me."

She knew he meant it.

For now.

Submitting to his plea even as she feared what it might later do to her, she kissed him back, let him in. She circled her arms around his shoulders, plunged her fingers into the damp hair bordering the nape of his neck until he possessed every piece of her body, mind, soul. They reached the peak together, seconds apart. She didn't let him leave this time—hooked her legs around his and held him tightly to her, taking his tortured groans into her throat and swallowing his raw passion.

If he even tried to leave her. If he did, it was a weak attempt.

Rolling to his back, he snaked an arm beneath her, pulling her into his side. She laid her cheek on his heaving chest, spent and, for once, speechless. The mantel clock counting off the seconds and their harsh exhalations were the only sounds. Finally, the crack and hiss of firewood disintegrating in a blazing hearth came to her. The call of a bird signaling the arrival of dawn. A cart rolling along the cobbles in the alley behind the terrace.

As she settled, her body cooling, her mind stilling, reality intruded.

She parted her lips, preparing to say something, *anything*.

Don't run from this, was the argument that kept coming to mind.

When she turned to him, king of the mean streets, the Limehouse Prince, smuggler and incorrigible scoundrel, it was to find his dark lashes dusting his skin, his lips parted in endearing slumber.

Sex had never been fun before.

Macauley stood on decidedly shaky legs beside the bed an hour later, scowling down at an exhausted Pippa, his feelings skipping around like a damned waltz. Joy, extreme satiation, fear, annoyance. He'd never been *annoyed* after sex. In a rush to leave, certainly. Thinking, *well, that was better than my hand,* sure.

But never angry.

He tunneled the cheroot from his waistcoat pocket and jammed it between his bruised lips, fully dressed but wavering. All he could smell on his fingertips was her, not his bloody expensive tobacco. Standing by her bedside like a lovesick fool, contemplating climbing back beneath the sheets.

Letting the servants find them and being forced into what he mayhap truly wanted.

Because this night had been close to perfect.

When he didn't *require* perfection. He didn't need a woman telling him she would murder his father for hurting him, then tupping him to within an inch of his life. He demanded simplicity and agreement regarding the rules he'd set for himself long ago. Mature relationships involving physical release and gratification. Manipulated by both parties, not the spontaneous *wonder* this had been. A tawdry token given when the deal was done. Possibly flowers, which Pippa didn't even like. When he'd never been a flower giver.

Truthfully, he had no idea where to go with this. Aside from deciding to either use the servant's staircase or the towering oak outside her bedchamber window to get out of here. His gaze flicked to the bedside table. Her knife, done with slicing cheese during their impromptu picnic—another first. *That* gift, she'd liked. As he'd known she would.

Dazed, he rubbed his chest, drawing the damp stealing in the open casement into his lungs. His body felt tight, like it did when a threat was imposed upon it. When he was in the middle of a boxing match or striding down the streets of Limehouse. On guard.

His shoulder ached, and he didn't know where his cravat had gotten. The firelight had dimmed to a dull flicker, an amber splash stealing over her delectable body. He trailed his hand down her arm, unbelievably tempted. Curling a lock of silken hair around his finger, he gave it a playful tug. Possibly hoping she'd wake and demand he stay. He absolutely *loved* her hair. It was a shade lighter than the enticing thatch between her thighs.

How many nights had he come in his hand wondering that?

He'd never had anyone fondle his cock to bring him to climax after he withdrew. A release that had about taken him out. At the end, his partners were usually concerned with their own bit and not worried overly about his.

He'd actually never considered this dismal truth before.

The frightening piece was, Pippa was a woman with expectations. High as hell ones. She would look him right in the eye and ask why he was leaving. Why he wasn't planning to do this again. Why, why, *why*. This mutinous chit—fascinating despite the turmoil surrounding her— was coming to mean more to him than any woman ever had.

He should have realized the trap he was stepping into. Smugglers were usually cautious.

His lips compressed around his cheroot. He recognized her ploy. She was fooling all of London with her wallflower ruse, but she'd never once lied to *him*. On the contrary, she'd told him exactly what she wanted. The most honest person he'd ever had the exasperated pleasure to meet. Which, in its own way, was like a shackle circling his wrist. Or his heart.

When *he* was the one lying.

Except, he'd told her about Ollie. About the scars. About his fucking father. *Deep waters, Mac*, he thought, a chill racing down his spine.

I loved it, she'd whispered before falling asleep in his arms. He'd expected a little timidity when she'd been content as one of Streeter's lazy felines, snuggling against him and practically purring. Telling him *yes* without a whimper when he mentioned tying her up. Something he'd only done once, long ago, then found the act made him feel too vulnerable.

His courageous girl was up for anything. No pretense, no fantasy, only real *her*. She was game in the best of ways. A situation that allowed him to be himself. He recognized, despite the challenges—their difference in age, her status, his lack—that they were well-matched in stamina and nerve.

Well-matched *period*.

He glanced toward the door and the echoes of a rousing domestic staff on the lower levels. He had to get out of here. He didn't know what he wanted, what to do about her. Panic was compressing his chest, taking a full breath impossible.

Searching the room, he found his cravat lying in a twist on the Aubusson rug. He retrieved it, making an impulsive stop at the scattered chess pieces. Rook in his pocket, he returned to her side. Sighing over the gesture but certain he would make one, he wrapped the length of silk around her slim wrist. Then he tucked her arm under the counterpane, hidden from sight. He couldn't risk leaving a note and had nothing else on his person that wouldn't compromise her.

Leaning in, he kissed her cheek, lingering to take one last breath of bliss.

He decided on the towering oak as the safest method, shinnying down it while thanking the gods for his impoverished youth. Not many toffs could do such a thing to reach their woman.

But his heart was heavy.

If Leighton found out about this, Macauley wouldn't live to see another day. Pippa's future husband wouldn't be happy, either, to note she'd arrived with experience. Possession gripped Macauley, rage lighting his blood as his Wellingtons hit the packed earth of Roan's lawn.

This jealousy could not be, but it was.

Some things, as Tobias had advised, you couldn't control.

Chapter Sixteen

Where a defiant chit seeks to hide her transformation

Pippa went about her day enveloped in a sensual haze she hid well.

It wasn't only the physical changes, her skin sensitized as if she'd bathed with sandpaper, her body pulsing in strange and miraculous ways, it was the *images* rolling through her mind. Unrelenting and visceral, erotic waves lapping the shore. Macauley rising over her, his gaze hot, sliding inside her, whispering promises and warnings as he took her to another place. His teeth scoring her skin, his lips circling her nipple. His fingers driving her mad, touching her in ways she'd not known he could. His cock—

She smiled behind her teacup, hoping to hide the reaction before anyone noticed. *Cock.* A new word. He'd whispered this in her ear when she wrapped her hand around him.

He'd liked that. She planned to do it again.

Although to have the opportunity *to* do it again might involve a fight.

All he'd left her with, besides an altered person and a missing rook, was his cravat looped around her wrist. A reminder of his lewd suggestion. One she'd consented to without question. Or a declaration that he owned her. A declaration he'd never *want* to make. If nothing else, she understood Xander Macauley. He wanted her but didn't *want* to want her. She was striving not to take that personally.

Nevertheless, her heart was light—or as light as it could be when she'd woken in a hushed bedchamber, the man she suspected she was in love with missing from the picture. Perhaps he was as helpless, their attraction as engrossing. Not what he'd planned and then some. Etcetera, etcetera.

He often said love was like an infection, and he didn't want to be infected.

She took a contemplative sip.

Thankfully, some things one did not choose.

"I received a note from Macauley," Roan said, jarring her from her musing. He sat at the head of the table in the breakfast room, a pressed copy of the *Gazette* settled by his plate. Helena was resting upstairs, the baby due any day. The household was running on enthusiastic anticipation and nervous energy.

She flinched, spilling tea on the tablecloth. "Macauley?" Her voice came out in a hoarse croak. He wouldn't, he didn't—

"Apparently, you've offered two staff positions in this household for his workhouse release program, as he's calling it. He sent the names around this morning and said to communicate them to you. That you were set to manage the 'details.' Whatever that means. I didn't think you two even liked each other, yet you're helping him with his charitable endeavors?"

Pippa set her teacup on the saucer, her temper sparking. The arrogant cur was willing to spend the night in her bed doing all kinds of wicked things to her, but he wasn't comfortable conducting *business* without alerting her brother.

"I overheard him telling Tobias Streeter about his plans. Helena is aware. As is the Duchess Society. Hildy has offered to do the training to prepare the applicants to enter service in a duke's household. Her Grace had been planning to branch into more philanthropic endeavors."

"It's fine, Pippa," Roan said, laughter lacing his words. "I'm not questioning your judgment. I'm glad you're working with Hildy and Georgie. They're positive influences. Macauley isn't, but that's neither here nor there. Certainly nothing for you to worry over."

She traced the floral design trimming her plate, wondering if this was a trap. "That's good, I suppose." Macauley a bad influence? *Gads*, if he only knew.

Roan smoothed his hand across his newspaper and bit into his buttered toast. "We need capable staff more than ever. Helena has the shipping enterprise and will never be overly concerned with household projects. I didn't secure that kind of duchess. Too, I located a cast fossil in the Dutch East Indies, and I'm coordinating shipment. And we have the new baby arriving any day. Our lives are about to be upended once again." He grinned, obviously thrilled. A most excited papa. "You're growing up, Pippa. It's time you take responsibility for managing the household in part. In preparation. Someday, you'll have your own."

His voice rose at the end, asking a question she wasn't prepared to answer. No one in London was certain if the Duke of Leighton's incorrigible sister would ever have her own household to manage. By marriage, that is. A spinster, given-a-home scenario was definitely possible.

She hated to tell him, but no one in England wanted to hear another word about his fossils.

However, Pippa felt she should clarify the issue. In case she needed the justification at a later date. "I *am* grown. Many of my contemporaries in society are married with children, Ro. I'll be twenty-three on my next birthday. I think you can't get this fact through your head."

He hummed a reply which was no reply. She realized he would always think of her as a little girl, which could be an issue after last night's activities. "Samuelson is arriving in an hour for that jaunt through Hyde Park. Itching to show you his new phaeton. Take your maid, please."

Pippa sank low in her chair. *Samuelson.* How was she to entertain one man with the scent of another still clinging assiduously to her sheets? To her skin? His cravat was currently resting in a secreted fold beneath her pillow. She'd been counting the minutes until she could run upstairs and press her nose to it.

"Pippa," he warned, drawing her gaze and her ire. "You accepted the offer. Now you have to go. We can't leave the poor sap standing in the foyer with a fistful of roses and no companion."

She grunted and pushed her teacup around the saucer. All she could picture was Macauley lying on his stomach in her bed, his arm locked possessively over her waist, the other curled around her pillow. Dead asleep. The sleek ridges of his muscled back, his round bum barely covered by the sheet. His lips parted in sleep, without the grimace he so often carried tightening them.

He was a different man with her. The jaded libertine was nowhere in sight.

He'd been... *sweet*. Understanding. An ardent lover. But gentle, too. They'd laughed. He'd told her his secrets. Surely these things meant *something*.

She'd not fully expected what happened to a man during the act. *Ah*, her knees trembled beneath the dining table to recall. Her skin burned; her heart was thumping. Macauley had ignited like a pyrotechnic and lost his mind for a few moments both times. If he'd transported her to another world, she'd also transported *him*.

"Pippa?"

She glanced up to find she'd waylaid the conversation and was spinning her teacup in furious circles atop the saucer. At times, her heart ached for Roan. He acted more father than brother because of what had transpired with their parents. And he didn't even know the half of it.

But Macauley did.

Roan coughed into his fist and needlessly refolded the *Gazette*. "You know you can come to me about anything, Pippa. Anything at all. Or Helena. I love you, and I only want what's best for you. More than anything, I wish you to be happy. Like I am with Hellie. The tough piece is, you have to open your heart, just a little, for love to be able to slide inside."

Would he give the same advice if he knew the man she wanted? Roan respected Macauley. They were partners *and* friends. But her brother had strong ideas about who was good enough for her—and who was not.

Would Roan accept her choice if her stubborn smuggler ever let her make it?

Macauley saw her twice (and read about her once) before he surrendered to temptation.

Two days after their interlude, he was crossing Bond as she shopped with her sister and that crooked maid who could be bought for two shillings. Pippa didn't see him. Instead, she and Theo were huddled together, laughing at something they'd seen in a haberdasher's window. She was wearing a plaid spencer, her glorious hair caught up in some intricate pink bonnet laced with feathers. He instantly wanted to *touch* her. Drag her into his carriage around the corner, tear her gown from her body, and make them see stars.

Breathless, he'd halted on the sidewalk while a swarm of people cursed and stepped around him. Her dance card burned a hole in his waistcoat pocket. Making it worse, like a lovesick chump, he dropped his folio into the muck. Thank God only Viviette noted his clumsiness from her place trailing behind the sisters, her gap-toothed smile as loose as her ethics.

Apparently, Pippa hadn't been searching for him on every street corner as he'd been looking for her. She wasn't chasing him. She hadn't sent a note other than two scant lines to let him know she'd be in touch about training for the scullery maid and junior gardener.

He hadn't sent a note, either.

What was there to say?

I miss you. Your laughter, your wit, your courage. I wake with dreams of you on my lips, choking my breath. The fantasy of you is with me every day. Pressing you against the wall of windows in my flat, your cries ringing off the ceiling. Your emerald gaze darkening with desire as you come. Chess and picnics. Waltzes. Your rook holds a special place on my bedside table.

I'm confused. Lost. Lonely.

The second encounter three days later was more satisfying.

The Duchess of Leighton had finally given birth to a strapping baby boy they'd named Chance, after a favorite uncle of Helena's who'd owned a public house in Brighton. Macauley smiled when he heard it; the *ton* would *love* that story. He stopped by before the gaming hell opened the next afternoon to deliver flowers and check on the family. If he ran into Pippa while being a good friend, it couldn't be helped. He wasn't going to change his routine simply because he'd spent the most splendid night of his life just down the hall and two floors up.

In any case, Pippa was out when he arrived. Although Leighton was there, beaming like a besotted new father. They'd lingered over scotch in his study, Macauley checking his Bainbridge timepiece, Leighton talking nothing but babies until he was forced to shove to his feet with a reminder he had a gaming hell to manage.

Pippa was walking into the foyer as he was leaving.

Their gazes collided seconds before their bodies. He gripped her elbow to steady her, pulling her into his chest. Though he did an excellent job concealing it, touching her rocked him in his boots. His cock stirred, his heart skipped, both saying what she had, *yes*. Her eyes gleamed in the sunlight shimmering through the window at her back. Her lips parted, and before he could lean in to kiss her—because somewhere in the absurd yearning thumping through him, he'd been about to—Theo and the shady maid tripped in behind her. Those two, for some uncanny reason, missing little.

Not knowing what to say, what not to say, how to ask her, how to *tell* her, he'd botched the entire thing. Tipped his hat and stalked from the townhouse, wondering when he'd ever tipped his hat to a woman.

The third event, a day after the hat-tipping, resolved his quandary.

The incident was brief but jealousy-inducing. *The Times* society column, which Macauley had avoided reading until Pippa managed to twist his drawers in a knot, spattering inked drivel about Lady Philippa Darlington and Lord Samuelson's marvelous jaunt through Hyde Park. The duke's sister was lovely in chartreuse. The dashing lord had even let her take the leads at one point.

Word was, the betting book at White's was running high in favor of a winter wedding at the duke's country estate.

Macauley tossed the broadsheet in the hearth and stalked to his desk. Insolent *fop*. He scratched a note on foolscap and folded it with a tight crease. He'd had a wild notion circling his mind for days now.

An idea he'd known she would like, but he'd not had the courage to suggest.

Up for another adventure? Midnight. Dress casually. The mews behind your townhome.

Then he went in search of a servant in his household willing to deliver a missive to a certain bribable maid of Pippa's.

Chapter Seventeen

Where a midnight jaunt causes more chaos

D*ress casually.*

Pippa smoothed her hand down her faded day dress, hoping this was what he'd meant. She wore this garment for gardening or cooking. The fit was pleasing, the material quality but aged. Unfortunately, there was a hole in the skirt and a stain on the sleeve. Macauley thought she was too good for him, so she didn't want to show up for their next adventure in a gown fit for a ball.

Which would prove a point she didn't wish to verify.

The alley alongside Roan's townhouse was sprinkled with moonlight and fog. The night was balmy, and she drew a breath to calm her racing pulse. Excited did not accurately describe her feeling at the moment. She'd only seen Macauley once in a week, that charged encounter in the foyer of her home. Bemused, she laughed behind her gloved fist and did a little dance on slick stone. He'd been about to kiss her; she knew he had. And crazy, crazy, crazy, she would have let him. In front of everyone.

Pippa heard the clip of horse hooves before she saw the curricle rounding the bend. Macauley was cloaked in mist and his standard jet-black attire, a specter in the night. Halting before her, he tossed the reins to the seat and leaped to the ground.

"You're alone?" he asked hoarsely. His gaze swept her once, head to toe, his fingers fisting at his side.

She nodded but didn't have time to reply before he captured her face. Turning her like in a waltz, he bumped her against the carriage, kissing her until her knees quaked, threatening to release her to the cobbles. Until light exploded behind her lids. Until her body melted, seeking closure only he could bring. A familiar pulse started thumping between her thighs. Sliding his hand to her lower back, he brought her against him. He was hard and ready, like he'd been that night in her bedchamber.

She wove her fingers through his hair, knocked his hat to the ground, and gave everything she had.

They knew each other now. Seconds time enough to enter the fray.

Panting, his lungs churning, he pulled back to see her face. His eyes were burnished silver, dark and compelling. "I didn't come for this. Or not only. Ah, *Christ*, Pippa, I've bloody missed you." Then he dove in again, pressing until there was no room to maneuver, his muscular body capturing hers against the curricle.

The sound of laughter and glass breaking in the distance forced them apart. Then going to the balls of his feet, he reached over her and into the carriage, coming back with a tattered coat and a lifeless lump of a hat.

"Put these on." He worked the cap on her head while she shrugged into a garment that hit her at the ankle.

She tried to contain her smile. Her adorable smuggler looked so serious, tilting his head to see if anyone would recognize her in this sad outfit. Her heart did something in her chest that signaled decisions were being made. "I assume this is my disguise."

He grunted, coming back to himself, realizing how preposterously he was acting. She could always tell when he got embarrassed, shifting from boot to boot, searching for a cheroot. "I couldn't risk a coachman, and I bought this silly conveyance, one I can drive on my own. The hood is up but open still if some meddlesome bloke really wants to see inside."

Pippa peeked from beneath the brim of what had once been a groom's hat. It stunk of horse and hay but felt as delicate as a diamond tiara because Macauley had placed it on her head. "What if I decide to kiss you? You'd have all of London say you were seen with a young man draped over you in the seat of your curricle one fine summer night."

He handed her up with a gust of laughter, giving her bottom a squeeze. Then bending down, he grabbed his hat from the cobblestones. "To protect you, Pip, I would let them say any deuced thing they cared to."

He circled the curricle and hopped up beside her with admirable grace. His body was a marvel. Long, lean, muscular. Ideal in every way. She could scarcely believe he wanted *her* when he could have any woman in England. As if he sensed her thoughts, he pulled her against his side while working the reins, sending them down the alley and into the night at a fast clip.

He drove like a man born to it. He was athletically gifted, even if he couldn't play chess worth a hoot. He banked turns, murmuring to his mounted team, reminding her with a chin dip to hide her face from anyone they passed.

She stole a glance at him when they entered Hyde Park, a shiver of recognition working its way down her spine. Did he know about her drive with Samuelson? A tedious afternoon, all told. Could he have possibly read that meaningless tattle in the broadsheets? She'd about choked on her tea this morning when *she* had.

She didn't understand where he could be taking her until she caught sight of the Serpentine shimmering in the distance. Sliding his arm away, Macauley maneuvered the curricle and the black bays leading it into an alcove sheltered by a grove of elms and dense shrubs. Little used. Private. Hidden.

She bit her lip and turned to him, joy pumping through her. "This is where you used to come with Tobias Streeter. Where you swim."

"Wild thought, innit?" He laughed, snaked his coat sleeve from his arm, and then tugged on the other. Extracted a pistol and a nasty-looking knife from his pockets, placing them on the seat. "Two boys on the lamb, frolicking in the blue-bloods' water."

"Are we..." She gestured to the lake. "Without..." She pressed her hand to her bodice. Shrugged stupidly in the oversized coat. *Goodness*. When she challenged the man to find escapades for her enjoyment, he considered the request seriously.

Macauley's lips kicked up. He folded his coat neatly over the seat and started on the bone buttons of his shirt. He'd chosen not to wear a waistcoat, clever chap. "Swimming's easier without all the trappings your set loves so damn much. Get down to your drawers. And the chemise, I suppose. That should do it."

Feeling scandalous but more comfortable with Macauley than anyone in her life, Pippa undressed as best she could. He stopped what he was doing when she got stuck, helping with ties, wiggling sleeves down, gown over hips, down legs. She'd left her petticoat and corset at home. Casual dress didn't require accoutrements.

And less was better for undressing in a hurry. She'd learned the value of bare skin the other night.

When they were left in his drawers and her lace-edged chemise, they stared, the air surrounding them denser than the vacuous fog rolling off the Thames. He was aroused. His fast breaths and stout erection were irrefutable evidence. Her pointed nipples and burning cheeks, her tell.

Amused but patient, he held out his hand, waiting for her to decide. Of course, she accepted, letting him lift her from the curricle. He slid her down his body, teasing her. When her feet hit the ground, he linked his fingers with hers and led her to the water's edge. She dipped her toe in. Cold but not too. A muddy bottom, slick.

She couldn't quite believe he'd shared this with her.

"Going to do it, Little Darlington? Or too much of an adventure, swimming with the Limehouse whatever it is they call me in your filigree underthings?"

"Where else do you swim?" she asked for lack of a punchier statement and waded in without looking back, his joy a jubilant, chuckling echo as he followed. The chill eased until the submerged part of her body felt warmer. Knees, hips, chest. She wasn't going to renege on this wager. She could swim well, thank you very much.

They frolicked. The sound of splashing and the wind knocking branches together were the only reminders they weren't inhabiting a dream. The faint knicker of his horses as they munched on grass.

Macauley flew past her with long strokes, desiring to place himself between her and the deepest part of the lake. Like he did when they walked down an avenue, he'd taken the lane closest to the street and the chance of being spattered by mud. A protector to the end, even if he didn't realize it. The waves he created lapped against her breasts, creating a longing in her belly and lower. The muscles in his arms and shoulders popped and shifted—and all she could remember was him towering over her, sliding inside and possessing her.

Moonlight and water rippled off him when he stood. He slicked his drenched hair off his brow and shook his head, droplets flying. A pagan god rising from the sea.

"Where else do I swim?" He threw a pensive glance at the sky, questioning how much more to tell her. "I have an estate I bought off Viscount Anders-Dale. Hampshire. Hunting grounds in his family for centuries, his financial ineptitude forcing him to sell for mere shillings. I couldn't say no, and someone was sure to take it. Ruin it. He was gambling it away at a hazard table last year. It's enchanting, although I have no real use for it. When I first stepped into the place, I was met at the front door by the majordomo, Spencer. He was quite put out to be overseen by a rookery thug. I think those were his words before I relieved him of employment." He moved close enough to touch her but didn't. "Maybe I'll go there this winter. Hire new staff. Get Stanford away from the city for a bit. At Christmas, to avoid the spate of gatherings the Leighton Cluster will invite me to, children running amok. Jam-covered hands, sticky fingers." He shrugged at the end of the speech, ostensibly lost.

Take me with you. Make a place for me in your life. I respect you even if all the Spencers in the world don't. Though she didn't dare utter a word of it.

Instead, she went where he'd follow. "Are you going to touch me, Macauley? Or is this merely swimming?"

He slanted his head in consideration. "Are you going to let me, Pip?"

She closed in until their bodies bumped, the water swirling around them. Their skin was chilled, their clothing clinging. "When have I said no?"

His raw exhalation pierced the silence. "*Never.* Which makes it tricky, this deal."

"Tricky?"

He brushed his lips over her cheek, her jaw. His hot breath washed over her. His teeth caught her beneath the ear and worked hard to make her quiver. "Complicated."

She trailed her finger down his chest, seeking gold. "Can't it be easy?"

He grabbed her hand before she reached her destination. "Not with you, Pip." Then he proceeded to haul her from the water, her two steps matching his one as she stumbled along behind him. "Never with you."

"Where are we going?" she breathed as they sprinted across the dew-covered grass, moonlight casting shadows around them.

He threw a blistering glance over his shoulder. "I'm thinking to tup you silly in my shiny new curricle. Presently, that's *my* grand plan. Clue me in if you have another."

She giggled and raced ahead of him, but he caught her, laughing as he hoisted her effortlessly over his shoulder. His hand was on her bottom, between her thighs, doing wicked things. Winded, he climbed atop the buggy, settled in the seat and turned her atop him. Ripped her chemise down the front and feasted on her breasts. Her heart began to pound, obliterating the sound of their gasps filling the night.

The inclination was immediate. He'd promised, after all.

She was on her knees, kneeling between his spread legs before he could stop her.

He tried to draw her up. "*No, Pip.*"

She hummed and pulled his damp drawers down, not letting him control this for once. His cock sprang out, shocking even after their activities a week ago when she thought she'd learned everything. Long and hard, the thatch of dark hair surrounding the base was in stark contrast to his tawny skin. He was built like a god.

She didn't know what to do, so she started at the crown, swirling her tongue, pressing soft kisses down his shaft. She did what seemed to make them both feel good. He dropped his head back with a guttural sigh, submitting for the first time. His hand fisted lightly in her hair, though he exerted no authority over her movements. His other went to the rounded edge of the squab, fingertips digging deep. Knuckles paling. His hips lifted, body tensing, his groan ripping through the night.

His excitement ignited hers like tinder to dry wood.

There was power—and pleasure—in driving someone mad with desire. She understood now why he loved doing this to *her*. Bringing Xander Macauley to his knees was the most erotic delight of her life. The act was awkward and somewhat crude, licking and sucking him, his taste flowing through her like lava. But it was also splendid—and put any intimacy she'd dreamed of to shame for its unadulterated simplicity. Drawing him deep, she used her hands and mouth, his murmurs, curses and promises guiding her. Her hair was a shroud around them, protecting the privacy of the deed.

She glanced up once to find savage hunger lighting his gaze.

He apologized, or she thought he did, and yanked her into his lap. Dragging her tattered chemise to her waist and spreading her legs, he settled her atop him. There were no words, only shifts of each other's bodies to accommodate, groans and murmurs as he fit himself at her entrance. Stroking fingers tunneling inside to ready her.

Grabbing her hips, he thrust, capturing her guttural moan in his mouth.

Curling one hand around her waist, he dictated the rhythm, his other diving into her hair and shaping the kiss into one made for ecstasy. She gripped his shoulders and rode him, a suggestion he'd whispered in her ear before. He shuddered, tilting her head back. She opened her eyes to find his locked on her. Silver with shades of black. Brows touching, they moved. Slowly, grinding, her core pulsing around him. Leaning, he took her nipple between his lips, sucking, ratcheting her yearning higher.

"I can't hang on much longer, Pip," he whispered, his voice frayed. "Come with me." With a groan, he slid down on the seat, changing the angle, rubbing against her. Hitting that pleasure nub. Drawing his strokes out until they were languid, penetrating.

Teasing. Persuasive.

"*There*," she said, unable to say more. *There*.

He brought them home seconds apart.

She shattered, gripping the back of the squab, his shoulder, fingers twisting in his hair. Frantic. Mindless. He followed, thrusting deep, panting, mindless murmurs leaving his lips, staying with her through his release.

She collapsed atop him, gasping. His delectable scent invaded her lungs, warming her entire being.

Tears pricked her eyes, but she held steady. They didn't fall.

Yet, the moment's intimacy wrapped silken strings around her heart, chaining her to him.

Chapter Eighteen

Where plans change in an instant

Macauley practiced his speech to Leighton on the ride to the gaming hell.

I want to ask—that is—I am—I don't know if you realize—Pippa and I—

Swearing beneath his breath, he wiggled a damp cheroot from his coat pocket and jammed it between his lips. Pippa nestled against his side, mumbling faintly. She'd put the pathetic hat and coat ensemble on, making her seem tinier or younger, something that kicked his protective instincts in the gut.

Somehow, she'd finagled her way into coming to the Devil's Lair, instead of dropping her home as he should. She'd looked at him with those glistening green eyes, promising to leave before dawn. Twisting a lock of his hair around her finger and cooing. Maybe even going so far as kissing him. Assuring him she was safe after another bribe to her maid, this time five shillings. He couldn't quite recall.

He'd still been inside her when he agreed.

What man made a satisfactory decision then?

"Quit brooding," she whispered sleepily, her head draped on his shoulder, her arm looped through his.

Bonded. Attached. Connected.

They couldn't keep their hands off each other, which signaled doom any way you looked at it.

He tucked her tighter against his side, slightly panicked. Mildly concerned. Reasonably vexed. After perhaps the most crushing orgasm of his life and all the bloody *feelings* arriving with it, his cock between her lips, *finally*, he'd about decided he was in love with her.

Terrifying, overwhelming, impossible love.

Love. He ground his teeth together and yanked on the leads. The horses danced a step in response, the curricle skidding on the cobbles. He bloody well *knew* that love would snatch him up if he continued to associate with this damned group, the so-called Leighton Cluster.

He was now one of the afflicted. A feeble duckling and Pippa Darlington held the hunting pistol.

Tobias and Markham were going to laugh their arses off. While Leighton was simply going to put a bullet through him.

Pippa kissed his cheek, not helping one bit. "You're still brooding."

"I have masculine things to worry about."

She laughed, her breath streaking across his skin and making his belly clench. "Masculine things?"

"*Things,*" he repeated with no further explanation. He turned into the alley backing the gaming hell with the finesse of a maestro. He understood with a fierce jolt that he'd never stop wanting to impress the woman currently draped over him like a shawl.

This realization made him blindingly angry.

"From brooding to cross," she said on a languid, leggy yawn.

"I'm not— " He halted mid-denial, a disturbance ahead causing him to rise to a rigid sit, his arm drawing away from Pippa. "Pull the hat over your eyes, Pip. Right *now.*"

He should have taken her to Mayfair, where nothing dreadful ever happened. Or not Limehouse dreadful. Macauley was weak, and now Pippa was in danger.

The differences in their standing were being hammered home by circumstance.

The scene unfolding was familiar. A patron of the hell who'd lost more than he could afford to wager returned after the club closed. Lord Neeley, a low-ranking baron with fast-dwindling funds and a hopeless future. He'd been ejected earlier in the evening. Ousted last week, too, if Macauley remembered correctly. Neeley was shouting, unsteady on his feet, jagged glass from a bottle of what smelled like gin strewn about his feet.

Making the situation worse, the man trying to talk sense into him was the Earl of Stanford. A bloke who, despite his harsh façade, believed in the best in people when he was usually shown the worst.

Neeley said something Macauley missed and bent low, coming up with a shard of glass, thrusting it in Stanford's direction with a snarl. It glittered menacingly in the dim moonlight.

Macauley halted the curricle a distance away and vaulted from the rig. "*Stay put*, luv. Right here. The pistol is under the seat, fully loaded. Just don't shoot my brother or me if you can help it."

She'd once caused her own mischief. Now he was bringing her into *his*. This fact did not go unnoticed in Macauley's heart or mind.

He strolled to the men with a careless swagger, playing the game. They'd seen him arrive. A panicky entrance helped no one.

Neeley turned with a rush of fetid breath and desperation. His glance skimmed the curricle before returning, wild-eyed, to Macauley. "Your whore arriving for the night, I see. Hate to interrupt the festivities, but there's a situation with my blunt and your shady establishment. Somehow, the back entrance is being manned by a bleeding earl. Returning soldiers make efficient sentries, is that it?"

Macauley laughed, his gaze never leaving the jagged shard glistening in the baron's fist. He wanted Neeley's attention off Pippa, off his brother. He'd gut the man if he touched either of them with so much as his pinkie. "I don't think you want the fight you're begging for. So run along, back to the posh borough you're presently able to afford. And I do mean now. I'm not an enemy you want to gain this night, mate. Spot of trouble bigger than you need, innit?"

Neeley swallowed and licked his lips, fingers twisting around the glass. Macauley's heart sank. The baron's clothing was in disarray, his sparse gray hair knotted. Cheeks ruddy from months of drink and despair. Macauley wouldn't be surprised if the man had also secured himself a fine case of pox. He had the crazed look of disease. Sadly, this wasn't the first time Macauley had confronted a man with nothing to lose.

Neeley jabbed the shard in the air. "I'll leave when I have my hundred pounds returned to me, you thieving bounder. Trick dice on the hazard table, I tell you! This is what I get for mingling with thugs."

Macauley shifted on the balls of his feet, preparing. His mind fixed on protecting his family. Seeing his readying gesture, Neeley shrieked and lunged.

It happened quickly. Like when he'd been a boy, and he'd stepped between Tobias Streeter and a boozy sailor intent on gutting them both. Had it been glass then, too? He'd nearly died in a pool of blood by the docks, *that* he recalled.

This time, however, his brother stepped between him and a madman.

Stanford took Neeley to the ground without much effort, knocking his feet from beneath him, twisting his arm behind his back, and shoving his chest into the cobbles. But the baron got in a Machiavellian swipe that earls weren't trained for and barons usually didn't employ.

And he'd thought to call Macauley a thug.

Macauley went down, pressing his knee to Neeley's throat, the baron's gasping breaths sickeningly enjoyable. He frowned. There was blood. Mixed in the milky street grime, spattered across his boot, across Stanford's, staining his cuff. Macauley reared back, grasping his brother's shoulder. "Ollie, did he get you?"

Stanford rose to his feet, stumbling back. Blood leaked around the hand he held to his cheek, trickling down his jaw in trails to color his collar crimson.

Pippa, *not* in the curricle as he'd ordered but thankfully still in disguise, dropped down next to him, searching his waistcoat pocket without invitation. "Your handkerchief, Xander."

He yanked it out, debating whether to squeeze the life from Neeley. They could get rid of the body without too much difficulty. The many ways to do it flashed through his mind.

Pippa put her hand on his wrist, her gaze understanding. Of everything. Another piece of his heart broke away, racing to her. Although his rage for getting her into this mess hit new heights.

"*Don't,* Xander. I'll summon Dash, get Stanford inside. You take care of this rubbish."

Macauley yanked his arm from her. "Do you see the destruction I bring? I tried to tell you. Your life is not meant to be tangled with mine." He gestured to his brother, his eyes stinging. The scent of blood and coal smoke choked him. He was cursed, tragedy following him. He wasn't going to wrap her up in this misery. "I tried to tell him long ago. Part of the reason I kept away. Any association with me is deadly."

Pippa ignored his ominous declarations and went to work. Pressing the handkerchief to Stanford's cheek and murmuring to him. Calm in a crisis, as Macauley had guessed she would be. Dash was there in seconds after being alerted to a situation in the alley, leading Stanford and Pippa inside the gaming hell. Two burly former stevedores muscled through the doorway seconds later. They took Macauley's order to get the baron home but make it as unpleasant a trip as possible, with vacant agreement, dragging Neeley, lurching and shouting, to the hell's waiting carriage.

While Macauley simply hung his head, emptiness invading his chest.

In the end, Macauley made the best choice for the group, even if said choice meant his love affair with Pippa would be exposed and subsequently destroyed. Additionally, as repayment for his transgressions, he would undoubtedly have to allow the Duke of Leighton to beat him to a pulp.

The carriage, one of two assigned to the Devil's Lair, the other in route to a locale Baron Neeley better not crawl from for *years*, pulled to a stop in the mews behind Leighton House. The exact spot where he'd picked up Pippa five hours prior.

Servants were ready, forewarned by a runner Macauley had dispatched once he'd had a moment to grasp that the worst thing for

Lady Philippa Darlington was being found, in any state, in the gaming hell of a known hoodlum. Unfortunately, he didn't have enough money to keep the rumors from floating free should she stay amidst this disruption.

He was honest about his social standing and this rank predicament.

Macauley sighed into his fist as he saw *two* dukes haunting the servant's entrance when he'd only needed one. Leighton paced while the Duke of Markham held the door and his remarks as they hustled Stanford inside the townhouse and to the waiting doctor. Macauley was fairly well-versed with injuries of this nature. His brother's wound was going to scar. A jagged cut from his temple to the edge of his mouth. Their only hope for it not to scar horribly was a capable hand stitching him up. A physician of such majestic caliber, he would only be on all-hours call to a duke. Macauley would have had to wait hours to find anyone willing to come to the stews under cover of darkness. Even if he'd paid the sawbones a devil's fortune. He could have found a midwife. He'd had a seamstress patch him up once.

Later that evening, she'd patched him up in another way altogether.

Feeling a surge of guilt recalling a woman whose name and face were lost to time, he glanced to the chit he'd *never* forget, who sat fretting in the corner, hidden in shadow. As if that would save her. He glanced out the window, noting that Leighton continued to pace, waiting for the remaining inconvenience of the night to unload itself on him. "Go ahead, get out. This ruse is blown. We have to face your brother sometime."

Pippa scooted across the seat until a splash of light from the carriage lamp caught her tenacious expression. "I'm going to tell Roan everything."

Macauley patted his chest, realizing he had no cheroot and no flask. "Bloody hell, Pip, are you mad? I have enough going on with my brother without yours hearing your bald version of our truth. Let me handle this, will you? I'll present it softer."

She knocked her cap, a pathetic piece he'd pilfered from his groom, off her head. Her magnificent hair tumbled about her in damp, curling glory. The color of her eyes was close to the shade they'd gone when she'd come while sitting astride him earlier this evening. "My version of the truth is that I'm in love, Xander Macauley." She poked him in the chest. "With *you*."

There it was. *Love*. Macauley scrubbed his hand over his eyes, his heart tripping over itself to get to her. "Can we talk about this after I let Leighton thrash me?"

"You don't have to marry me. I merely want *you*. I don't care how that happens."

Macauley's breath twisted in his throat. If he'd ever felt like crying, this would be the moment. "Pip, luv." He grabbed her hand, linked his trembling fingers with hers. Fought the urge to bring them to his mouth, to kiss away their troubles.

"I would if I could. If it was best for *you,* I'd fashion you off to Hampshire and never come back. Toss your skirts up daily in every house we occupied for the rest of our lives. But you see, the things I've lived through, I can't forget. Those things change a man. They'll stain you. Ruin you." His fury mounted when she continued to stare unblinking at him. She wasn't backing down, giving in. Instead, she looked hopeful, damn her. "You need a man with a blank slate. A man without enemies. Do you see what happened to my brother? The blood splattered on my boots, my shirt, my hands? How do you think they'd treat my *wife*? I'd seek to guard you every second. I fear my situation will only worsen when my connection to Stanford comes out, and it's going to eventually."

She gazed at him long enough to see he was serious about rejecting her. Snatching her hand away, her expression went stony. No tears for this hellion. "Do you realize what you're destroying? What you're losing if you turn away from me?"

Agony rippled through him. "Ah, luv, I do."

She thrust a furious breath through her teeth. "Retreat to that palace in the slums. Be alone when I was offering to happily be there *with* you." She yanked his overcoat off and tossed it at him. "Oh, wait, as the scandal rags frequently report, you're never alone for long!"

"Dammit, Pip, don't leave like this." Batting the coat away, he reached for her as she scooted past, his shoulder giving a painful twinge to remind him it wasn't completely healed. Only, Roan was there, grasping her arm to assist her down the carriage steps and away from him.

Which is what he wanted.

She popped her head back inside the conveyance, tears shimmering in her eyes. "I'm not giving up my project with the workhouse. I've already installed the beneficiaries in this household. The Duchess Society has begun their training, and I shall not interrupt it. Don't think you'll stop me once I've gotten started."

Then she was gone in a tide of female fury, her tight bottom swinging beneath wet, clinging silk.

Leighton didn't follow her. No way Macauley was getting that lucky.

"Get out here, Macauley! Right bloody now!"

Like he had a choice. Enraged lover. Injured brother. Furious friend. Macauley lumbered from the carriage, half expecting to be knocked on his arse before his Wellingtons hit the ground. He held up his hand, staying the execution. "Can I go check on the Earl of Stanford? Then you can soundly trounce me."

"Who is he to you? And where the *hell* have you been with my sister?"

Macauley halted, memories of Pippa swirling like mist. She'd stalked off with part of his heart, and he wasn't sure he was going to reclaim it. Two years ago, he'd stumbled upon her sniffing his coat over a forgotten chessboard, and he'd known they were both attracted. The first time *he'd* known had been years before that, at a dinner party when she'd been far too young, an impossibly lovely nineteen. He'd stared at her all evening, hating himself for finding her so appealing.

An untouchable temptation he'd eventually touched.

For her reputation and safety, their affair couldn't continue. Although he'd never forget a second they'd shared. Games of chess in scant clothing, impromptu picnics before a blazing hearth, her eyes going dreamy as she pulsed around him. Her impassioned moans streaking past his ear. Her luscious body curling around his. Her smile. Her wit. Her laughter.

The last would be the hardest to surrender.

No one had ever made him as happy as Pippa Darlington.

He could lie. But by God, he was tired of lying. So striding through the doorway on his way to becoming a proper brother, he threw over his shoulder, "I took her swimming in the Serpentine."

Oliver Aspinwall, the newly disfigured Earl of Stanford, woke to find someone sitting by his bed.

A female someone he'd never met before. A domestic in the Duke of Leighton's household Stanford instantly assessed. Ragged fingernails. A streak of dirt on her chin. Her clothes the standard service-issue black. Standard issue *men's* clothing with an overlong coat and trousers, a tattered cord for a belt, and a threadbare hat she'd pulled low to cover part of her brow. However, the gentle curves beneath the layers were anything but masculine. And she smelled faintly of nutmeg.

He turned his head to get a better look because something was stunning about her, even in the dim candlelight. He groaned as pain radiated across his cheek. His stitched skin itched maddeningly. *Christ,* that drunken sot had gotten him good.

"It's not as bad as it looks, sir. The sawbones did clean work. Scars make a man, and you're going to have a right flashy one. If you ever wanted not to look posh, you have your wish," she whispered and applied a cool cloth to his cheek.

He lifted his hand to touch it, but she stayed the movement.

"Lucky for you, he missed yer eye. My ma was a healer of sorts. A midwife, too. She treated various knifings. Though your attacker used glass, which creates an angrier wound. Jagged. A dirty rotten fighter is what you faced. I soaked this cloth in feverfew tea, you see. I had a wee garden in a ratty spot behind the workhouse, but the patch grew nonetheless because I have the touch. The herb will help heal your skin if you use it. Every day. I'll leave enough for a month. Alas, no addlepated medical man is going to recommend it. Don't even think to ask. I knew they'd toss me out if I suggested it. I saw them bring you in." She shrugged as if this made perfect sense. "So here I am."

"My lord," he murmured weakly, unsure why he'd think to correct someone coming to his aid. This titled rubbish was hard to overcome.

She was clever, her gaze narrowing, catching his meaning. He had trouble looking away. Her eyes were an unusual shade. Almost amber. Like the last drop of whisky at the bottom of a glass. "My high-in-the-instep lord then," she said and squeezed the rag into the bowl she held. But her touch was tender when it returned to him. She evidently wasn't one to hold a grudge. "Marquess, ain't it?"

He breathed through the pain. "Earl."

"Why no laudanum, earl? No bottles by your bedside."

He shook his head as best he could without jarring his wound. *Can't.*

"Ah." She dipped the rag again, then pressed it gently to his face. "Troubles with the opium dens. Happens to heaps of returning soldiers. Happens to lots, actually, where I come from. Passed out in the alleys, stepping over them like waste. Stumbling out of flash houses. The world is often a depressing place."

He blinked, bringing her into sharp focus. Her face was ethereal. Truly fetching beneath the grime. "How much do you know about me?"

"Everything they print in them naughty broadsheets. We got 'em at the workhouse. Days old, stained and wrinkled from another's use, but serviceable just the same. Latest rumor is, you and that hulking bloke who rescued me are related. The smuggling one who owns half of London. I believe it, you being brothers or cousins perchance, after spying him pacing the hall outside this chamber for an hour before he upped and left. He has sad eyes, and those eyes don't lie. Not another set like them that I've ever seen outside yours. The jig is up should you have thought it wasn't."

She waved off his unease, sensing a delicate topic. "Don't worry, my lord, I waited until after to come in. I know my medicinal intervention wouldn't be appreciated by the upper level. Seeing as I'm assigned to the gardens and all. That daft majordomo has shot cross stares at me since I arrived."

Stanford swallowed, wondering vaguely if they'd given him laudanum though he'd begged they not. He felt woozy, and this filthy little urchin wasn't clearing up the picture. Though she didn't smell nearly as filthy as she looked. "Who *are* you?" The majordomo was likely trying to determine how to tell her that her ruse of dressing as a man wasn't working.

"Necessity Byrne of the Shoreditch Byrnes. It's actually Josephine, but my pa called me his little Necessity, and it stuck. My ma called me Josie. She was educated, even had a governess of sorts when she was a babe. Her father was a cobbler of some import in Beaconsfield. We could read, and she didn't allow us to talk like we'd crawled from the gutter."

"The Shoreditch Byrnes," Stanford murmured, oddly charmed. Her cockney *was* on the light side.

"All deceased now. Cholera. Leaving me at twelve to manage on my own, hence the workhouse. I survived by my skills with herbs, mostly. Buying and selling from that grubby plot I was telling you about in the stews. I dressed as a lad for those years. I know you're wondering. Protection, if you get my meaning."

"Getting harder now, though, isn't it?"

She glanced at her body with a faintly betrayed expression. "Quite."

She'd rattled off her dismal history with impressive steadiness. Not one flicker of her eyelid or twitch of her hand. Her voice was as steady as if she'd been ordering bread from a shop down the way. He had a feeling this had taken lots of practice.

She stood, giving him another shock. Tall and slender, coltish. If not for the delicacy of her features, those plump lips, the curve of her breast beneath her linen shirt, she might have been able to pass for a lad.

"I left the feverfew there." She nodded to the bedside table. "I'll be in the garden should you need more. I'll have a lovely herb patch by fall. Use it every day until the wound closes and the tenderness dissipates."

Stanford lifted to his elbow, staying her. His cheek throbbed in time to his heartbeat, but his curiosity about this chit was weightier than the distress. His desire not to be alone even greater. "Xander Macauley placed you here? Working in the garden?"

She halted at the door, whipped her sad excuse for a hat off, and spanked it against her thigh. Her hair rolled out like lava, dense and inky black. Arousal swam to his toes and back, filling his chest with a fierce yearning he hadn't experienced. "It was the lady he has eyes for who placed another lucky soul and me. Lady Philippa. I seen him look at her earlier, hot as a brand. One second enough to know. She hasn't told anyone the apprentice gardener is a woman, even him. Or her brother, the duke. We're waiting to spring it on them until it's too late. I'm golden in the green, you understand, anything I touch growing wild, so much promise they won't be able to let me go. My plan, my lord earl, is to become the most famed gardener in England. Next to Capability Brown, of course."

With that ludicrous declaration released to the universe, Necessity Byrne strolled from the Earl of Stanford's borrowed bedchamber with the grace of a rookery queen.

Leaving a scarred earl transfixed.

Chapter Nineteen

Where a smuggler assesses his bleak future

Macauley prowled Leighton's study, anticipating a dressing down or a thrashing, he wasn't sure which. Unfortunately, he'd determined long ago that fighting a man you loved like a brother wasn't enjoyable.

However, when you'd compromised his sister, your choices were limited.

He touched every fossil on every shelf, riffled through the duke's desk drawers (more fossils, a book *about* fossils, and what appeared to be a velvet garter of Helena's), searching for anything to pass the time. Not many situations in his lifetime had made him fidgety. Or sick at heart, which he absolutely blamed Pippa for. When the duke arrived, after letting Macauley stew for an hour without so much as a glass of liquid persuasion, he had reinforcements in the Duke of Markham and Tobias Streeter.

And thankfully, a bottle of gin.

Macauley began to see the picture.

Markham, the pacifist, had alerted Streeter, the negotiator, to calm Leighton, the hothead.

"She's still a girl," Leighton snapped, the door he'd whipped open banging against the wall. "And get your bloody hands off my brachiopod!"

Macauley took a breath and counted to five, staring at a spider crack in the duke's ceiling he wasn't going to alert His Grace about. "She's not a girl, mate." *She came to me*, he wanted to add but would never. That was between him and Pippa.

Tobias and Markham circled Leighton, caging him in.

Macauley braced his fists on the desk and leaned over it, the hulking piece of furniture between them. It wasn't a fighting stance, but it *was* a stance. He'd take his punishment, but he was also setting the truth out there.

"You left her to me to protect after running off to Bath. That headstrong, reckless chit was wandering this town like it was her playground." He gestured to the shoulder that currently ached like the devil. "How the hell do you think I got involved in that catastrophe at Talbot's, anyway? Little girl that she is, Pippa was in the middle of the melee, investigating a man for the Duchess Society while fending off inappropriate passes"—he held up his hand when Leighton snarled—" unbeknownst to Hildy and Georgie. She was cavorting in Talbot's garden when I got there, hiding behind a statue, a couple engaged in a rather shocking activity on the bench across from her."

Leighton's expression—confusion, rage, panic—was comical. Or would have been had his sentiments not involved a woman they both loved. "How did you know where she was?"

Macauley dragged his finger over a bloodstain on his cuff. This is where it got fiddly. "I knew she was trouble. Or going to be soon sunk in it." He scrubbed his hand across his eyes. "I had her followed. Fetching simple, innit? I reckon someone had to. The most troublesome baggage I've yet to meet."

Markham shoved a glass in Leighton's hand and scooted another across the desk to Macauley.

Leighton tossed back the gin in one punch. "Like knows like."

Macauley's grin was immediate. And a costly tactical error. "Aye, that's it exactly."

Leighton scrambled over the desk and tackled Macauley, sending them to the floor in a tangle of fine wool, pressed linen, and masculine pique. Markham and Tobias were there but not in time to stop the duke from landing a jarring blow to Macauley's jaw that had him seeing stars.

"*Enough*," Tobias growled, he and Markham rushing to pull them apart.

Macauley shook off his friend's hold and shoved to his feet. Grazed his hand across his lip and came away with a dab of blood. "That one I'll allow. Deserved, mate. No question. But no more without my stalwart participation. Shall I roll up my sleeves?"

Leighton rose with a swift exhalation, not attempting to put his disheveled clothing to rights. The man liked to brawl like no one Macauley had ever seen. Although only one of them looked beaten. "You don't know her."

"Pip?" Macauley used the nickname, his temper riding high for many reasons. For one, leaving her with tears in her eyes. Two, having her brother look at him as if he wasn't worthy. Which he *wasn't*.

Life was unfair. He knew this. Fate's way of playing a joke to make him finally want someone. Someone he couldn't have.

Leighton's head snapped up, his fingers curling into fists at his side. "Pip? *Pip?*"

Markham rolled his eyes, moving in front of Leighton.

"*Stop* it, Mac," Tobias whispered, his arm blocking his friend should he think to dive back into the scuffle.

Knocking him aside, Macauley made a rambling circuit of the room, his heart skipping, his pulse dancing. "She chews on her thumbnail when she's nervous. She plays a vicious game of chess. Cooks after hours in your kitchen, and some hag of a society matron helps her deliver the foodstuff to a church in Cheapside. Chit's as daring as any gambler who'll stumble into the Devil's Lair this evening. A risk-taker in skirts. She's kind. And honest, which baffles me considering the poisonous bunch you have her associating with, someday tying herself to for life."

Macauley paused, realizing the room was buzzing with shock and silence. They'd never heard him give a speech like this. He'd never imagined he would. "She wants to change her world. Senselessly, she wants to change mine."

He halted before Leighton, exhausted and melancholy, his heart in pieces, his shoulder smarting deep in the joint. He'd probably have to go back to using that blasted sling. "Hit me again if that will help solve this mess," he murmured, meeting his friend's troubled gaze. "But don't say I don't know her. Or that she doesn't know *me*. I told her things I've never told another soul. I protected her for a short time. Now, it's your turn."

Leighton's lips parted, closed, parted. He buffed his hand over the nape of his neck. "Are you in love with Pippa? Xander Macauley? In love? The man who thinks marriage is worse than a raging case of the pox?"

Macauley stumbled to an armchair before the hearth and threw himself into it, dropping his head to his hands. His vision was spotting, his breath backing up in his lungs. *Love.*

Hearing Leighton say it rocked him.

Love.

Love was *bollocks*.

Leighton continued to process, beginning to pace the room himself. "You love Pippa. Xander Macauley in love with Philippa Darlington. I can't wrap my mind around this."

"Hell's teeth, if I do, you're not the first person I'll tell." This admission elicited groans from Tobias and Markham. "That's right, perfect husbands and lovers, I never told her."

"Pippa. My sister. You never told *Pippa*."

Tobias retrieved Macauley's glass and slapped it in Leighton's hand as he passed him, liquor splashing on the Aubusson. "For pity's sake, Ro, how many others are there? Drink this, will you?"

"Theo," the duke murmured, still dazed. "I have two now."

"No risk with Theo." Tobias perched on the desk's rounded edge, wiggled a toothpick from his waistcoat pocket, and slipped it between his lips. His successful effort to stop smoking as his darling wife had requested. "According to Hildy, Theo's shooting for a professor. The most intelligent and dullest man in the room. Fella like that won't race her off for midnight swims in the Serpentine. The marital journey promises to be a joy with sister number two. Your only concern is young Dash, her new student, who's about the handsomest bloke I've ever laid eyes on. But he's as far from a professor as one can get, so you should be safe."

Leighton's gaze pierced Tobias's. "You *knew*. Besides, he's too old for Pippa."

Markham sighed and straightened a truly ghastly painting of a deer entering the forest at sunset. "From one duke to another, anyone paying attention knew, Your Grace. He's not too old. Younger than you, I believe."

Leighton turned to Macauley in a fury. "You're marrying her!"

Woefully, Macauley shook his head. "I want to, but no, I'm not. In any case, I've hurt her, and she's so deuced stubborn, she wouldn't agree now if I begged. I was actually practicing my speech to you on the ride to the Lair. Then we arrived and Stanford, the blood, the shards of glass glittering on the cobblestones. My life, this existence, sweeping over me. I can't protect her in my world, not that incorrigible hellion. That's why I'm leaving her with you instead of taking her with me. With all the knowledge I can impart to ensure her safekeeping.

"A sentry traveling with her when she leaves this townhome isn't a terrible idea. Someone who can shoot and carries a knife in his boot and is not afraid to use either. She's going to continue to deliver food to that church even if you tell her she can't, but she'll agree to the guard if you let her keep this activity in place. Also, she's helping the Duchess Society with my workhouse release program. You already have two foundlings installed in your household. Protection should be provided for anything related there as well."

Leighton collapsed in the chair next to Macauley. "I don't know her. That's becoming clear."

"She's growing up, finding her own way, mate. Customary, innit? Only healthy swallows leave the nest." Macauley dabbed his bruised lip, Pippa's teary eyes swimming through his mind and landing in his chest like a punch. "When they find out the Earl of Stanford is my brother, they'll tear her apart for their amusement while I watch. I can't have that. It'll mean me waging war on this city and everyone in it, and the earl, he's not strong enough to deal at the moment. Struggling to keep him out of the dens is my current venture."

"*Brother*," the dukes breathed in tandem.

Macauley pressed on, needing Leighton to understand. "No one outside our little family knows about us. Me and Pippa. Dash, who I trust. Pippa's maid, I can't recall her name, something starting with a V. A chit whose been bribed so often and so well, she'll never talk. You might want to reinforce that arrangement, though, to be sure. We've been discreet is what I'm telling you."

"It's unfortunate there was a need for discretion, *mate*."

Macauley rolled his head to look at Leighton. The firelight tossed amber flashes of heat across them, adding tension the night didn't require. "Shall I tell you who approached whom?"

Leighton grunted and closed his eyes.

Macauley did the same, his heart leaden.

He didn't think so.

Pippa sat before the chessboard she'd found Macauley agonizing over two years ago. The night he'd caught her with his coat in her hand, her face buried in his velvet collar. His teasing scent cascading through her like sunlight, warming her in places she'd not known he would someday *own*.

He'd acknowledged his attraction that night, although it had taken years for him to act on it.

She'd never be the same after this experience. No way around it. Maybe that was the gift he'd imparted. One step closer to becoming who she was meant to be.

Her heart his—but her future *hers*.

Pippa flicked the blade of her birthday knife across the base of a rook, the emeralds embedded in the handle winking in the candlelight. She'd never been sure before, but now she suspected they were real.

She remembered what she'd thought of Macauley then. Grimacing killjoy. Cocksure bounder. When he was none of those things. Her understanding made their parting practically unbearable.

Nevertheless, he'd warned her from the start. *Don't think because I break the rules, I don't know them.* It was her fault she hadn't listened.

He'd broken the rules... but he was not taking the girl.

The door to the game room opened. A heavy tread, tentative. She knew it was her brother before he settled in the chair across from her.

"Did you hurt him?" She raised a tumbler of brandy Roan better not complain about to her lips. "His shoulder is still a mess."

He nudged a pawn needlessly about the board. "It's decided, then. You love him."

She sent liquid fire down her throat. Her mind was finally getting fuzzy around the edges, thank heavens. "No one of any import knows, Roan. Calm down. I'm not sorry, and I won't lie and say that I am to anyone that matters."

"*I* know, Pippa."

Pippa folded the blade in and wrapped her fingers around the knife. "I'm not attaching myself to a man who doesn't want me. So don't press the issue. I'll say no publicly if I have to."

Her brother swore, grabbed her glass, and took a healthy gulp. "Oh, he wants you. He just doesn't *want* to want you. I wish I could say I hadn't been there myself a couple of years ago with Hellie."

"That's mad," she whispered, her body melting at the notion.

"No, darling, that's a man."

Pippa chewed on her thumbnail, pausing at the arrested look on Roan's face. "What?"

He shook his head, downing the rest of her drink. "Do you know him, Pippa? In a way we don't? He seems to think he knows you, and I'm coming to believe he's right."

Pippa squeezed back in the chair until her spine hit the spindles. She parsed through what she could tell him yet not tell him everything. Her memories were hers. And Macauley's. "He was... sweet. Kind, considerate." Loving, oh, *so* loving.

"Sweet? Xander Macauley?"

Pippa shifted a knight to a new position with the tip of her knife. "He's not the same with me. He's funding an orphanage in Tower Hamlets. Did you know that? Moving children out of a workhouse and into employment, one at a time. He loves his brother. He loves you and Streeter and this entire cluster we've surrounded ourselves with, even if he's unable to admit it. You need to remember being high-born doesn't make a man, Roan."

The duke sprawled in his chair, thoroughly aggravated, hanging his head back to stare at the ceiling. "I know that. You act like I reserve friendship for those listed in *Debrett's*. When I didn't even *want* this title. Remember?"

Pippa sighed, wishing Roan hadn't finished her drink. "You mustn't let this ruin your friendship. Your business association." It would affect funds the Duke of Leighton and his starving estates needed more than Macauley ever would. She drew the letter M on the chessboard, her cheeks heating. The reaction hopefully hidden in the dim light. "It was my idea, you see. He waved me off for a long while before conceding. I can be very... *convincing* when I put my mind to it."

Roan swallowed thickly, his gaze not daring to catch hers. "Yes, he inferred that. Very diplomatically. A gentleman to the end, our cunning hoodlum."

"Macauley *is* a gentleman. I know that's hard to hear when you're outlining ways to defend me. However, I believe his decency is why he's making these choices. The selfish option isn't this one."

Roan finally looked at her, a searching study. As if seeing her for the first time. "Aren't you furious? You're not getting what you want. The Pippa Darlington I know doesn't like that very much."

Pippa propped her chin on her fist, the tears she knew were coming threatening to spill. Her chest felt hollow. "I think I'm just sad."

Roan covered her hand with his, turning it over and staring at the knife she held. "I'll bring him to heel if you wish. I can make that happen. Honestly, I'm not sure he doesn't want me to. I love you, and I want you to be happy. If Xander Macauley is central to that happiness, then he's central. He's already family, all told."

A spark of fury flared in her belly. Pippa was relieved there was anything aside from grief. Slipping the knife into Roan's hand, she wrapped his fingers around it. "Return this to him, will you?"

The Duke of Leighton stared at the knife as if she'd put a rattlesnake in his hand. "I have a feeling this is going to make him angry."

Pippa smiled, her eyes stinging. "Me, too."

Roan shoved the knife in his coat pocket, and she had to bite her lip to keep from asking him to give it back. "Seven days before he returns and starts begging. That's where I'd lay my blunt."

Pippa stilled, her heart dropping. "Returns?"

"He's fleeing to Hampshire with Lord Stanford as soon as the earl can travel. Tomorrow morning, likely. A man I suspect you already know is his brother. Whatever's in Hampshire that he's running off to, I can't say. No good fossils anywhere near there, so I won't be visiting. He's leaving that boisterous young Scot to run his gaming hell. And me. Streeter. Markham. Like we have time with all these children and dukedoms and such to run a gambling den, too."

"Hampshire," Pippa murmured beneath her breath. His estate. *Coward.*

"The glower on your face is genuinely frightening, Pippa." Roan yanked his hand through his hair, leaving the strands in disarray. He'd had quite a day, her beloved brother. "I can't believe I'm saying this, but when Macauley comes crawling back, because he will, most men do, go easy. I'm beginning to feel sorry for the bloke."

No. She was going to go hard. To the mat, as Gentleman Jackson liked to say.

Xander Macauley had broken her heart.

She would win this round *and* the blasted twenty pounds they'd bet on who would get married first. Just see if she didn't.

Chapter Twenty

Where a lovestruck smuggler seeks to correct his bleak future

T he last straw was receiving Pippa's birthday knife.

Via a runner Leighton had sent to Hampshire at rather exorbitant expense. The duke's note had clearly stated as much. He'd added that he couldn't leave the return of something so personal to the post and chance losing what neither Macauley nor Pippa wanted to lose. His final request? It would suit him if they could get their heads out of their arses.

Meddlesome bastard.

Although everything His blasted Grace had written was true.

Macauley was lonely. On the edge of miserable. Books? Uninteresting. Work? Tedious. Women? Over for him except for one.

It had been exactly ten days since he'd last seen Pippa.

Ten agonizing days where he'd completed a host of duties to keep himself from jumping in the river that ran behind the estate and letting it carry him off. The list included hiring staff, installing new thatch on the chapel roof *and* the stables. Paying numerous invoices in the village that the viscount he'd purchased the place from had left to hang in the wind. Rebuffing a blunt offer from a comely widow.

Digging a trench in the side garden that he could have left to a servant. He'd toiled from dawn to dusk, then returned to have late supper with Stanford before collapsing in a bed big enough to sleep seven. It was so high off the floor he needed a step stool to get into it. A medieval wonder like the rest of the place.

A bed he'd imagined tossing Pippa atop and staying in for a month. Just the two of them. What he desired with every beat of his heart. What he'd chucked aside like yesterday's rubbish.

When he'd only set out to *protect* her. His world was not the one she should inhabit.

He'd been too exhausted to take himself in hand for the first time in recent history, fantasies of her bringing quick release. Which helped him sleep. Well, he'd *mostly* been too exhausted. Not every night, at least, which was his norm.

And he'd gotten word. She wasn't pregnant.

Which should have been the news he *wanted*.

This message had come from Dash. He'd confirmed the intelligence with Pippa's shady maid, whom Macauley had covertly discussed the topic with before he left London. A babe would have changed everything, and he couldn't count on Pippa to tell him. So, he'd made another contribution toward Viviette's fripperies fund. Dash didn't even know the question he was sending an answer to. Macauley couldn't chance the note being intercepted or anyone aside from the corruptible personal maid of the lady in question being involved.

It was a simple *no* scratched on foolscap that had sent him into a boozy spiral for no sane reason. Stanford had scraped him off the library floor that night—a chamber gorgeous enough to make him weep once he finished restoring it—and poured him into bed.

Surprisingly, Stanford had proven an able caregiver, once given a chance to care. Although, his brother was currently claiming he was never returning to London. Aside from asking about the girl Pippa had placed in the gardens, he seemed uninterested in life when Macauley knew a grubby lad had taken that position. His future. Their partnership.

The broadsheets had picked up the story of Stanford's injury, in part. Although thankfully, without any mention of Pippa. The

Scarred Earl, they were calling him. A hero of some sort. A survivor of war atrocities returning home to save someone from an attack that had never actually happened. Or had not occurred in the manner described in the *Gazette*. Macauley didn't think hiding out in Hampshire was the path to a sound mind or body, but at the moment, he wasn't going to push. Ollie needed to get used to his changed appearance before he returned to confront the wolves. The news of their relationship was surely the next scandal to be published.

Macauley had cornered him on the back lawn on their third day at Hampshire when Ollie had finally decided to leave the house. His face still covered in bandages, he'd been carrying a telescope Macauley had seen covered in a dusty tarp in an upstairs bedchamber. It was closing in on nightfall, and Macauley was eternally grateful his brother had found something of interest to take his mind off his disfigurement.

He hadn't been able to keep himself from asking. "Why did you step between the baron and me that night?" The scene had kept Macauley up at night. His brother's blood spattered across the cobblestones, a hiss of pain shooting past his lips. All because Ollie had been protecting him when he'd never had anyone protect him before.

Ollie had glared at him and stormed away, leaving the telescope on the lawn, the answer evidently obvious to him. It was an error in judgment that had left grief burning a hole through Macauley. Once again, he'd ruined the situation.

So, he had an ailing brother to worry about. A love affair to mourn.

Consequently, Macauley's wrath was running high. So when he'd received the bloody knife in a cigar box that smelled of rotting fossils, he checked on Stanford, then climbed in a carriage bound to London.

Enough was enough with this woman.

"This could be a boon," Georgie, the Duchess of Markham, whispered from her spot on the sofa of her lavender receiving parlor. She and Hildy Streeter sat next to each other, whispering in low tones he could hear without issue. "I always thought him beyond the Duchess Society's ability to transform. Yet, life changes. Newfound brother to an earl. Marriage to a duke's sister. A *love* association. It would move us away from mere matchmaking and into miracle territory."

Hildy Streeter assessed Macauley with a skeptical eye, searching for imperfections she could swiftly repair.

"I'm paying you for a romantic consultation, ladies. I have my own team of solicitors should we move into arbitration. I need a proposal even a considerably exasperated woman will not refuse. Not redesign of the man. I realize that's what you two chits love to do. Take them apart and put 'em back together like broken crockery. I've seen the unfortunate saps stumble out of here, head in their hands." He chewed on his cheroot, having no intention of telling the Duchess Society contingent he no longer smoked. "Pippa likes me the way I am, sorry to inform you."

Georgie smiled. Winsome and a tad scary. "Are you sure?"

Actually, he *was*. However, Pippa had rejected the notes—*five*—he'd sent in the two days he'd been back. What Leighton called the 'grand gesture' was required. Dukes and their fancy ideas. He'd suggested Macauley call on the Duchess Society as they seemed to understand the mysteries of the female mind.

Although Macauley was seeking answers about the *heart*.

"Flowers," Hildy mused, the arm of her spectacles caught between her teeth.

He swallowed a curse they wouldn't appreciate. "If that's the best you can do, I'm doomed. I thought you were famous for this nonsense."

"Chess set. She loves to play."

He shook his head. "Not good enough. Trite and uninspiring, in fact."

"You're known to frequent a jeweler on Sackville." This from the duchess, her fearsome smile still in place. "But no mistress for close to a year, which is commendable."

His boots hit the floor with a thump. "Have you had me investigated?"

The ladies shrugged in guilty tandem.

"Pip's not a jewelry kind of girl. Not alone with nothing else to back it, that is. I need to know how to find my way inside the castle if you get my meaning. Pip's drawn the bridge up over the moat."

Georgie giggled behind her teacup. "We thought your success with that venture was part of the problem."

"Not *that* castle. Ever heard of a metaphor?" He frowned, his cheeks, unbelievably, going hot. "What a lewd mind you have, Your Grace. I'm stunned to my boots and back. Posh upbringings don't curb naughty natures, do they?"

Georgie rolled her eyes, used to Macauley's mockery. Perhaps stunned herself that he knew the definition of the word metaphor. Did they not think he could *read?*

"What does Lady Philippa want? Aside from you. We suspect you understand her better than anyone. For example, how did you know she'd welcome potentially ruining her reputation by taking a midnight swim in the Serpentine?"

He narrowed his gaze on the lovely duo across from him. The hair on his neck lifted like it did when he negotiated a business contract, and the conversation was getting fierce. "She wants freedom. Adventure. *Purpose.* She doesn't want anything society gives her. The duke's sister bit. She wants her unique slice of the world. Closer to mine than hers, which scares the stuffing from me."

"Give her your world, then."

Macauley stilled, the cheroot tumbling from his lips. He caught it with a fast snatch before it hit the carpet. "My world is dangerous." He jabbed the smoke in Hildy's direction. "You know. Streeter's out of it but not all the way out. You're not as bloody reckless as Pip is, though. He's loaded you down with enough cats and children to keep you busy."

Hildy's indigo eyes glowed as they did whenever anyone mentioned her husband. Macauley wanted that dreamy look to steal over Pippa's face when someone mentioned *him.* His gut churned with envy and newfound intent.

"Isn't there a saying about keeping your enemies close?" Hildy asked as she needlessly pleated her skirt. "Couldn't that apply to the people you love? You can protect her better than anyone. She'll be more honest with you about her dicey activities than she will be with her brother. Instead of giving Leighton advice about ways to protect her, give her this slice of your world she wants, then keep her. Help her find her purpose."

He slid the cheroot into his pocket, his brain buzzing. "Purpose finding *is* a rather grand gesture, innit? Life-changing and all that. A man's world, so she needs me even if she doesn't *want* to need me."

Hildy opened the folio at her side. "I have faith you'll find the key to unlock Lady Philippa's heart, Xander Macauley. And her castle. The job was tailor-made for you." She put a bound set of papers on the table and smoothed her hand across the top. "Now, about those marital contracts."

Pippa had the odd feeling someone was following her.

Not Aston, the hulking brute assigned to her, a stipulation she'd agreed to after Roan had threatened to terminate her runs to the church to deliver food. Blast that Xander Macauley! While getting pummeled by her brother, he'd apparently spilled her secrets.

She giggled behind her gloved fist. Well, not *all* her secrets.

Going to that dreamy fantasy place where Macauley alone resided, Pippa halted on the stoop leading from the Westminster terrace of William Blair, MP serving the Banbury constituency. It took her a moment to catch her bearings and recall where she was. Blair's wife, Lavinia, was interested in upping her charitable game after hearing that another MP's wife had agreed to place two "graduates" of a Tower Hamlet orphanage into her household.

Which gossip had allowed everyone in London to understand was the Duke of Leighton's sister's pet project.

This was Pippa's third tea this week.

Aston gave her an inappropriate wink from his perch at the bottom of the stairs. "Ma'am," he said, correct use of names and titles beyond him, a man seemingly delighted to squire a hopeless eventual spinster around town. If looks could kill, her guard's would lay one out flat. Not from beauty but from pure terror. His nose was smashed from repeated attempts to break it. His ebony hair was held back in a queue at the base of his neck. His jaw was cut by a scar that would conceivably rival the Earl of Stanford's.

This thought brought Macauley front and center when she'd managed to go a solid minute without thinking about him. She was sick of cycling through emotions—fury, misery, heartache—on a second-by-second basis.

The carriage slid in behind hers in a neat tuck and skilled driving. A lacquered black box pulled by two bays of impressive breeding. No crest or coat of arms.

When Aston nodded to the coachman atop the box, Pippa's temper began to boil. Of all the—

She marched up to her guard, poking her finger in his chest. When Aston remained silent, she gestured to the carriage. "Who is that?"

He grinned, gap-toothed, enjoying her outburst. "He told me you were a real pisser, ma'am."

"Did Xander Macauley hire you?"

He blinked, lips parting in uncertainty. "No, that be the Duke of Leighton. But Macauley sent me to him. I've known Mac since he was a lad roaming the docks in tattered breeches. We came up together, I reckon you could say."

Later, Pippa wouldn't recall her trip to the carriage. She only remembered beating on the door, the luscious voice she'd missed with all her heart sneaking through a crack in the window and inviting her inside.

"Get in, Blondie."

Pippa was speechless. Furious at him (arrogant bounder) and herself (weak-willed chit) for wanting to scramble inside his darkened conveyance without another breath passing from her lips. She knew she was encouraging a scene on a public street because Macauley didn't care. Suddenly, she didn't, either.

She was off, turning on her heel, away from the man who owned her heart and the sentry who'd known him since he was in tattered breeches.

Macauley caught up to her easily, before she'd even crossed to the next block. Further aggravating her because she was winded, and he was not.

Don't look, Pippa.

Then she did, stumbling so clumsily that he had to cup her elbow to steady her.

Heavens, he was stunning. Windblown. His jaw shadowed with the faintest hint of stubble. So tall she had to rear her head back to take him in. His mahogany hair curling around the brim of his beaver hat. And those eyes. Silver as a knife's blade in the misty afternoon light.

He also looked exhausted. Dark slashes a violent streak beneath his eyes. His bottom lip chapped from pulling it between his teeth, which he did when he was perplexed. His cravat needed a woman's hand to correct it.

The urge to kiss him right there nearly buckled her knees.

"Don't pull the wretched man routine on me." Then she started down the street with a huff, realizing she was walking *away* from Mayfair.

"Wretched man," he murmured on what sounded like a laugh.

"My guard could be doing this, following me." She popped her head with her hand, knocking her bonnet askew. "Oh, la, you know all about him. *And* having me followed."

Macauley matched his stride to hers and strolled alongside her for two blocks before continuing the conversation. "Don't be angry about Aston. Your brother doesn't have the wealth of resources at his command that I do. Jawbreakers and lawbreakers, that's my specialty."

"What do you *want?*" Pippa seethed, dodging a pram being pushed by someone who recognized her. The lady gasped and turned as she passed them. Lady Digby and her governess. Not the best group to see her arguing with the Limehouse Prince.

"I have a business proposition," he said, uncaring if they had an audience.

She snorted. "Sure you do."

He gripped her elbow to stop her. Pedestrians flowed around them, an island in the city.

She made the mistake of looking into his eyes. Gunmetal silver, like the moon on a stormy night.

She wanted to touch him. She wanted him to beg. She wanted to never see him again. She wanted to rip his clothes off. The world revolved while she tried to pick the safest option. A gust carried his enticing fragrance to her, forever altering her with one breath.

He crossed the line for them both, tucking a stray strand of hair behind her ear. She shivered in response, struggling to hide it.

"Is that devious maid of yours present, Pip?"

"Viviette. In the carriage."

Macauley tunneled his hand inside his waistcoat pocket, coming back with a slip of paper. She recognized his bold penmanship from reading his personal papers above the gaming hell that night. "Meet me at this address. My carriage will follow if that's agreeable."

Pippa took the note and tucked it inside her glove. She would review it in the privacy of her carriage—although she was dying to know where he was inviting her. This seemed like another adventure, which she loved *and* loathed. Talk about devious. "Your plan all along, I'm sure."

"Ah, *cor*, Pip, haven't you missed me at all?"

She'd been in the process of leaving the man she loved on the street. Slowing, she glanced over her shoulder. Her heart skipped, sending black swirls across her vision. Xander Macauley was rightfully the most magnificent specimen in England. Toe-curling, thigh-melting male beauty. "Miss doesn't quite describe it."

He swallowed, a sluggish sigh stealing past his lips. "Same, luv. Same."

"I'll meet you." Pippa tapped her glove and left him standing there, staring.

Chapter Twenty-One

Where an incorrigible young lady is given a choice
(and a smuggler makes a grand gesture, Xander Macauley style)

The squat building was located in Holborn, an area settled strategically between Macauley's world and hers. As she descended from the carriage, Pippa wondered if the choice was intentional. It had been a shop, perhaps a haberdashery, but now sat vacant. The trim was a charming shade of green, flecked in spots, begging for restoration. However, the door made nary a squeal when she opened it and stepped inside, the scent of linseed oil proclaiming a recent cleaning. The bay window's glass was spotless when she glanced at the carts and buggies traveling along the lane. The space was flooded with light and would be pleasant on London's rare sunny days. She could just picture it.

The entry room was tight but cozy, with a narrow hallway leading to a larger paneled antechamber at the back.

That was where she found him. Resting his hip against a massive desk she immediately identified as Gillows, a piece that was more expensive than the lease on this entire building for a year. Ten years. A rug beneath him that was clearly Axminster. He had an open book in his hand, and he didn't look up. His hair was a disordered tumble across his brow, as if he'd repeatedly raked his fingers through it. He wore a pair of silver spectacles, a detail that made her heart sink to her slippers. She smiled for the first time in days to see him so engrossed in his text that he didn't hear her enter.

She quietly crossed to him, having left Aston and Viviette in the carriage. The desktop was littered with objects. Her knife. A stunning chess set as costly as the Gillows. A leather riding crop with a lavender tassel. A colossal vase of wildflowers, not one rose in sight, sharing their boisterous aroma with the room. Lastly, leaning against the desk was an oblong, wrapped package.

He glanced up as she closed in, his subtle show of pleasure bringing out the dimple she loved. Light glimmered off his lenses. "You came."

"You knew I wouldn't be able to resist a chess set that looks medieval."

"It *is* medieval. Found in the ruins of a monastery. Collectors consider it priceless."

Priceless. Of course. She crossed to the other side of the desk, putting the length of glossy mahogany between them. Macauley was dressed in his customary black, and he smelled like heaven. Leather and bergamot with the slightest hint of labor. Add to this, those blasted spectacles. She needed a hulking bureau between them to resist the urge to ask if the piece would support them. It looked sturdy enough.

Delight curled his mouth. "It would hold up, luv, if you're wondering. I made sure before I purchased it."

"I wasn't wondering." She frowned, a horrible image coming to her. "*How* did you test it?" If he'd touched another woman on this desk, she would murder him.

He plucked a violet petal from a coneflower and tucked it between the pages of his book. Slid the volume to the desk and, bracing his hands, leaned in. Getting closer than she wanted. And his stance. It spoke of action. Her blood flared in her veins. "I sat on it and rocked around a bit."

Pippa's laugh spurted free. Flustered, she trailed her finger over the petals of what she thought was a snapdragon. It was an unusual assortment. Still, Macauley owned a shipping company and had access to the best of everything. "These are extraordinary."

He hummed a vague response, his cheeks tinting a delicious, rosy hue. "Those were Hildy's idea. I know you don't like flowers. I've never been a man to give them. Although they do brighten up the room. And they smell nice."

"Diamond pendants seem more your style." She breathed in the luscious scent, astonished but willing to overlook his reaction. Imagine, Xander Macauley *blushing*. "Maybe with the right giver, I'd like flowers."

His shoulders lowered a notch, his throat clicking as he swallowed.

She studied him. He was *nervous*. This realization shouldn't have made love for him overflow the banks of her heart.

But it did.

Disconcerted, she picked up her knife and turned it in her hand. "So... this place."

"It's not simply a place, it's an offer. A business proposition."

"For me?"

His gaze tracked away as he reopened his book and flipped through the pages. "I want to start a formal apprenticeship program for the workhouse and the orphanage. I can't run it. If I add another feather to my load, I'll drop from the weight. I don't have room in the warehouse, and I'm trying to get these souls *out* of Limehouse. Not have them staying in a finer building down the street while mingling with the same shady elements. This location is a mix. Safe enough but not sparkling bright."

"Like Mayfair."

A smile tiptoed across his face. "Like Mayfair."

Her breath caught. *Oh*, she wanted to kiss him. Crawl atop this desk he'd tested and have her way with him. They didn't have to disrobe completely. *That* was information he'd given her that they'd been, as yet, unable to put to proper use.

He exhaled gently and glanced back to his book. "An assistant could sit in the front room. This office would be all yours. The entire building, in fact. Look past the dust and neglect. Dream and dream big, Little Darlington. Streeter's drawing up plans to restructure the upper floors as temporary living quarters while the students, for lack of a better term, transition to their full-time positions. It'll be showier than Carlton House when Street's done spending my blunt. You see, I want staff situated in homes all over England. Not just London. And not merely housed with the nobility. True apprenticeships with cobblers, seamstresses, and the like. I have a thousand and one contacts from the shipping venture I don't have time to chase down. You should involve your brother at some point. Markham, too. Maybe they can host a gala to announce the effort and ask for support. It can't hurt. Everyone loves a duke and their deuced galas."

She came off the desk, rocking back on her slippered heels. "You want *me* to manage this?" She should have known Macauley would take their molehill of an idea and make a mountain of it. The man feared nothing. She was in awe of his courage and determination.

And frankly, his *faith* in her.

He fluttered the pages of his book, playing with her now. "You don't think you can? With a modest staff at your disposal? Two dukes supporting you?"

"I can do it," she blurted before she had time to be sure.

His gaze was heartfelt, his delight genuine. "I think you can, too. Next week, a high perch phaeton and two of the finest mounts in England are being delivered. Fastest model on the market. You'll need your own transport. With Aston seated beside you every time you leave this place. He's your personal sentry from now on. We agree, or this doesn't happen. I won't budge on this point."

She picked up the riding crop. "I begin to see how your mind works." Then she gave the desk a little slap that had his lips parting, air sighing out. "A lot of things one could do with this."

"If you're trying to drive me mad, luv, it's working."

Her gaze dusted him. His shaft was hard and full beneath his trouser close, not a typical part of his business discussions, she guessed. A bolt of heat drifted lazily down her body to pool between her thighs.

"And this?" She toed the wrapped package, her mind replaying indecent memories. She wished she hadn't worn petticoats. Wished Aston and Viviette weren't waiting in the carriage.

Wished Macauley would step around the desk and kiss her already.

He paused, his chest rising with his deep breath. He let the book close. Nudged the spectacles high on the bridge of his nose. "That's the big question, luv."

Oh. Running the philanthropic division of Xander Macauley's business wasn't the question. Her own phaeton. A chess set worth a fortune. The return of her beloved knife. A hothouse of wildflowers.

Or not the *big* question.

He gestured, impatient. "Go on. Open it."

Pippa laid the crop aside, placed the package on the desk, and unwrapped it. Inside were two signs, large enough to hang over the front door. *Macauley Enterprises* both stated in bold crimson lettering. The name beneath held the difference. The question.

P. J. Darlington, Proprietress.

P. J. Macauley, Proprietress.

She traced her finger over the letters. Darlington or Macauley.

Darlington or Macauley.

"Leighton told me your middle name. Though I don't think you sound like a Jane. I reckoned the initials better suited you, but we can change it if you want. I kept off 'lady' and all that because I truly don't even know what's correct. I like the sound of P.J. myself."

"Jane was my grandmother's name," she whispered, fearing she would faint. Instead, what sounded like a church bell was ringing in her ear. This was a *proposal.* Macauley's understated, slightly bashful, full-hearted, extravagant proposal. Flowers. Chess set. Knife. Phaeton. Building. Purpose. *Life.*

Wife.

A burgundy velvet box with a gold crest on the top slid into view at the edge of her vision. "I didn't want to miss anything," he murmured, sounding uncharacteristically cautious.

She grasped the box with a hand that shook. Her heart was beating in a frantic rhythm. *Say yes. Say no. Kiss him. Tear his clothes off. He'll let you.*

The ring was lovely. Simple yet not. A circle of pearls surrounding a glittering emerald.

"Like your eyes," he added, the words so low she had to struggle to catch them.

Say yes. Say no. Kiss him. Tear his clothes off. He'll let you.

"Can you please say something, Pip? I'm starting to panic."

Her gaze lifted. He looked impossibly young standing there, flipping pages, worried and weary. How had she ever thought him too old for her? Wrong for her in any way? "You love me?"

A tiny wrinkle settled between his brows. He sketched a circle around his heart with his finger. "Macauley loves Pippa. Desperately."

"You want to marry me? Without a kiss to seal the offer?"

He sighed, closing the book, making no move to touch her. "I could kiss the answer out of you. The one I want. Fetching simple, innit? Persuade you in that way. Have you tangle me up like only you can, where I forget what I was asking in the first place. The way we are together..." He dragged his hand through his hair, searching. "We're remarkable. Being with you, I've never, it's never been this good. This *complete*. Everything about being with you works for me. Love, pleasure, passion, laughter, friendship. I want to bend you over this desk so badly I'm about to rip through my trouser buttons. We haven't done that yet. It's on my list, of course. But it's dirty dealings if I do. Because I want the rest *more*."

"More," she whispered. *More.*

He forged ahead as she concentrated on staying upright and not slithering to the floor. "I'm not who you're supposed to marry, luv, I get that. For all the mysteries of life, nevertheless, you're who I *want*. You're it for me. I'll figure this out"—he gestured to his tented trousers —"if you choose business only. I want your partnership. Your mind is keen. You'll do what needs doing with a cleverly hidden, thoroughly devious bent. Better than any man alive. You're honest but not so honest you beat someone about the head with it."

"*Macauley*," she whispered.

He held up his hand, stopping her. "You need purpose, and strangely enough, I'm finding *I* do. Dash is a natural with the gaming hell. His temperament, controlled but deadly, is well-matched for a dangerous endeavor. Where I'm lost. I want to save my community, and I need you to do that. I'm not dealing with the Duchess Society.

That's your plank to walk. I want control, at least in part, of where these people *land*. You'll be an able negotiator once we smooth away your tells." He tapped the Darlington sign. "I'll accept it if you say no. But I won't be happy about it. *Ever*. I don't like to lose. And my life won't be much without you in it."

"My tells?"

"That's the crucial point you pick out like a splinter?" He braced his hands on the desk, leaning close again. His dimple was winking, tempting her. Amazingly, he looked almost professorial in the spectacles. "Ah, Little Darlington, you have all manner of tells. I can read them like one of my blasted books. I want to spend a lifetime detailing each and every one."

"We could run the charitable business and remain as we'd been until—"

"*No*," he whispered, fury threading the word. "I'm not selling part of myself. Or you. Hiding this anymore from the people we love. I told you, once I decide, I'm not a man to accept half measures."

Pippa popped the velvet box onto the desk. "I'd like to have a moment to think, thank you!"

He gestured to the ring. "You don't like it? I could have gone for a sapphire, but an emerald was the only reasonable choice with those eyes of yours. The bloody jeweler disagreed, but what does that silly nob know about it?"

She trailed her finger over the sparkling gem. "I love it. It's perfect. I love the priceless chess set and the thought of driving my very own top-of-the-market phaeton through London like a beast, Aston hanging on for dear life. The flowers are gorgeous. I've never received any that pleased me more. You're *gorgeous* and generous. Kind. The brightest man in the room, and no one has any idea. I love you with everything *in* me." He started to round the desk, but she stopped him with a whispered oath. "You're also the most arrogant man I've ever met. You simply expect me to say yes. Change my life in one second without a moment to review the deal. You say no half measures, so I bend to your will without examining my own."

"*Deal?*" He took a step back, yanked his gloves off, and whipped them against his thigh. "This isn't a wager I'm proposing. A twenty-pound gambit on who gets married first. Don't think I forgot about that! This is *life*. Mine and yours. Together. One name. Macauley. Babies. The whole deal. All I claimed I was running from. I'm letting you catch me, so catch me already."

"Is this winning, Xander? Or is this *me*?"

Swearing, he stalked across the room, his gloves clutched in his fist. "Stubborn chit. You have to make me bleed. Fine, then, go about it." Turning, he stabbed his finger in her direction. "Aston knows where to find me when you're ready. He sticks to you like *glue*. Don't test me on this."

He prowled toward the door, then turned back. Came to her and shoved something in her hand, then he swept from the room in a categorically theatrical exit.

Pippa looked down to find her dance card from the night of their first kiss sitting in her hand. Her heart skipped a hard, fast beat.

He'd kept it all this time. She'd think Xander Macauley was a romantic if she didn't know better.

Watching him leave, Pippa swiped her knuckles beneath her teary eyes, taking two steps to follow him before she halted. She'd hurt his feelings when all she'd wanted was a *moment*. He hadn't even told her he loved her. Not conventionally.

Oh, Pippa.

Who wanted convention when a man drew a circle around his heart? Shuffling to the desk, she popped open the velvet box and wiggled the ring on her finger. Tilted her hand in the light, green facets dancing along the wall.

So he didn't do things the way any other man in London would have. She loved that about him, she decided, glancing at her gifts. He *knew* her. He understood she wanted excitement and purpose—and he was prepared to give her both. He would let her deliver meals to any church she wanted, as long as she had protection. He was offering her a piece of not only his life at home but his life at *work*. No spouse aside from Hildy, Georgie, and Helena had been offered such a thing. Tobias Streeter, the Duke of Markham, and her brother, Roan, would have it no other way.

Macauley wanted a real partnership. With his wife, P.J.

She spun around her office, joy a dizzying rush. Of course, she was marrying the conceited cur. Another woman wasn't getting her hands on him.

Xander Macauley was *hers*.

Pippa smiled. She was *it* for him, after all.

And he was *it* for her.

PART THREE

JUDGMENT

Chapter Twenty-Two

Where a smuggler gets his answer
(and then some)

"**A**re you engaged, then? Shall we have a wee dram of a toast?" Dash asked absently, not bothering to glance up from his ledger as Macauley stomped into his office. The lad had an incredible gift for calculations and counting cards, but his reading skills were shaky, hence his lessons with Theo. Macauley planned to have him assume responsibility for the Devil's Lair shortly, as he'd discussed with Pippa. A man who managed the most successful gambling den in London needed to be able to read everything put before him. Contracts, promissory notes, correspondence. Or he'd be milked blind.

Macauley threw himself into a leather armchair, the sounds of a thriving gaming hell drifting to him. The aroma of macassar oil and cigar smoke stung his nose. By midnight, he wouldn't be able to wade through the main hazard room without gasping for air. "Obstinate bit of baggage. Has to make everything more difficult. I'm not engaged, mate. Not yet, anyway."

Dash smothered a laugh with his fist. "She'll come round. Dinna doubt it. I have a feeling."

"She wants me to beg. When I came bearing gifts. Every kind I could think of. Flowers. A chess set that cost more than we secure in a month. You should see the phaeton. Men will *weep* when she tears down Rotten Row in that buggy. Add to that a very satisfactory building I'm redesigning. Streeter was more excited than I've seen him in months when I showed him the place. Actually, I enjoyed shopping for the willful chit. A little. Depressing, innit, how low I've sunk?"

Dash paused, his gaze meeting Macauley's. "Gifts but no beggary? No lass will say aye to a proposal without a spot of petitioning. Make a fool of yourself if ye want a wife, guv. Every bloke kens this doctrine. In Scotland, we deuced expect it. Our women are believers in a brawl before agreeing to most anything. I've never understood forever-afters, myself. I say look for pleasure for one night, especially with so many pleasures to choose from."

"I didn't believe until I met *her*." Macauley propped his chin on his fist, feeling sorry for himself. He'd hoped to have Pippa naked by now. He was getting tired of coming without her. Tired of *being* alone, period.

A knock sounded on the door. Macauley flicked his fingers carelessly. "You need to start telling these women not to distract you at work, lad. After hours, if you please."

Dash grinned, more offers than he could handle a dream rather than the nightmare it would become. "They come to me. I dinna invite a one of 'em. Some are old enough to be me ma. Ain't that grand?"

Macauley grunted, thoroughly disgusted at the moment. "I wouldn't welcome the trouble your comely mug is set to bring. Even if looking in the mirror is a delight."

Dash shrugged and scribbled an entry on the page. "Nothing I can do about being near the handsomest bloke many have ever seen. I ken it's like receiving a straight flush on the first deal. Not being snooty, they've told me so. Blimey, don't act like ye havena tunneled through your fair share. There ye go, rewriting history because you're in *love*." He muttered the word with utter disdain.

Exactly like Macauley used to.

Macauley perked up as Aston peeked around the door, his heart giving a crazy skip. "I escorted Miss Pippa to your private suite, boss. She insisted, and well, like you advised, better to go along if she ain't risking harm to herself. Gel has a quarrel ready for every blessed thing. It ain't proper, but if she's gonna be your missus, there's no threat, I suppose."

Macauley was up in a flash and racing for the staircase.

Dash's voice rang behind him. "She dinna even make ye wait an hour. That's a chit in love."

He took the stairs two at a time. Winded, he bounded through the door to his bedchamber and closed it behind him. Gave the key in the lock a turn.

She was pacing before the hearth. He looked closely. The ring was on her finger. He could see the stone glimmering in the firelight.

"Partners," she said and turned to him. "You won't go back on your word. Expect me to be a typical wife? I want your promise."

Taking a step forward, he yanked his coat sleeve from his arm, tugged on the other, then let the garment slip to the floor. "I won't go back on my word. I don't want typical. I want *you*. You know my offer. Pick a sign, Pip."

She raised her hand, holding him back. Her gaze darkened when she realized he was disrobing. "And—"

"Two minutes, luv," he interrupted and started on his cravat. The knot free, he let the silk strip dangle from his fingers before dropping it to the carpet.

She licked her lips, sending his cock into a painful press against his bone buttons. "Two minutes?"

He slipped his Bainbridge from his waistcoat pocket, checked the time. "Actually, one minute, thirty seconds."

"Until?"

He advanced a step. Worked his waistcoat buttons free. "Until I lift your skirts to your waist and fuck you until we can't see straight."

She backed up, coming against the wall.

Reaching over his shoulder, he grabbed a wad of linen, yanking his shirt over his head. "That's a fine spot. Stay there. Your legs around my waist, your luscious little body jammed between me and the wall. Perfection."

"Xander," she whispered and edged to the side, looking for a way to escape. When he didn't think she wished to escape. Her color was high, her breathing staggered. Her gaze dripped over him like hot wax.

She wanted him as much as he wanted her.

And he wanted her badly enough to want it a little rough.

They had *years* for the slow stuff.

"Bed or wall." He nodded to the other side of the room. "Or desk. You pick. Dealer's choice. I'm happy to oblige."

She huffed, giggling, sidestepping to put a settee between them, the darling girl. "I don't have any cards."

He laughed, too, loving this about them. They liked each other. When had he ever *liked* a woman he'd been with?

Vaulting the settee like a puddle, he pulled her into his arms. "You have all the cards, luv, every damned one of them."

The kiss was brutal. Tinged with love. Trust. Faith. He'd never experienced another like it. They circled much as they had during their waltz, kissing, murmuring, moaning. Her hair falling down her back, hairpins tumbling. His hands full of her.

The back of his thighs hit the bed, and he went down, Pippa crawling atop him. It was a flurry of motion, panting, grasping *need*. Her gown and chemise wrenched high. His trousers ripped open, a button spinning away from them and bouncing off the floor. He was inside her, at her direction, before he had time to fully prepare.

She was wet, eager, hungry. He couldn't have said *no* had someone held a knife at his throat.

He grabbed her hips to coordinate her movements until they were steady, relentless. Their rhythm was a mastery. He whispered her name against her lips when she leaned to kiss him. Released agonized pleas against her collarbone, the top of her breasts pressing against the edge of her bodice. Her fingers in his hair, tugging the strands as she rode him. Their scent mingled, teasing his senses and invading his memories. She tasted of cinnamon and tea. Passion and glory.

In the end, he tried to tell her. "I can't. Wait, Pip."

She only increased the pace until he was blind from desire, arching his back, pulling her down onto his pulsing shaft. The waves of pleasure ripped through him like an angry tide, starting at the base of his spine and rolling north. They gasped, grinding, releases seconds apart. Skin moist, burning.

He wasn't sure if he'd helped her or if she'd helped herself. He could only lie there, gasping, Pippa draped over him, marveling that it got better every time he touched her.

Aside from their churning breaths, the tick of the mantel clock was the only sound. In the distance, if he tried, he could hear the gaming hell kicking into high gear.

Pippa rolled to her side, exhaling long and hard. "Black dots." She pointed to her eyes.

He shifted, realizing he still had his boots on. "Roll over."

She complied, giving him her back. He undid laces and stays, allowing her room to breathe.

"All these silly layers. You don't have to do this when we're at home." *Home*, he thought, tears pricking his vision. Home.

She collapsed face-first to the mattress. "Dying."

He laughed, drew her back against his front, and wrapped his arms around her. They were a sticky, glorious mess. "If this is dying, sign me up."

"I pick the Macauley sign, by the way."

"Brilliant choice."

"I love you," she whispered into the counterpane. Then she released a not-so-gentle snore.

"Love you more, Pip."

His lids drifted low. One minute, maybe two, then they would talk. About marriage, the future, where they would live. About that twenty-pound bet.

Happiness claimed him at the same time as sleep.

Epilogue

Where a blissful couple realize sleep is a commodity in short supply

Two years later
A Hampshire estate housing a growing family

Macauley awoke to a piercing cry.

Wrestling to his elbow, he yawned and blinked, his bare feet hitting the floor before his mind fully roused. Stumbling, he made his way across the bedchamber and down the carpeted hallway to the nursery. Thankfully, moonlight lit his path as he crossed to the babe, giving him a glorious one-second opportunity to gaze upon his son, Christopher. Creamy skin so like his mother's. His hair a replica of hers, too, the color of wheat and candlelight. A pert nose he and Pip couldn't determine the origin of.

Christopher recognized his father, and his smile was a bubbly, spit-filled wonder. His arms came up, indecipherable chatter streaming from his rosebud lips. Macauley often questioned how a body could stand such a burst of love streaking through it.

Knee-weakening, life-altering *love*.

"Kit, my boy," he whispered and reached for him.

"Da," Kit chimed in a sing-song tone—as if he said it every day.

Macauley held his son up to look in his face. His heart pinched, rocking him where he stood. "Yes, I'm *Da*."

Kit socked him in the cheek with a gurgle, the rest of his speech babble.

Macauley caught her scent before he realized Pippa had followed him to the nursery. Her arms came around his waist, and she snuggled against his back. "The Limehouse Prince is the most caring of fathers. You raced in here before I could even locate my dressing gown. I know of some men in London who don't see their children but twice a year, Birthdays and Christmastide."

Tucking his son in his arms, Macauley gazed at Kit, unable to fathom living that existence. He and Pippa hadn't even wanted a nanny to assist in the early months. However, falling asleep during two meetings with district leaders due to lack of sleep had made him recognize the benefits of a modest nursery staff.

He and Pippa gladly did most of the caregiving, however. Nappies, feedings, baths. His son, aside from his wife, was the greatest joy of his life. Macauley didn't want to miss one second.

"I can't believe you made it here before me," Pippa said drowsily.

"I'm still half asleep myself, luv. You had to climb into bed last night and do that trick of yours. You know it drives me wild."

Pippa laughed, her warm breath snaking down his spine. He wore only drawers, and her plump breasts pressing against his bare skin was causing a noticeable effect. Which was ludicrous, considering their activities well into the night.

"It's not a trick. I only asked you to show me something new. You know more than I do about this topic, and while I don't *love* how you came by your knowledge, I find myself willing to take advantage of it."

"I told you that footstool wasn't going to hold you once we got going. Though it did lift your bottom up nicely." He sighed in dreamy remembrance. "Perfect height, actually. You pressed against the wall, fingers spread on the paneling as I came up behind you. I don't think I'll ever forget the sight."

Pippa did another delicious wiggle against him. "I have a burn from the carpet on my elbow. And my knee. Those take days to heal, you know."

Macauley chuckled and pressed a kiss to his son's forehead. "Apologies. Next time you tumble off a stool while we're close to completing, I'll have us finish on the bed, not the floor."

"Deal," she said and brushed her lips across a sensitive spot beneath his shoulder blade. "Kit has the Macauley grays. It's official. I knew the blue was turning. I only wish the *ton* wasn't calling them that, which I'm sure Stanford doesn't appreciate considering he's an Aspinwall."

Macauley loved that his son's eyes were his, but he didn't wish to broach the topic of his troubled brother. A subject sure to wreck his peace. "He said 'da'."

Pippa came around, peering into her son's face. "He did *not*. Kit's going to say 'mama' first."

Macauley threw an arm around his wife and pulled her close. "I'm sorry, Little Darlington. Your son has chosen his favorite."

"It can't be. You misheard. You said yourself you're half asleep."

"Come on, Kit. Say 'da'."

Kit glanced between them, his chubby grin growing. A line of spittle dribbled down his chin.

Pippa went for the box of rags they kept in every room. "He's teething. One is coming in on the bottom, I think. Soon, he'll be running."

Macauley glanced at the babe, trying to imagine it. *Running.*

His life had radically changed since he'd married Pippa nearly two years ago. They moved between London and Hampshire, depending upon business in town and the season. The charitable endeavor had grown to four associates working under Pippa's strategic management. She'd somehow turned the inclusion of a Duchess Society/Macauley Enterprises trained staff member into something of a fashionable circumstance. Markham and Leighton had worked the angle, too, holding balls that were exclusive to the charity twice a year.

Macauley was not above using society's fascination with their bloody standing for his personal gain. Gain that now meant helping people claw their way out of the slums.

"This is the perfect time to discuss what's troubling you, Xander. The semi-darkness of our son's serene nursery. You can look on while I feed him. I know you like that."

Macauley sighed, needing to pace if they were set to discuss delicate matters. He handed Kit to Pippa and started his trek from window to door, glancing back as she settled in the nursing chair, slipping her gown from her shoulder and guiding the babe's mouth to her puckered nipple. Motherhood had done miraculous things to her body. Widened her hips. Plumped her already gorgeous breasts. He could barely keep his hands off her. He was a randy lad around her, which she seemed to like.

"Spill," she said in her no-nonsense way.

Macauley made the trek two more times, halting at the window to nudge the velvet curtain aside. The moon was high, almost full. The verdant land stretching to the horizon, his. The scent of baby and Pippa and something unique to this place surrounded him.

And they were his as well.

Possession gripped him. Elemental possession. He became more connected to Hampshire with each hour spent here. The village. The tenants. The house and estate. He'd sunk his hands, his heart, in deep. Blood, sweat, and tears, as they said. He wanted his family to thrive in this very spot.

"I know Ollie had to leave. That it's a significant step in our relationship. Healthy swallows leave the nest, I always say. We'll be brothers no matter where he is, where I am. I've told him this a thousand times. The estate in Derbyshire is his legacy, whether he desires that legacy or not. Can't manage it from here. Or from London. Not with the work that calamity of a property is going to need. And honestly, the city offers too many temptations for a man not yet sure of himself." He let the curtain fall, his temper rising. "I should have killed the baron when I had the chance. Such a low point to bring a man lower. I'll never forget the glitter of glass that night. And the blood. Never."

Pippa adjusted Kit's fit on her breast while Macauley stared in open fascination. "Ollie's strong, darling. Physical labor on this estate for two years, working like a dogged servant alongside you. No opium, no drink. A widow or two in the village to keep his skills sharp. Streeter, Markham, and Roan sparring with him every time they visited. Why, he'd trounce anyone who tried to provoke him now. He's put on at least two stone. His scar is intriguing rather than repulsive, at least to a woman."

Macauley tunneled his hand through his hair. A spider crack on the ceiling caught his eye. With a groan, he added it to his mental repair list. "I butted in, where I usually don't. Not my typical mode."

Pippa stilled, this bit of news enthralling. "Excuse me?"

Macauley crossed to the shelves holding the books they read to Kit every night. Books made Macauley feel *safe*. "I hired Necessity Byrne. She's leaving for Derbyshire tomorrow."

"Oh, darling, you didn't."

Macauley scowled and wiggled out a book about a dancing dog that Kit particularly enjoyed, then popped it back into its slot with a thump. "The gardens at Aspinwall House are a disaster. You saw them when we visited last year. Vines overtaking the fruit trees. The conservatory windows shattered. The bloody place looks like it's haunted. What happened there with our father, I worry that Ollie's returned to face those memories before he's ready. Anyway, he knew Byrne was a woman masquerading as a man before I did. So, I thought maybe it meant something."

Pippa's laughter caused Kit to stop feeding and giggle along with her. "That's not saying much. Her role-playing was a farce until it was a farce even she couldn't maintain. Her attire is still horrid, but she's wearing gowns, so we're making progress."

"The lessons with the Duchess Society?"

Pippa shrugged. "I posed them as a sure way to grow her business. Polish off the rough edges, move in society in at least a business sense. You know that's all she cares about. Dirt and plants. Being invited to teas to discuss society dragons' gardens was the only way I got her into a dress."

Macauley grunted and examined another book. This one about a flying pig. "Streeter has her working on the landscaping for his new terraces in Islington. Should have enough blunt to purchase her own manse soon. Getting quite a name for herself."

"And securing a reputation as an oddity."

Macauley trailed his pinkie along a cracked spine. "She *is* an oddity."

Pippa hesitated. Macauley looked back at her. "Spill, luv."

"Did you see the latest *Gazette*?"

He dropped his head to his hands and massaged his temples. "Dash overturned his phaeton. Racing on St James."

"It's that deuced book. He's taking too many risks. Women, gambling, racing. Thinks he's invincible."

Pippa propped Kit on her shoulder for a burping session. She patted his back with a tender touch. "One can't argue with success. The Devil's Lair. That face. Now a book on gaming that everyone in England has read or is clamoring to. A boy from the stews being invited to speak at society events must be thrilling."

"Disconcerting is what it is. None of it is real. He should have kept up his lessons with Theo. She was grounding him, somehow. Whatever falling out they had, well, that's all done."

Pippa smiled when Kit burped. "Theo is almost engaged to that professor of hers."

"Pompous arse, you mean."

"Edward is very nice. Perfect for her. Talks about history non-stop. They're coming in two weeks with Roan, Helena, and the children. You didn't expect Theo to attach herself to someone remarkable, did you? She likes the brilliant dullards."

Macauley grunted. "Edward is as dank as muddy rainwater. I think he likes being connected to a duke more than he likes being connected to *her*."

"You're protective. It's sweet."

Macauley crossed to his wife and dropped to his knees. His arms going around her, he put his head in her lap. He was more vulnerable with her than with any person in his life. "I love you both with all my heart."

"You caught the infection."

He smiled, the soft muslin of her dressing gown caressing his cheek. "But good."

She danced her fingers through his hair. "I love you and Kit more than life. I knew exactly what I was fighting for. Don't ever imagine I didn't."

He drew his family into his soul. His clever girl was right. More than life.

THE END

Thank you for reading *The Wicked Wallflower*!

Next in line is Macauley's troubled brother, the Earl of Stanford, in *One Wedding and An Earl*. Who do you think he'll end up with? After that, I'm excited to write Dash and Theo's love affair in *Two Scandals and a Scot*. A dull professor is not going to be her fate after all.

In the meantime, have you read Hildy's and Helena's, as well as Georgie's story in *The Brazen Bluestocking* (book 1), *The Scandalous Vixen* (book 2) and *The Ice Duchess* (prequel)?

THE DUCHESS SOCIETY SERIES

While waiting for book 4, check out other books by Tracy Sumner or dive into one of WOLF Publishing's latest releases: The sexy and fun Victorian romance by **Sydney Jane Baily**: *Clarity*!

DIAMONDS OF THE FIRST WATER SERIES

Acknowledgments

I have so many wonderful friends in the romance community. Too many to list here! But I want to send a special **thank you** to Estela Niedo-Williams and my reader's group, The Contrary Countesses, for their continued support, encouragement, and friendship! I love you guys!
(And sending a warm shout-out to The Brazen Belles, too!!! You rock!)

Also by Tracy Sumner

The Duchess Society Series

The Ice Duchess *(Prequel)*

The Brazen Bluestocking

The Scandalous Vixen

The Wicked Wallflower

League of Lords Series

The Lady is Trouble

The Rake is Taken

The Duke is Wicked

The Hellion is Tamed

Garrett Brothers Series

Tides of Love

Tides of Passion

Tides of Desire: A Christmas Romance

Southern Heat Series

To Seduce a Rogue

To Desire a Scoundrel: A Christmas Seduction

Standalone Regency romances

Tempting the Scoundrel

Chasing the Duke

About Tracy Sumner

Award-winning author Tracy Sumner's story-telling career began when she picked up a historical romance on a college beach trip, and she fondly blames LaVyrle Spencer for her obsession with the genre. She's a recipient of the National Reader's Choice, and her novels have been translated into Dutch, German, Portuguese and Spanish. She lived in New York, Paris and Taipei before finding her way back to the Lowcountry of South Carolina.

When not writing sizzling love stories about feisty heroines and their temperamental-but-entirely-lovable heroes, Tracy enjoys reading, snowboarding, college football (Go Tigers!), yoga, and travel. She loves to hear from romance readers!

Connect with Tracy: www.tracy-sumner.com

Made in the USA
Columbia, SC
18 April 2022

58901425R00162